THE ICARUS CONTINUUM

STORIES FROM THE FILES OF THE DOMESTIC THREAT EARLY ASSESSMENT UNIT

A STANTON CHRONICLES ANTHOLOGY

BY THE SAME AUTHOR

The Cannon and the Quill, Book One: We All be Jacobites Here*

The Cannon and the Quill, Book Two: Princes of the World*

The Cannon and the Quill, Book Three: How to Be a Proper Pyrate*

The Cannon and the Quill, Book Four: All the Devils Are Here*

Three Gothic Doctors and Their Sons*

Sherlock Holmes and the Mystery of M*

Minor Confessions of an Angel Falling Upward*

Jester-Night (Book 1 of the Ambir Dragon Tales)

Non-Fiction

Watch Out For the Hallway: Our Two-Year Investigation of the Most Haunted Library in North Carolina (with Tonya Madia)

Roommates from Beyond: How to Live in a Haunted Home (with Tonya Madia)

*Part of the Stanton Chronicles

THE ICARUS CONTINUUM

STORIES FROM THE FILES OF THE DOMESTIC THREAT EARLY ASSESSMENT UNIT

PART OF THE STANTON CHRONICLES

JOEY MADIA

New Mystics Enterprises
Leavittsburg, Ohio

ACKNOWLEDGMENTS

These stories have seen many iterations, going back a decade:

To the actors who read the original audio drama scripts on which some of these stories are based—thank you for your time and enthusiasm as we gathered around the fire in "the Holler."

To Knight Berman, Jr., for making the Message Man come to life for the Page to Stage versions of the Planner Forthright/Michael Stanton monologues on www.newmystics.com.

To Bob Teague, who read later drafts of the audio drama scripts on which these stories are based—your feedback made them considerably better.

To readers of the Kindle Vella versions of these stories—you have my deep appreciation.

DEDICATION

To all of the Truth Seekers and Message Bringers I have the honor to know and work beside: the COMMIIC is making it harder to bring the message thru. So let's work all the harder to keep on shining the light.

TABLE OF CONTENTS

SERIAL SECAUCUS

Sometime in the not too distant Present

Lucky Red's Tavern, the oldest bar in Secaucus, New Jersey, enjoyed the patronage and praise of dozens of loyal locals, as well as considerable traffic from commuters and tourists traveling Wood Avenue on their way to the Lincoln Tunnel and the heart of New York City, located five miles away, across the Hudson River.

Founded in the winter of 1866, five months after the end of the American Civil War by Liam "Lucky Red" Ryan, former first sergeant, Battery A, New Jersey's 1st Light Artillery, the tavern was still the place to be to trade stories of "ya best an' woysta days, boyo!" as Liam had shouted to patrons until the day he died.

"Lucky Red" got his nickname when a twelve-pound smoothbore "Napoleon" he was crewing took a direct hit from one of Johnny Reb's own at the Battle of the Crater, part of the siege of Petersburg, Virginia, Saturday, the 30th of July, 1864. While the rest of the crew were killed on the spot or later succumbed to their wounds, "Lucky Red" got away with the loss of "only" the middle and ring fingers and pinky of his hand.

"An' it ain't the one I sign the checks wit', me lads! An' here's another wee bit a' truth… a pinky don't count as a finga!" he'd shout, when the whiskeys he'd been downing between pours had at last coerced him into reminiscing about the Brothers War as the evening came to an end.

Ever since Lucky Red had poured the initial round of to-the-rim shots and pints of whiskey and ale in the winter of 1866, an unbroken line of Ryans had been helming the oak and maple bar that was the tavern's central feature. Through bull and bear markets, two world wars, and the embarrassments of Korea, 'Nam, and Afghanistan, Lucky Red's had been a symbol of stability—of the city of Secaucus itself. No matter the name of the town in which it sat—it was part of North Bergen at the time "Lucky Red" had first hung a bright red horseshoe over the entryway, and another over the bar, until the change in 1900—the tavern *was* the town, and everybody knew it.

On the December night on which our tale begins, it was the great-great grandson of "Lucky Red," Daniel Patrick Ryan—the first of the Sons of Ryan to do without a nickname—who was working behind the glass-ringed, beer-stained bar. His bright red apron tied tight around his waist and ubiquitous towel with the bright red Ryan horseshoe emblazoned upon it draped like a talisman over his shoulder, Daniel was watching the Seton Hall Pirates take on their Big East basketball rivals from across the river, the formidable St. John's Red Storm.

Having graduated with a business degree from Seton Hall six years earlier, Daniel was one of the Pirates' most rabid fans, shouting at the television for "Better defense!" and "Some big ole' hustle now, fellas!" until he was exhausted and hoarse.

If you didn't root for Seton Hall, you weren't welcome in Lucky Red's on game night.

And if you made the mistake of wearing a rival's colors, you were sure to be asked to leave. *For life*.

"Our boys in blue and white are lookin' good tonight, ain't they Danny Boy?"

"Hell yeah they are, Pops! Say... you wanna get up and give me a hand back here? They're spillin' out the door!"

Daniel's father, Patrick "Iron Balls" Ryan—a retired Navy warrant officer, Vietnam veteran, and former Golden Gloves welterweight champ who got *his* nickname for his refusal to wear a cup during boxing matches, remained on his favorite stool at the corner of the bar, where he perched himself six nights a week. Instead of getting up as Daniel had asked, he raised a pint of Guinness Dark and shouted with a put-on Irish accent, "Me days a' servin' are long dayd an' gone, boyo! Sink er swim, me darlin' little Nancy!"

While pouring two more pints and a trio of shots, Daniel was searching his mind for a fitting comeback when he spied an off-kilter figure pushing through the crowd of Christmas shoppers on the Wood Avenue sidewalk. As his target entered the tavern, Daniel shouted, "Uh-uh!" Leaving the glasses where they sat and moving to the section of the bar closest to the door, he added, "You turn yourself around, Lola, and take your street-walkin' ass right the hell outta my bar! I warned you last week... You show yourself 'round here again, you syphilitic bitch, and I'm gonna pull out and piss on each and every one of your cheap-ass hair extensions!"

Daniel could feel his father's hands taking hold of both his shoulders.

"Hey now, Danny Boy... why don't ya take a bit of a breather and back yourself offa this thing? You're makin' a helluva scene here, son. This rantin' and ravin' don't do you nor the business any good."

"Don't muscle me, Pops," Daniel whispered, standing his ground. "I didn't get my business degree, and join the Chamber of Commerce and four other business and service organizations to watch the downtown go to shit 'cause of drunken whores like her!"

Forcing her way between two bleach-blonde co-eds wearing Seton Hall jerseys and little else, Lola leaned over the bar until her nose was inches from Daniel's. "Oh yeah, you faggoty limp-dick leprechaun? A Walkin' Lady's money's all of a sudden worthless in your trashy piss-ass tavern just 'cause Lucky Lola don't let the bartender–owner cop a feel or fuck for free? *Fine*—there's plenty other joints in which to lay my coin. And they don't smell like *puke!*"

Grateful his father's hands were still on his shoulders so he couldn't raise his arms, Daniel shot back, "Walkin' Lady? You all call yourselves whatever it is you want... you're hookers, plain and simple. And don't be tellin' people I wanted to cop a feel. I wouldn't touch your body with the hands of the St. John's center. And that 'lucky' nickname a' yours... You ain't fit to have it! You ain't decent people! You're lousy for the city of Secaucus is what *you* are! Now get outta my bar before I shove your ass down a storm drain!"

Three hours later, the bar closed up and Wood Avenue starting its five hours of sleep before dawn, Lucky Lola emerged from the shadows of a side alley, pulling a tube of bright red lipstick from her purse. While things were quiet, she was planning to inscribe her thoughts about the Ryans and the rest of their corned beef and cabbage cronies front and center on their lit-up storefront window.

Popping the top off the tube and twisting the bottom so three inches of the lipstick-cum-marker were protruding like a thumb, she leaned into the window, writing in her best middle-school cursive the letters *F* and *U*.

Then she realized she wasn't alone.

"What the hell *you* lookin' at?" Lola asked, making no effort to hide her handy work. "Oh, um... sorry, uh... *officer*. Didn't see your badge. Saaay... is that a nightstick in your trousers? You lookin' for some thunderous, top-shelf lovin'? What? Nuthin' to say, Mista Law-n-Order? You the strong, silent type or what? Come around the corner, Johnny Law, and I'll show you all the reasons why Lola's livin' large."

Certain she'd hooked her prey, Lola abandoned the window, her message to the Ryans forgotten, the heels of her bright purple FMPs echoing off the tall brick buildings around them as she headed for her favorite spot in the alley, beneath the spill of a single naked bulb, 'cause Lola liked to watch. Taking up her usual position as Johnny Law approached her, Lola smiled.

"Alrighty now," Lola purred in his right ear as she hiked up her leopard-print mini-skirt. "No one's gonna bother us here in this spot. It's Lucky Lola's own private hidey-hole. Good one, huh? *Hidey-hole?* I got a few of those for sure... But each one costs you green. The rarer the hole, the bigger the bucks. So, what'll it be, Mister Shiny Badge? Oh, now—here he comes... That's right... lean in here against me. That's right... Lucky Lola's—"

"A degenerate piece of filth. A vile little pustule. Now you'll be delivered. The Master judges not."

The voice that Lucky Lola (real name Loretta Vera Parks) heard before she died could hardly be called human. It sounded awfully close to what Pastor Richardson at the First AME Church of Poughkeepsie, where Loretta once prayed a child, had described as *Satan's own.*

Not that she could hear much of it at all. By the time her killer/deliverer finished the second sentence, Lola was choking on her blood from an opening in her neck that stretched from ear to ear.

As her lifeless body slid to the alley's concrete surface, Lucky Lola's soul tugged away from her chest, heading to somewhere at least a little better than the downtown streets of Secaucus. As her soul flew farther away, the movement of the knife as it cut the fabric of her neon green tube-top sounded to the thick surrounding silence like the whispering wings of the angels Pastor Richardson had often told her would accompany Loretta wherever it was she went, as long as she said her prayers and refrained from embracing sin.

Twelve hours later, in a borrowed autopsy room an hour's drive up the Jersey Turnpike from where she lived and worked, Doctor Ruth Anne Marsh put on a fresh pair of gloves and pressed the record button on the digital recorder mounted on the adjustable arm of the lamp above the stainless steel table holding the target of her attention.

Clearing her throat after covering her mouth with her green-gloved hand, she placed her goggles over her eyes and started her report, as her professors and supervising doctors had taught her at Robert Wood Johnson Medical School and during her residency at the Jersey Shore. "Preliminary report by Doctor Ruth Anne Marsh, on assignment from the Department of Forensic Science, Eastern

Pinelands University, to the Federal Bureau of Investigation, Hudson County office, by special request of the Domestic Threat Early Assessment Unit based in Langley, Virginia. It is two-thirty p.m. on December sixteenth. Victim is 26 years of age. Name, Loretta Vera Parks, professionally known as Lucky Lola. The body was found with the left arm placed across the left breast. The right breast was removed and propped upright against the right side of the ribcage. Both legs were bent, with feet flat on the pavement, knees turned slightly outward. The head is almost completely severed from the neck, which was cut from ear to ear, left to right by a blade approximately nine inches in length, indicating that the perpetrator is most likely right handed. The same instrument was used to inflict thirty-nine distinct stab wounds and then to eviscerate the victim, including removal of the intestines, liver, and uterus, which are missing. The surgical precision evident in these tasks indicates a skilled—"

Ruth hit pause on the recorder at the sound of someone knocking on the gunmetal gray doorframe. Looking through the wire-reinforced glass window in the center of the door, she waved the visitor in.

FBI Special Agent in Charge Kevin Connor entered the room, looking damned embarrassed to be there.

"Sorry to interrupt you, Doctor Marsh," he said, making a point to avert his eyes from the naked figure on the table. "Looks like you're hard at work…"

Always amazed at how a man with Connor's experience with grisly murders like this one went out of his way to not set his eyes upon a corpse on the autopsy table, unless it was necessary in order to do his job, Ruth placed a sheet over Loretta Vera Parks's mangled, dismembered body and removed her goggles and gloves.

Turning to face her visitor, Ruth said, "Sometimes an interruption is exactly what I need. I'm several hours into the examination, although I was just getting started on recording my report. I'm surprised the locals already called you in on this one, Agent Connor. Or, considering I am *also* already here, maybe I shouldn't be at all…"

Connor shrugged his shoulders. "The Domestic Threat Early Assessment Unit's got a lot of pull right now—last month's thwarted chem attack on Port Authority made a lot of people on both sides of the river look damned good for a change—so we're on everyone's positive radar and when we got the call, I knew I needed the best."

Ruth smiled, feeling guilty for doing so considering where they were. "I'll try to prove that's true. So far, though, I don't have anything that could help, but I really just got started. I intend to be very thorough… extensive tox screen including the latest exotics, inch-by-inch examination to ensure I don't miss a needle prick or some other easily overlooked mark, and deeper assessment of exactly why the body and its dis-attached parts were arranged the way they were. That's going to take some time."

Connor nodded. "Understood. I just wanted to see how you were settling in and thank you in person for making the drive as soon as you did. I know exams are in full swing, and you should be looking forward to the start of Christmas break rather than dealing with carnage like this."

"I appreciate that, Agent. Although, after spending time with the body and reading the victim's history several times, I am more than happy to let the Christmas festivities wait. This killer is not typical at all. And, despite your refraining from saying it, I know that this will not be a simple one and done."

Looking like a little kid lost in the mall late on Christmas Eve, Connor mumbled, "It already isn't. Got a call as I pulled up… The unsub got a second one. Probably two hours after the first. I can't say too much at present, as insane as that might sound. I'm on my way to the crime scene. All I know is, it's bad. Look… there are lotsa powerful people looking our way on this one, Doctor. We have to get this right. So let me leave you to your work, and I'll get back to mine."

As her visitor turned to exit, Ruth asked, "Can you tell me why you were brought in on this case so soon, Agent Connor? Secaucus PD has a reputation for being *uber* territorial and the local FBI office is the best they have in the state. Yet they chose to call in a specialist. The county ME's apparently super pissed that they released the body to me instead of to him, and I can't say that I blame him…"

Without turning around, Connor answered, "I'm sorry you're feeling uncomfortable. After you file your report, we can talk about the background. Expect the second body soon."

As Connor was closing the door behind him, Dr. Marsh was removing the sheet, turning on the digital recorder, and continuing with her work.

The sooner she knew what this assignment was all about, and why Connor was involved, the happier she would be.

Eugene Gorman Howe always felt most at home when he was below the ground.

Not that this rented basement in a Hoboken brownstone, with its rusting pipes and dripping water and constant sounds of angry machismo from the Hispanic man who lived above him—directed toward the *hijo de puta*'s wife and trio of children—could compare to his warren of rooms beneath a sprawling Queen Anne Victorian in rural West Virginia.

He could not wait to finish with his mission and get back home to New Haven, just in time for Christmas.

Patience, the Voice of the Beast reminded him, whispering the message deep within the ear on the left side of his head—which was the one that Eugene could not hear *human* voices, or anything else *but* the Voice, out of because of a man like the one upstairs.

That particular piece of shit was a fourth-generation Italian coal miner, whose non-English-speaking great-grandparents had been duped by agents of John D. Rockefeller's Colorado Fuel and Iron Company, who lured the couple—and thousands of others like them—from Ellis Island with one-way train tickets and promises of prosperity the agents never planned to keep.

Fuck them. Fuck them good, Eugene thought. Their garlic Guido great-grandson had met with an unfortunate *accident* involving a grinding wheel in his shop out back of the house when Eugene was barely twelve.

That was Eugene's initiation, after an introduction to the Voice of the Beast in a cave half a mile from the house, which his mother—a liquor-lover who sold herself when she wasn't giving it away for free—had inherited from Eugene's grandparents. A cave where he used to hide when that fucking dago WOP was in the midst of one of his rampages.

On that particular day, Eugene was trying to cope with the white-hot, blinding pain of a busted eardrum, caused by a blow from a metal meat mallet delivered with prejudice when the shitting *scifosa* thought the dishes Eugene had washed were not quite clean enough to suit him.

Although it was the first time Eugene could hear it, that long ago day in the cave, the Voice of the Beast sounded to him like it was coming from a friend. The first one Eugene had had in his entire shit-soaked life. After delivering a long, inspiring speech on Eugene's rights and privileges as future inheritor of the house and land the Guinea had *invaded*, while Eugene's ear kept aching, causing him to vomit from the pain until he thought that he would die, the Beast made a *suggestion*.

Eugene should wait until the next time the lousy bastard was working in his shop.

Then he could make things right.

Two days later, with the Beast entrenched within him, providing details of what to do, Eugene did the doing and laughed at the mess it made.

An uncalculated result of that particular tormentor's demise—*live and learn*, the Voice of the Beast had said—was the arrival of his mother's sister, a pious puss-bag of a Bible-thumping busybody who made Eugene's life a different kind of Hell for the better part of a year.

That is, until she *slipped*, falling end over end—all knees and ears and elbows—down the warped and far too narrow set of half-lit cellar steps.

The Italian fucker had said he would fix them, but of course he never did.

As for his mother, she died a decade later—of what a medical examiner deemed, after an autopsy, *natural causes*—when Eugene was old enough to inherit the house and entirety of the seventeen acres.

Including the cave.

Patience, the Beast had said.

Patience Eugene had.

And, as an unanticipated bonus, he was a natural at masking his kills.

The Hispanic bastard's tirade was now punctuated by a series of gunshots from somewhere up the street.

Hoboken, Hudson County, New Jersey, and America… all were going to hell in a bushel basket due to the degradations of immigrants, Welfare Queens, and corrupted politicians.

Eugene's job was *Reclamation*. A sacrifice at a time.

Picking up his custom-crafted knife—exactly nine inches long, one for each of the donors his mission would embrace—and a long leather strop, he began to move the blade rhythmically back and forth, staring into the flickering flame of the only source of light in the basement—a handmade beeswax candle.

This ritual, which he had learned from the Voice of the Beast many years ago while performing a set of similar sacrifices in San Francisco in the middle of his twenties, put him in a trance state, allowing his beloved Mentor–Master to more easily instruct him.

As the sounds of the shouting *cabrón*, and all other earthly sounds, faded into the distance, Eugene whispered, "I'm going out again tonight. Icarus crawling from the Darkness to soar to the black-coal Sun. To collect the blood required. I revel in my reasons—the bitches *have to* suffer—but it is not *my* arm, *my* hand, *my* heart that births the holy hacking or feels pleasure in the pain. Talk to me, my Mentor. I see you past my eyes... the flicking of your tail, the curvature of your horns, laughing in the cracking, warping mirror of my focused, fecund mind. Guide me in my kills, that I may meet your needs." Eugene shrieked in anger as a familiar, hated filmstrip started to flash and flicker on the cave walls of his skull. "Why do you not trust me! Why, after all my years of loyalty, do you nightly choose to show me my skank-whore of a mother and my Jesus-freak-fuck aunt, my dead and buried tormentors as they rise like ghouls from their graves! Why subject me still to righteous auntie's rants on pink and virgin flesh and the scalding, spewing impulses those delicacies provoke? I am *not* my mother's child! Tell me why I have to suffer for her endless, ugly sins? Why is it *her* face I see on every bitch I kill?"

You came from her womb, did you not?

Eugene stroked the knife a little harder along the leather. "The womb from which I come is *not* my mother's filth! That is what you taught me. That is why I'm yours. I've been baptized in the blood. I have fostered bestial births. Helpless Eugene was replaced, as he was crying in his cradle, a Changeling from the faeries laid there in his place! Give to me your strength. Treat me as a brother, as your long-ago London Master once deigned to do for you."

The Voice of the Beast was laughing, its unearthly tonality twitching Eugene's spine as its breath brought forth a storm. *Two is the number of whores that you shall take tonight. Choose your message-laden locations to further the larger mission. Slit one's lying throat but otherwise leave her intact. Do the other good. Carve the look of smug contentment off her dull and vapid face. Carve and collect her whore-parts—all of them this time. Take your time and tap the Vel. I shall once again protect you. Invisible as a spectre, invincible as a God. The chalice must be cleansed, and the cleanser must be pure.*

Eugene Gorman Howe, stroking his knife along the leather until he felt his balls release, shouted into the whirlwind, "I shall be your servant! I shall be the Passage. I shall be the Door. I am ready now, my angel. My knife is nice and sharp."

As the Beast continued to laugh, Eugene lumbered up the stairs.

A dozen hours later, SAIC Kevin Connor, who had built his career and reputation amidst the carnage of serial killings, mass shootings, and religious and cult crimes across the United States, looked out over the gathering, chitchatting group of beat cops and homicide detectives crowding into the staff room of the Secaucus police station and felt his jaw begin to tighten.

Thinking back on his days as a starting tight end for the Fighting Illini, Connor knew that there were plays where you ran down the field, with a chance to make a catch, score a touchdown, and be a star. On most downs, though, you were blocking like a lineman for the back field.

He wouldn't be doing any running down the field with hopes of catching the ball and making a touchdown today.

These guys and gals were the quarterback and running backs and it was his responsibility to cut them a path so *they* could get the win.

As the final stragglers sought out seats in the back, Connor dropped his crammed-full, dog-eared day planner on the desk so it rang out like a gunshot and said, "All right, everyone." Still the chitchat continued. *Fine*, he thought, *you're gonna make me earn it. Not a problem. I've been in this spot before, plenty of goddamned times.* "I said all right!" he proclaimed a little louder. "Everyone settle down."

Nothing but mumbles, grunts, and a sharp peal of laughter from the back as one of the detectives shared the punchline of a joke.

Okay, assholes, he thought. *You want me to be the heavy? So then fucking be it.*

"I said LISTEN UP!" Startled by the power and volume of his voice, everyone did as he said. Taking a breath and saying a silent prayer of thanks, Connor continued, just loud enough so those by the door could hear him, "As most of you know, I'm SAIC Kevin Connor with the FBI's DTEAU out of Virginia. I've been brought in to help you catch the serial killer you've got working in your town. I just picked up a forensics report on vics number one and two. I'm awaiting delivery on a more detailed report on the two that he got last night. The crime scene photos and prelim from forensics are enough to get us started."

A uniformed cop with a wide swath of grey in his hair stood and waved his hand. Not waiting to be called on, he asked, "Were they cut up to the same extent as the first two?"

Glancing down at a stack of color photos, although he had them memorized, Connor replied, "There is a definite pattern emerging. If you recall, the first vic had her throat slit and the unsub had mutilated her torso and taken some of her organs. Victim two, throat also slashed, though her body was even further mutilated. Both breasts were removed and placed between her legs. Vic number three had her throat slit, but the unsub went no further. We believe someone interrupted him. And yes, we are pretty damned sure it's a male. Victim four… her throat was slit like the previous vics, but this time he went further with the pelvic region. He didn't just gash the genitalia or take trophies. Her intestines were on her shoulder. And he did what an initial on-scene examination indicates was a radical hysterectomy."

A wave of murmurs and variations on taking the lord's and his virgin mother's names in vain washed hotly over the room. Connor noticed some of the younger officers turning pale.

"All of you settle down. This kind of situation—the frequency of attack, the brutality—are thankfully rare. But Secaucus drew the short straw, which means that this is the situation put before you, and you'll have to toughen up. I know some of you were first responders after some of these attacks. And I know you all want to get this guy as badly as I do, so let's keep focused and find ways to work together."

The station captain, Conrad Saunders, who had initially called the FBI's Hudson County office to make the request for assistance when Lucky Lola was killed, stood up and moved to the front of the room. "SAIC Connor is correct. This is graduate school, kids. They don't teach this in the academy, but here we are. And it sucks."

"I got a question, Captain." This came from the front row, from a grizzled-looking detective with a gin blossom and the start of a gut. "How'd you know this was gonna go serial? I mean… you had to, for county FBI to call in this guy here—no disrespect—who brought a forensic specialist who's been holed up in the lab ever since delivery of victim number one."

Expelling a coffee-tinged breath of frustrated air, the captain looked at Connor. "You wanna field this one, Agent?"

Connor nodded. Best to get it behind them. "Absolutely, Captain Saunders. I don't know how many true crime aficionados we have sitting here among us, but this was, from the start, obvious copycat. Or close. Let's call it inspiration and homage with some very specific markers."

A female detective in the middle of the room asked, "You thinkin' Zodiac?"

A female officer followed with, "Or maybe Trailside Killer… Bastard's name escapes me…"

Connor put up his hand to prevent another round of vocalized, off-the-mark guesswork. "David Carpenter. This is not their style, either one of them. But it's nice to know you have some inkling about America's most notable serial killers."

"Who then?" a senior sergeant asked.

"The killer named Jack the Ripper."

Knowing he'd get a good bit of laughter, wise-cracks, and astonished stares at the mention of arguably the world's most famous serial killer, Connor let them come.

"Talk about some bullshit..." Gin Blossom said with a groan.

"You think so? The wound patterns match the documented Ripper killings. The first vic was stabbed 39 times, same as Martha Tabram."

"Who may or may not have been Ripper..." This was from the female officer who had guessed the Trailside Killer.

Connor stood his ground. "The unsub's saying she was. I didn't know for sure until I talked to my forensic specialist, Doctor Ruth Anne Marsh, but the intestines on the fourth vic's shoulder, the missing uteruses, the thirty-nine stab wounds and removal of the breasts—it's a Ripper fanboy for sure."

"So that was your theory from the start, Captain Saunders? Lucky Lola was done up like a Jack the Ripper showpiece? That it?" Gin Blossom asked, confrontation in his voice.

The female detective, in an attempt to break the tension and keep everyone's eyes on the goal, said, "If he keeps to Ripper history, there are gonna be more vics."

Connor nodded. "As I've said—and everyone needs to keep this in mind—he isn't keeping exact. He's mixing and matching, although vic three, with only her throat slit, is a match for Elizabeth Stride. An immediate, mutilated follow-up also matches the pattern."

"You think he'll go inside a private home for the next one, Agent?" asked a Hispanic female officer. "Like he did with Mary Kelly?"

Connor looked at Captain Saunders, who exhaled another puff of acrid coffee breath and, after a quick look at the drop ceiling's bright-white tiles, nodded to him to proceed.

"We don't think so," Connor began, carefully choosing his words. "If you look at where the four victims were killed, there is another pattern emerging. One that has nothing to do with Jack the Ripper." Moving to a hinged whiteboard a few feet away, Connor flipped it over, revealing a map of the downtown done in blue marker with four red marks and four names written in green. "This should be familiar to you. The red marks are where the vics were found. All four of these businesses labeled here in green are owned and operated by families who at some point migrated to America."

"What the fuck?"

Connor didn't bother to turn around to see who asked the question. The best he could do was explain.

"Vic one... Lucky Lola. She had a confrontation with Daniel Ryan at Lucky Red's Tavern a few hours before she was killed."

"Hey!" a red-haired cop yelled from the center of the room. "Don't be sayin' nothin' against the Ryans... especially Danny. That kid works his ass off for Secaucus. Can you blame him if he don't want whores in his place? She wrote F U on their front window that night with her *lipstick*..."

Connor turned around, trying to keep his temper. "No one—for the moment—is accusing any of the business owners or any of their employees, Officer... Ryan. I interviewed Daniel and his father. I also interviewed the owners of Kim's Korean Barbeque. And when we're finished here, I'll interview the Khatris from the Dollar or More Mart, and the Portuguese family that owns the Pastel de Nata bake shop."

"So this unsub despises immigrants... no surprise. We have plenty of that," said a Black detective in his forties. "But he isn't killing immigrant shop owners. He's killing prostitutes near their storefronts."

"And disrupting the immigrants' businesses, at least in the short term," the captain added. "Just in time for Christmas. Let Agent Connor continue."

Instead, Gin Blossom said, "Hold a sec. Aside from the wound patterns, and some probable coincidence—given the high number of immigrant shop owners in the downtown—you've got nada. No witnesses, no motive. And he's using the MO and signature of a guy long dead and gone. A guy they never caught, so everything is theory."

Plenty more mumbles and murmurs rose up in the room.

Connor raised his hand to calm his audience down. "The detective here is right. To a point." Grabbing a stack of stapled papers from the nearby desk, Connor began to pass them out. "I've put together the start of a profile with the help of the DTEAU's lead profiler, Maggie Sorrus, and Doctor Marsh, who is on loan to us from Eastern Pinelands U. Read it over carefully. Then read it all again. And several times more, until you've got it memorized. There's target age, probable job, stressors... Get this guy burned into your brain. I'll be available for questions 24–7. Don't hesitate to call. My number's at the top."

As most of those assembled began to look it over, the female Hispanic officer raised her hand. When Connor nodded in her direction, she said, "Detective Chase said MO and signature. Can you explain the difference?"

So that's Gin Blossom's name.

Sitting on the edge of the desk, Connor said, "The MO, or modus operandi, changes. The signature, though... never. It's what the unsub has to do to be fulfilled."

Chase added, uninvited, "It's how he gets his rocks off."

Followed by Officer Ryan. "So for him, it's gotta be carvin' up whores."

"Prostitutes, Liam. For chrissakes," the Hispanic female officer corrected.

"And he will definitely strike again," Connor said, anxious to end the increasingly chaotic meeting. "He's not spreading them out like the Ripper. Four in a little more than twenty-four hours is an unusually rabid pace. For some reason we have yet to figure out, he's in one helluva goddamned hurry."

"Maybe he wants to be home for the holiday."

Nodding his acknowledgment at the officer who said it, Connor asked the room, "Anything else before we close?"

"Yeah, actually," Gin Blossom/Detective Chase said, standing up. "You ever heard of the Zapruder–Patterson film, Agent Connor?"

Knowing he would immediately regret engaging, Connor replied, "I have not, Detective Chase."

"It proves that Bigfoot killed JFK."

Barely able to focus her eyes to check the time on her smartphone, Dr. Ruth Anne Marsh pushed the exit button on the ME office's main entrance doors and waited impatiently for them to release her into the cold night air after a difficult thirteen hours of autopsies and analysis.

Glancing up from the phone, she noticed a dark blue Prius hybrid blocking her way. Leaning against it was a fit-looking man her age, his leather-jacketed arms folded and hiking-booted feet crossed confidently at the ankles. He had his head down, so all she could see was an unruly mass of medium brown hair.

"Do you have any idea what time it is, young lady?" Leather Jacket asked, not adjusting his cocky posture.

"As a matter of fact, I do," Ruth answered, amazed at how comfortable Leather Jacket looked, despite the nearly freezing temperature and a steady fall of snow. "I just checked. It's fifteen minutes past midnight."

Leather Jacket chuckled. "Dangerous time of night for a young woman to be out and about in Secaucus."

Slipping her hand into her pocket, Marsh grasped a compact canister of Mace Pepper Gel. "You should get in your car and drive away from me," she warned.

"Or what?" Leather Jacket asked. "You're going to Mace me?"

As Marsh pulled the canister from her pocket, Leather Jacket looked up, the streetlight above his head illuminating his face.

"Are you kidding me? What are you doing here, Uriel?"

Still not changing his posture, the man smiled. "Waiting for you, of course."

"Does the police department know you're here, or the ME's office? If they knew I was talking to a reporter... An out of town reporter, no less..."

Uriel unfolded and spread his arms in an alluring combination of surrender and assertion. "So don't tell them. And, just so you know, the *Eastern Standard* is fast becoming a *mid-Atlantic* paper of no small consequence, so how 'bout a little respect?"

Marsh looked thoroughly unimpressed.

"Look..." Uriel continued, "you're obviously exhausted and want nothing more than to get back to your hotel room ASAP to sleep, so I'm gonna be direct. I'm not here for an interview, or to try to use our history—such as it is—to get a scoop or an exclusive."

Her interest further piqued, Ruth asked, "So why then *are* you here?"

"It's about my twin brother, Michael. He's been getting these messages. Of the super-realistic, yet freakishly nightmarish, psychic variety. And they really have him rattled."

A little disappointed that Uriel's visit wasn't purely personal—a reaction she chalked up to being overtired, stressed, and lonely— Ruth took a few steps closer. "You certainly have my attention."

"Great. What do you say we sit in the car? I can run the heater. You look like you're freezing."

Nodding her agreement, Ruth replied, "And you look like it's summer in Savanna."

Opening the passenger-side door before she could change her mind, Uriel answered, "My mind's on other things. You know my brother's backstory. He's got a lot of mental problems, but he's also, for lack of a better word... gifted."

Once they had situated themselves and the heater was blasting away, Ruth asked, "Wasn't Michael forced into full-time psychiatric care six months ago after he called the FBI field office in Newark about an imminent assassination attempt on the governor of New Jersey?"

"Yeah. Even though he pretty much saved the governor's life. It's a cruel, cruel state, New Jersey. Seemingly so modern, but stuck in a distant past. No one believed that he *dreamed* the details he shared. That his 'guardian angel,' as Michael calls him, gave him the who, the where, and the when. They assumed he was part of the plot from the start and had suddenly chickened out. We're still in the stone ages, Ruth, and we really should know better than to dismiss these kinds of phenomena."

"Where is Michael now?"

Uriel pulled a pamphlet from his sun visor. "Up until a week ago he was in an assisted living facility in Storm Haven. A fairly decent one. Near the ocean, which he likes. Our father arranged it after Michael's mandatory ninety days on the psyche ward, just before he left for one of his digs on the Amazon River."

Ruth sat up in her seat. "Michael went AWOL a week ago? Okay, Uriel... let's not play around. Does this have anything to do with why I'm here in Secaucus?"

"Yes. Michael called me from a pay phone this morning. Apparently, he's holed up in some converted room above a garage. Not sure where. And he's been having these terrible dreams... all about serial killers. Well... one serial killer who takes on a lot of different looks and signatures. Nasty stuff. Slit throats and extensive mutilation. Especially of prostitutes. The kinds of things that—"

"Jack the Ripper did. I mean, that's what you were gonna say. Am I right? Jesus, Uriel... you two freak me out... You always have."

Slapping the steering wheel, Uriel said, "Our keen ability to freak you out aside... Yes... Jack the Ripper was *exactly* what I was going to say. You know about my great-grandfather Uriah's uncle, right? Judah Philemon Stanton?"

Marsh nodded. "Newspaper guy. Uriah's inspiration for starting the *Eastern Standard*."

"Yes. And..."

"Son of a bitch, Uriel! He investigated the Ripper murders in London!"

"Correct. For the *Pall Mall Gazette*. And he had this crazy theory..."

"I read his book about them when I was doing my residency," Ruth said. "I actually read all three of his books. Crazy doesn't even begin to cover the stuff he claims is true..."

Adjusting his position to face her, Uriel said, "I'm flattered on his behalf that you read them. But let's leave my great-great-uncle Judah's maybe not so crazy theories aside for the moment. If you knew I was gonna say Ripper, then Michael's dreams are actually coming true, as they almost always have."

Ruth suddenly wished she hadn't gotten into the car. "Am I a part of his dreams?"

Pulling a reporter's pad from his pocket, Uriel said, "Not exactly. It was more an insistent clue. Verbal instead of visual. It's the final thing he hears at the end of every dream. You ready?"

Planting her feet securely on the floorboard and exhaling a girding breath, Ruth nodded. "Okay. Yeah. I'm ready."

Although she really wasn't.

Opening the pad and flipping several pages, Uriel cleared his throat and read, "If you want to avoid the swamp, you'd be wise to seek the marsh."

Ruth glanced over to get a look for herself, mouthing the words as she read them. "Creepy, yet poetic. A hundred and ten percent Stanton."

Laying the open pad on the dashboard between them, Uriel shrugged. "That's how Michael describes his dreams. A weird blend of Artaud, Bergman, Lovecraft, and Poe. I'm worried about him, Ruth. When Michael goes off the grid like this, especially from a facility, bad things always happen."

Glancing again at the pad, Ruth whispered, "So I'm the marsh in the message? Logical assumption, given what you probably figured out from the police scanners and however else you reporters get your info."

Uriel leaned away. "Ouch! Since when do you hate reporters?"

Ruth tried her best to smile. It wound up looking lame. "I don't. And I certainly don't hate you. But I have spent the past two days alone with a quartet of very mutilated corpses. Mutilated to an extent I've personally never seen. The only thing that comes close are the photos of Mary Kelly. It has me rattled. And the beat cops, and Connor..."

Uriel grabbed his pad while pulling a pen from the visor. "*Kevin Connor*, you mean? From the FBI's DTEAU unit in Virginia? Of course... He's the one who brought you in... I should have figured that out..."

"Don't do a damned thing with that information, Uriel. I mean it."

"I won't. For now. I promise. But now you know why I came here... Why I needed to share what he said..."

Ruth nodded. "Let's say you're right... that I *do* understand, and further, that I take everything you've told me seriously. What do you want me to do? As much as I'd love to play Quincy to your Kolchak, I could lose my job... I can't let down those poor women lying under mortuary sheets upstairs."

"Losing your job is admittedly a possibility. But we could also stop this Ripper copycat and maybe save some lives. And get justice for those women whose deaths you couldn't prevent. So... here's what I'm asking..." Uriel removed a black business card from his pocket with his name and *Eastern Standard* printed in white on one side and a QR code on the other. "Scan this into your phone. If there's anything at all you think you can share, text me. Or, if it's safer, send me an email. I'll do the same. Michael's been calling me every morning. Anything he gets, I'll promptly give to you, and you can give it to Connor."

Holding her breath for a moment, Marsh nodded and took the card. "Let me see that message one more time."

Flipping back to the page, Uriel placed the notebook on the dashboard.

"If you want to avoid the swamp... What the hell is the swamp?" Marsh asked.

"I really wish I knew."

Nine and a half hours later, SAIC Kevin Connor—managing to somehow look awake and alert following a mere three hours of fitful, broken sleep—was doing his damnedest to "be a man and take it" as his father and football coaches advised after a hard-to-take loss, when he was determined to throw his pads in the river and quit.

"Listen to me, Agent," Mayor of Secaucus Paramita Laghari hissed, leaning over her desk with a hazel green stare that could melt a titanium I-beam. "I supported Captain Saunders when he invited you into our city. He had a hunch about the first girl, based on your books and presentations on serial killer history and patterns, and it seems that he was right. But I have to tell you, devoid of any attempt at bullshit—I have grown incredibly tired of taking the heat from the media, local businesses, and the families of the victims on this. Four mutilated streetwalkers in two days—two of them, less than half an hour apart, which happened on your watch!—and I've been told that you're telling our police force that the perpetrator is Jack the Ripper reincarnated! Are you serious, Agent Connor?"

Used to dealing with frustrated politicians sweating their public image, reelection campaigns, and daily polling numbers, Connor kept his cool. "*Reincarnated* was never part of my profile or my hypothesis, Ms. Mayor. But there are definite parallels between the Ripper and our unsub that are impossible to ignore. And yes, there are two horrific murders on my watch, but—and this is not an excuse, but a fact—our unsub's working quickly, there's a lot of ground to cover, and, as you know, a lot of girls to track…"

Grunting in frustration, Mayor Laghari slapped the desk with her expensively manicured fingers. Connor was surprised the force of the contact didn't break at least half of her dark red nails. "You mean to tell me that my impassioned public pleas, asking… *demanding*… that these girls stay off the streets 'til we catch this creep did virtually nothing at all? I swear to God they have a death wish. I've had the families of the victims outside of my office protesting for an hour already this morning. Women's rights groups from around the country are coming here in droves! Our business groups, including the Chamber of Commerce, are reporting a slowdown in traffic, reduced sales figures, and our immigrant business owners are talking about going elsewhere. We're a week away from Christmas… it's a terrible time for this!"

Connor resisted the urge to ask what a better time might be. Instead, because he got it, he said so.

It didn't appear to help.

"Prevailing public opinion says we haven't caught this psycho because we don't *want* to! That he's doing Secaucus a service! Some of these loudmouth bozos with a podcast or a blog have been saying that I went out on the Dark Web and *hired him* to be some sort of savior to solve our prostitute problem—or to force the immigrants out. Are they serious? My *parents* were immigrants from Bangalore who ran a shoe shop not three blocks from this building!" Taking a brief breath while gripping the desk until her knuckles went white, Laghari continued. "You ever get a 2 a.m. call from the governor, Agent Connor?"

Considering his options for a moment, the veteran investigator chose honesty. "No ma'am. Not in Jersey... But in several other states..."

What he *didn't* mention was that all of those calls were congratulatory.

"You're really missing out," Mayor Laghari said, having a seat and inviting Connor to do the same with a flick of her ring-less fingers. "She's not half as nice as you'd think a God-fearing Roman Catholic Ivy Leaguer whose parents came straight off the boat at Ellis Island without a penny to their name would be. I've heard rumors she came close to becoming a nun. But no... no love-thy-neighbor niceties when she called me late last night. Not when her bid to unseat the current president—the *previous* governor of New Jersey—as well as her current state agenda are suddenly in the shitter. And, again, because I am at the moment *utterly incapable* of bullshit—there's *my* re-election campaign, which is also in the shitter. *Further...* I don't know if you follow politics, but I'm in line to be her successor. You follow me, Agent? So let's return to this Ripper business. He did all four of these streetwalkers *exactly* like his hero did his?"

Connor could feel a change. He was making progress just by passively listening, instead of pushing back. Instead of embracing the need to *defend*. His supervisor would be proud. "Damn near. From the waist up, two of them look *exactly* like the 1888 autopsy photos—even the nicks on their faces."

Mayor Laghari leaned forward. "What about *below* the waist?

"It's ugly, Ms. Mayor. Even for me, and this kind of carnage has been my life's daily work for more than twenty years. Our forensics specialist, Doctor Ruth Anne Marsh, is working on it. Like I said—this unsub's unusually fast, but he doesn't sacrifice precision and artistry in his work... And I am almost positive he knows we've figured him out..."

Mayor Laghari leaned back in her chair, drumming on its padded arms with her inch-long pointed nails. "Artistry? You sound like you're impressed with him, Agent. Get love-struck somewhere else, or after you actually catch him when you write your latest book. He's still got one to go, am I right?"

Connor dreaded this question, no matter whom was asking. And nearly everyone was. "According to prevailing theory amongst the experts, Mary Kelly was Jack the Ripper's fifth and final victim, although some—myself included—believe there were anywhere from three to seven more. Regardless, we've already seen extreme mutilation in three of the four victims and we are not sure the unsub has any intention of venturing inside a home. The pattern, as you've mentioned, is immigrant-owned businesses in the downtown."

Glancing at her watch, the mayor stood, signaling the end of the meeting. "If he kills again, I'm finished, and believe me, Connor—I will take you with me, despite your Bureau achievements. Do whatever it takes. Bring in additional experts. Think outside the box, as Saunders assured me you can. That's why you're here. It's four to zero, bottom of the ninth. I'm not suffering a shutout. This twisted prick isn't gonna be my Zodiac, you read me, Agent Connor?"

Feeling his ulcer acting up, Kevin said, "Perfectly, ma'am. I will not let him win."

With her examinations and paperwork for the moment all caught up, Ruth Anne Marsh—knowing from experience that idle time's the enemy—decided what she needed most was to get back to her roots as a teacher. As much as a book and a bath—and a bottle of wine—was the go-to remedy for most of her colleagues and friends, Ruth instead called the graduate assistant who had been covering her Introduction to Criminal Forensics course and arranged to teach the day's lesson herself via a webcam in her room.

Her lecture began by giving her students an honest look at what forensic fieldwork was like—the adequate but in no way upscale hotel room, the grease-stained bags of discarded takeout, the darkened flesh beneath her eyes from stress and lack of sleep. While on the one hand television procedurals had done their part to fill the classrooms of forensics programs for the better part of three decades, they had also misled many of those programs' students into thinking they would be a Bones Brennan or Dana Scully, off on endless adventures accompanied by a tall, handsome, quick-witted partner. Her point quickly, visually made, Professor Marsh pulled up a PowerPoint, hit screen share, and reviewed the foundational principles of their field, hoping the refresher would not only help ready the class for the upcoming mid-term, but would spark a potentially crucial insight that might help her solve the case.

Deeply enjoying her lecturer's role—sharing the theories she continually tested and refined through their practical application in her fieldwork, making her better at both—Ruth felt her shoulders sag as she noticed she had almost exhausted her allotted ninety minutes. Although she wished she could keep the class for at least another hour, Ruth stopped the screen share function and said, "These twelve principles I've reviewed with you today are the foundation upon which all forensic science is based. At least according to me, and, even though I'm elsewhere, I'm still the one grading your mid-terms and final assignments this semester... Okay, then. That's all we have time for today, future do-gooders. Try not to party the weekend away... Review your notes on the study of the wound patterns of the Ripper victims by the early forensic scientists of the late 1800s and write up an analysis about what they might tell us about the killer. I expect them in my inbox by Tuesday. Good luck on the midterm that day. Happy Holidays."

Although most of the squares that held the faces of her students—or their chosen avatars—had started disappearing when the PowerPoint was finished, a few of them were still active. A student in one of them raised her hand.

Glad for an excuse to stay a little longer, especially for one of her most promising students, Ruth asked, "What can I help you with, Tina?"

"Just want to make sure you're okay, Doctor Marsh. We're hearing some whispers that your assignment is in Secaucus..."

Ruth smiled. She trained her students to be both diligent and diggers. "Is that so?"

"It is," answered another of the three remaining students. His name was Wally, and although he was less of an achiever than Tina, he was continually trying his best. "And now you're asking us to revisit the Ripper? My uncle has a body shop in Hoboken. Knows a bunch of Hudson County cops. He says the Secaucus killer's a copycat. A serious one."

"As opposed to a serial killer who clowns around with his copycatting, Wally?"

"No, Doctor Walsh. I didn't—have a good weekend Doctor Walsh."

Ultra-sensitivity and forensic science are not such compatible companions, Walter.

In the split second it took Ruth to formulate the thought as Wally disappeared, she noticed the third student had also disappeared. Only Tina remained.

"Is there any way I can help you, Doctor Walsh?" her star student asked.

"Just keep those girls in your prayers. And while you're at it, pray you never draw an assignment like this one."

After Tina's square had vanished, Ruth shut down the teaching platform and lay across the bed.

Within sixty seconds, someone was knocking on the door.

Resisting the impulse to tell whomever it was to go away, or better still, to just ignore the knocker until they left, Ruth got up and went to the door. "Who is it?"

"Uriel Stanton."

How did he know where she was staying? She had taken her own car back to the hotel two nights ago, after their meeting in his Prius.

He's a crime beat reporter, after all, she reminded herself. *And obviously tenacious.*

Unlocking the door, Ruth waved him in before anyone could see him.

"You shouldn't be here, Uriel."

"Sounded like you were teaching. And I heard something about Jack the Ripper."

Ruth motioned him to the desk chair and sat on the edge of the bed.

"Worth revisiting. Maybe they'll see something thousands of other students, MEs, detectives, journalists, and forensics specialists have missed. A few of them are pretty intuitive."

Uriel nodded. "Worth a shot. Listen, Ruth. Let me take you to dinner. You don't have to tell me anything. But I spoke to Michael this morning—he says these aren't random."

Ruth nodded. "He's right. There's a common factor I can't disclose that links the four locations."

"Not that," Uriel answered. "Something else. Something that can only be found 'in the marsh,' he said."

Shaking her head, Ruth answered, "This cryptic-messages-from-the-ether stuff is creepy."

Uriel shrugged. "Just give it a little thought. If Michael said it, it must be important. I have something else as well. I did some digging… Called in a couple of favors… I'll tell you what I know over dinner, and you can confirm or deny with a series of cryptic hand signals."

Smiling, Ruth said, "Intriguing as that is… I never work while I eat."

"Is that some sort of mystical art of Zen forensics thing?"

"Nope. It's a means by which to eliminate the possibility of reaching for a sandwich and winding up with a lung…"

"'Cause there will be lungs at the restaurant?"

"What I'm saying is—"

"Dinner is out. Okay, then. Maybe another time."

Surprised at what was coming out of her mouth, Ruth replied, "Wait a sec. What I started to say was that this case is off limits in our conversation, Stanton. But I definitely do eat dinner. So why not let me get showered and a little bit dressed up and you can meet me in front of the office supply store a couple of strip malls south of here at seven?"

Uriel smiled and stood. "I'll get us a table at Amato's. Their lungs marinara is to die for."

Ruth shook her head. "It's got to be takeout. And no Italian. All that red sauce looks like blood. I don't even want to talk about fettuccini and sausage…"

Uriel laughed as he headed for the door. "You're making this weird, Doctor Marsh. When I pick you up, we'll figure something out."

As Uriel grasped the door handle, Ruth placed her hand on his arm. "Wait a minute, okay? I'm not sure why I'm doing this… You talked about risk and reward. Maybe that's why. The killer's changing things up... mixing and matching the wounds of the original victims. And adding in some new things…"

"Such as?" Uriel asked.

Only hesitating for a second—she had already said too much, so what was a little more?—Ruth answered, "On the fourth victim, he did what amounts to a radical hysterectomy. With seasoned, surgical skill…"

Uriel raised a brow. "Radical is everything, right? The uterus, cervix, ovaries…"

Ruth nodded. "I'm impressed. Maybe that info will help. We need everything we can get. Yesterday morning, Agent Connor got a major dressing down in the mayor's office. More importantly, this psycho could strike again at any time. So continue with your digging, and I'll see you at seven sharp."

Carrera de Jordain (a pseudonym, of course) looked at her Bvlgari Serpenti Tubogas watch—gifted to her by a Saudi prince who had been across the river in Manhattan recently (and secretly) meeting with the US ambassador to the UN ahead of the latest climate change conference—and blew a lock of her auburn-dyed bangs out of her unnaturally emerald-colored eyes.

Custom-made contacts, of course.

The prince's family owned the hotel in which she was sitting, the White Horse Suites at Secaucus Square. And hundreds of acres of developed land around it.

Prime real estate. Just like Carrera de Jordain.

Raising her voice over the running water—what had it been, twenty-five minutes already?—she purred, "Will you be finished in there soon? Seems a shame to get so clean if I'm just gonna dirty you up. Hour one will be up before we know it. *I like to take my time* with my ultra VIPs…"

Which is exactly how Carrera had earned the expensive Bvlgari. That and a willingness to do the kinds of things the other A-list escorts wouldn't.

Sixty seconds later, the sound of the water stopped. As the door was opened, she saw her client for the first time, backlit and beautiful in a drapery of steam.

"You certainly like it hot, don't you baby?" she whispered, rolling seductively across the bed and coming to an alluring position that allowed her muscular, suntanned arms to push her ample, well-formed breasts up and practically out of her Audrey Hepburn dress.

In response, the client said, remaining in the doorway to the bathroom, "I am the Servant. You are the Blood. I am the Passage. I am the Door. I am ready now, my angel. My knife is nice and sharp."

In the split second that it took Carrera de Jordain—originally Gladys Walinski from Donnellson, Illinois—to realize what was happening, she was dead, her head nearly severed from her spine with a single vicious swing of Eugene Gorman Howe's perfectly sharpened blade.

As he set to work on the body, the Voice of the Beast instructed him about what he should remove or otherwise alter/adorn and where it all should go.

They had all the time in the world.

The following morning, December twenty-first, 7:30 AM, SAIC Kevin Connor was leaving the bathroom of his motel—with no drapery of steam to make him backlit and beautiful because the economy line of motels with which the FBI had its contracts kept the water temperature low—when his smartphone buzzed.

Scooping it up as it snaked across the nightstand, Connor read the caller ID and tapped the answer icon. "Good morning, Director Vance," he said, addressing his supervisor at the DTEAU with by-the-book formality until he could ascertain the reason for the call. After four years of working together, the two former All-American football players had worked out a plethora of codes to govern their conduct and honor the number one rule:

You never knew who was listening.

"Agent Connor," Vance replied, signaling that formality was the order of the morning. "I just got off the phone with Captain Saunders, Secaucus Police. He had me on speaker with an extremely agitated Mayor Paramita Laghari."

Jesus fuck and seven angels dancing, Connor thought. *Another murder.*

Connor could hear Vance exhale a long trail of smoke from one of his ubiquitous Marlboros. "I told them both that calling me before calling you was a little out of the ordinary. Do you know what they said, each using slightly different but equally vulgar language?"

"I'm sure you're going to tell me, Mister Director."

"They said that ordinary has no place in a situation where a high-end hotel room is used for dissecting a call girl—or otherwise ornamenting her—so that she has to be carried out in a dozen and a half medical transport containers instead of a body bag."

Connor took as much time as he thought he could get away with before answering.

"I told them I was confident he wouldn't go inside."

"Yeah," Vance answered, tension in his tone. "They told me. What in the name of Christ were you thinking? Your Ripper theory is sound and the Ripper went inside. So to say he wouldn't do that…"

"You know, sir," Connor said, admonishing himself for matching Vance's tension with his own, "I am getting tired of being misquoted by these people. I said I didn't think so. The pattern of the kill sites all being owned by immigrants…"

"Is also sound," Vance answered, his voice a notch less tense. "Because that pattern's been upheld. A Saudi family owns the White Horse Suites at Secaucus Circle, where the fifth vic was hacked into bits. And, although *they* didn't immigrate here, the White Horse's live-in manager is second-generation Argentinian."

Sonofabitch, Connor thought. *This fucker is kicking my ass.* "We are doing everything right and by the book, sir. We've got plainclothes dressed like hookers, as food vendors… We've got marked and unmarked cars in his operating area. It's like he knows and changed his stratagem."

"That's exactly what he did. He went high priced. Exclusive. An escort preferred by politicians and celebrities named Carrera de Jordain. Had an $18,000-dollar watch on her wrist—which was still connected to the hand with very little beneath it. And that hand, Agent Connor, was shoved inside—"

"I'll read it in the report, sir," Connor said. "I should be at the crime scene. Unless this phone call is to summon me back to Langley..."

Vance exhaled more smoke. "It is not to summon you back. But be advised—you are walking into a shitstorm. Last night, the *Star Ledger* and *Eastern Standard* each received Dear Boss–type letters from fantasizing wannabes. Details inaccurate, psychological analysis of the handwriting far afield from the profile of the unsub, which actually makes it worse. We've got enough hay to pick through already without this kind of chaff. And there's more... there are messages in chalk full of a lot of nonsense showing up in alleyways where the prior victims were killed. This guy's got Secaucus by the throat and all the serial killer fantasists are helping out their hero. You've got to get this guy."

"Doing my best, sir."

"So find a better best."

Then the line went dead.

Ruth had just described to Uriel what was on the other side of the hotel room's door when she spotted SAIC Connor pushing through a crowd of hotel staff and curious guests the police did not have the time nor patience to herd away.

"Agent Connor," she said, her eyes going wide and her cheeks getting red. "I know you know Uriel Stanton from the *Eastern Standard*. He was just checking up on me and was on his way to breakfast elsewhere."

Connor raised a brow. "Are you two an item? No matter... I want Stanton to stick around."

Uriel, pulling his pad from his leather jacket pocket, said, "That so, Agent? Can I ask you why?"

Ushering the doctor and reporter to the end of the hallway, where it was quiet and a bit more private, Connor said, "This is all off the record for now. Behave and that will change. We're getting our asses kicked by this guy. I need help. There are whispers about you Stantons... about your brother Michael specifically. I know he's helped several intelligence agencies now and again, on account of supposed visions or messages he gets..."

Pitying Connor, who looked uncomfortable, yet also admiring his courage for thinking outside the box in service to the case, Uriel answered, "They screwed him over recently... about the plot to kill the governor. But yeah, it's all true what you've heard. He's been getting messages about this case for several days..."

Connor stepped forward, his corneas filled with fire. "What? What kind of messages? How long you been holding onto this, Stanton? Christ Almighty and his chorus! Waiting to be certain what your angle's gonna be? Thinking Pulitzer maybe... The more girls dead the better?"

"Enough, Kevin!" Ruth hissed, stepping between them, arms outstretched. "He was sharing the messages with *me*. There wasn't much I thought you could use, and I didn't want to be dismissed from the case because you thought I was insane."

Taking a few steps back, Connor rubbed his chin. "Fair enough. Sorry, Stanton. We're all on edge and operating far from our best. I know you're halfway decent as crime reporters go. Some ancestor of yours worked the Ripper case, correct?"

Uriel, still bristly, answered, "Correct."

"So, what do you have from your brother?"

"Not much," Uriel said, grateful to get down to business. "Michael says the voices are getting louder but less specific. Ruth should have faith in herself. That'll she find the connection that exists between the girls..."

Connor again raised a brow. "A connection between the victims, besides being sex workers? How about it, Doctor Marsh? You found anything in that direction?"

Ruth nodded. "I actually think I have. I was going to share it with you before you decided to act like a professional wrestler flexing at the pre-fight interview." Pulling an iPad from the bag on her shoulder, she tapped the screen to wake it up. "I've been coming up empty on a forensic link between the victims... though my gut's been screaming that there is one, just like Michael's been saying. Now I'm positive I've found it. I've been doing blood analysis, including a prelim using a field kit on the call girl from last night. And yeah—just so you know... it's bad beyond description. He basically took her apart. But here's the thing... Turns out all of the victims are Vel-negative."

Connor shrugged his shoulders. "Which means what?"

Ruth went into her browser and opened a bookmarked page. "It's a very rare blood marker. There's a 1 in 88,000 occurrence of Vel-negative being present in someone's leukocytes. So, considering the general population of Secaucus, and the far reduced percentage that are sex workers, you're comfortably out of the realm of coincidence."

Connor backed up, leaning heavily against the wall. "How the hell is our unsub finding that factoid out? And, even if he is, coordinating their working near an immigrant-owned business... There's something not computing. And Stanton... We're still off the record, understand? You don't type a word about this Vel-negative blood marker, or I will personally destroy you."

Uriel nodded as he flipped the pages of his notepad. "Listen, Agent Connor. Considering you already dislike me, I have to let you know... I did some serious digging. Twenty-two years ago, in San Francisco, there was a Jack the Ripper copycat. You were barely out of the Academy and were an agent on the case. You never caught the guy."

Connor's eyes were again aflame, although he held his position against the wall. "You kidding me, Stanton? You going to print that too?"

Uriel shook his head. "Not in the early articles. Once all is said and done, and regardless of the outcome, I think that people should know. Don't glare at me like that... Believe me, Agent Connor, I'm cheering for you to win this. It's driving my brother insane. I need this rampage ended, just as much as you do."

"Okay then," Connor said, crossing his arms. "Our guy in San Francisco... He was pure copycat... every nick, every cut, every organ. He up and quit after he killed the fifth. Just... disappeared. In almost every serial killer case, when that happens, the guy is either dead or incarcerated. But San Francisco wasn't the first or only. I've been tracking cases with similar kill patterns for over a decade. Nebraska. Oklahoma. Virginia. Vermont."

Uriel resisted the urge to jot the states in his notepad. "California was the only case I could find..."

"Like I said, the others are simply patterns, not strictly copycat-Jack. He's imaginative, switching up his inspirations. Sometimes it's Gacy, sometimes Dahmer, once it was Richard Ramirez. In Nebraska, it was Ed Gein with aspects of Zodiac... Six months ago, there was a murder in Ingleside, near Langley. All the markers of Mary Nichols. A warm-up. A way to get my attention. How he lets me know it's him. It's the reason why I'm here."

Before Uriel could confirm what he thought that Connor was saying, a middle-aged detective with a gin blossom and a belly was interrupting them by clearing his throat.

"Sorry to disturb the pow-wow, little injuns, but we just got word, Agent Connor," Detective "Gin Blossom" Chase said, cracking a yellow-toothed grin. "Our unsub left us a triple… storage room in the basement of Giakoumakis's Gym and Health Spa, other side of town. Another bloodbath. Took advantage of us all being here, fucking around for hours like police academy first-weeks…"

Seven hours later, sitting in a rental car in the parking lot of his motel, scouring a map of Secaucus he had studied for hours every day for nearly a week, Kevin Connor was tempted to buy a bottle of something strong, head through the Lincoln Tunnel, and not stop driving until he ran out of gas.

If it wasn't for the knock on his window, maybe he would have done it.

The three masseuses that the unsub had hung upside down and bled like pigs in the basement of Giakoumakis's Gym and Health Spa were underage illegals most likely brought in on a boat and purchased by Nikolaos Giakoumakis to provide an array of "special services" for his customers away from prying eyes.

Now, in addition to the horrific slaughter of eight women, they had uncovered a sex crime committed by an immigrant, and the mayor was on a rampage.

When this case was over, Connor would be lucky if he could be a traffic cop in Iowa.

Pressing the button on the door to bring down the passenger-side window of the Taurus, Connor rolled his eyes as Uriel Stanton and Ruth Anne Marsh crammed their knit-capped heads inside the opening.

"Unless you have a bottle of bourbon and the name and address of the unsub, take yourselves elsewhere immediately."

In silent response, Uriel dangled a set of keys.

"Those to the unsub's house and car?" Connor asked, tempted to hit the button and send the window upward into their necks.

"They're mine," Uriel said. "Well… they were. Lost them a year ago. So I thought. My brother Michael had taken them… he must have. It was his writing on the overnight delivery package."

"Congratulations… I'm sure you and your keys are happy to be reunited."

Connor heard Ruth Anne Marsh release a frustrated grunt of air.

"I get it, Agent," Uriel replied. "Eight girls in less than a week and you're looking like an asshole. A lot of people are. The point of my keys being back is that this thumb drive hanging from the ring… this wasn't on it when I lost them. It isn't mine."

Connor was suddenly paying attention. "What'd you find?"

Ruth shook her head. "We wanted to find you first. Figured there might be a case-breaker on it and this unsub works so fast, we didn't want to delay."

Grabbing his laptop from the passenger seat and getting out of the car, Connor motioned with his head toward the entrance to the motel. "Let's go inside and see if your brother's really got the gift."

Ten minutes later, hot cups of coffee in hand, they sat around a table in Connor's room. Looking prayerfully toward the sky, he inserted the thumb drive into one of his laptop's 3x USB ports. He leaned forward expectantly as its tip began to blink.

Clicking on an icon, Connor said, "It's an audio file. Let me get the volume cranked on this government-issue POS and we'll give it a listen."

The voice that came out of the speakers sounded to Connor as though it had been electronically altered: *Chemo-bio warfare is as old as "civilized" man. Poisoned wells and arsenic sending children's souls to Moloch before the time of Christ. Bodies bloated with puss and pox launched in castle siege. Mist from sticks from the Hooded Ones in the days of Bubonic Plague. Small pox, gifted in blankets, to decimate the tribes. Wilfred Owen, World War One, writing poisonous pomes of mustard gas, which blinded hellbound Hitler, giving vision beyond art. Giving rise to Vril and Thule, which made a Fuhrer feared. Paperclip holds the pages of the secret, sinister projects, funded by the generals keen to kill in droves. V-series nerve agents. US corporate oligarchy helping Hussein gas the Kurds. Fluoride flooding waterways. FDA favors for Rumsfeld's dirty baby, Aspartame. Japanese subway Sarin. Newsroom anthrax daggers. Science and technology birth global mass-man death squads. Wuhan's Special Blend, 2020 through '22. Beware the shadow technic and the rook that roosts within. Industrial–intelligence Icarus flying saucers to the sun. In the dark of Winter Solstice the trio must be cut. Sacrificing prostitutes is portal-prying prelude. The ingredient is rare, the needed donors nine. After the Beast-thing seeks the swamp, the plague will be unleashed, and all the plagues of yesteryear will seem like sniffles and coughs.*

Connor stared at the wave amplitudes displayed in blue across the length of the sound file. "I want to send this to our tech guy at the DTEAU. I want to hear it and see the display without these add-on effects. The amplitudes are odd..."

"Those aren't effects, Agent Connor," Stanton said. "That is the voice of something else. Something that isn't human, though it can pass itself off as one. Something that comes from the place halfway between biblical Heaven and Hell that has been talking to certain male members of our family for many hundreds of years." Not getting a response, Uriel pushed back his chair and stood. "I'm sorry about this, Agent. I really, truly am."

"What the hell are sorry for, Stanton?" Connor asked, also getting up. "Your brother just gave us a win."

As the rented Taurus carrying the trio wove through Sunday's Christmas shopping traffic at an unsafe, nausea-inducing speed, a blue police light flashing and blaring from its roof, Uriel, gripping the back seat with both his hands, asked, "What was it, Agent? What in all that gibberish about the history of biochemical weapons gave you a clue as to where to go?"

Keeping his eyes on the road, with quick glances in his side and rearview mirrors, Connor said, "Most of it I can't divulge. The larger picture that makes that insane-sounding monologue make any sense at all is highly classified. Something we've been tracking at DTEAU for a while. Which means your brother *knew* I would be listening. He included certain references, certain code names we've been using, that were sure to get my attention, same as the unsub does. Whatever this being is that talks through your brother is giving us one last chance to stop the ritual that's in progress before whatever this rampage is *actually* about becomes considerably worse than nine dead Vel-negative prostitutes in downtown Secaucus, New Jersey."

Keeping his eyes toward the floorboard, Uriel said, "You don't seem at all unsettled by what you heard on that recording. I find that odd."

"I'm plenty unsettled, Stanton," Connor shot back, glancing at his dashboard-mounted GPS and making a hard right turn. "For starters, the bit about the trio on the Winter Solstice. Your brother and his ventriloquist collaborator *knew* those kills were coming. Yet they chose to send an audio recording via overnight shipping rather than make a timely effort to stop them. Why the hell might that be?"

For the first time since entering the Taurus, Ruth joined the conversation. "You can't hold Uriel accountable for that. His brother's mentally ill. Functional at times, but trying to unpack his rationale is all but impossible to accomplish. Maybe they knew only that it would be three, and the date. Talk about a needle in a haystack…"

Uriel put his hand on the doctor's arm. "Thanks, Ruth. But he's right. Michael had been calling me every morning. He called me Saturday, which is the day he sent the keys with the thumb drive. If I had an explanation, even a theory, Agent Connor, I would gladly share it."

Taking a last minute left, Connor said, "Fair enough. For now. You asked me what gave me a clue as to where we needed to go." Easing a bit off the accelerator, the agent made an unexpected right, throwing Uriel hard against the door. "See for yourselves."

As Connor hit the brakes and killed the engine, Stanton was out of the car and looking over an embankment in the city park where the Taurus had come to a stop. As Ruth Marsh joined him, Uriel shrugged his shoulders and looked to the agent for answers.

"Look at the sign right there," Connor said, cocking his head to the left.

Finding the sign with his eyes, Uriel read it aloud. "Southwest Amphitheater. I honestly still don't get it."

"I wouldn't get it either," Connor said, "except for this." Pulling the map of Secaucus from his pocket, he pointed to a brown semi-circle in a little patch of green. "See that writing there?"

"I'll be damned."

On the map, in red letters, was the abbreviation SW Amp.

They had found the swamp.

The sun was about to set on the twenty-fifth of December when Eugene Gorman Howe spotted his final victim sitting on a bench by a stand of oak trees next to the amphitheater, just as he knew she would be.

As much as it had frustrated him to have to wait for so many days before he could make the ninth and final kill, he understood the reasons laid out for him each day with unusual patience and detail by the insistent Voice of the Beast.

Making law enforcement wait after the series of rapid strikes was bound to keep them guessing if their target had gotten away. The media was rabid and the blue-boys looked inept. Their operation was costing the city, county, and state chunks of their overall budgets they could not afford and the businesses in the downtown had taken a massive hit to their profits it would take them at least two years to recoup.

Many would not survive. Some were already planning to leave.

That ambitious bitch, Governor Amorata DiMuri, and her probable successor, the immigrant lapdog Mayor Paramita Laghari—the reason the Beast had chosen Secaucus—were never going to recover from the humiliation of eight dead prostitutes the week before Christmas with nary a suspect in hand.

Never mind a ninth on Christmas day.

The Beast had pre-rewarded Eugene for his patience. With the White Horse hotel room rented through the night, the privacy and hours it afforded made the high-end hooker Eugene's ultimate masterpiece, while the three illegal immigrants doing "massages" at the health club were all about the Happy Ending and more.

Three on one was their specialty.

Steel on bone was his.

Stopping thirty feet from the bench where the final sacrifice was sitting, Eugene whispered, "Speak to me, Beast. We've made our last arrival. Wading into the swamp. Shall I dice this waiting whore? The chalice must be cleansed… The Vel must be collected, so the sauce can be concocted, so the plague can be released."

Make quick and vicious work of her, my Changeling. Apply the skills you have been taught. Then you are done with whores. New work must be done. Your model shall be Rader. You will torture, bind, and kill.

Pulling his knife from its sheath, which he'd adorned bit by bit over the years with hair and teeth from his kills, Eugene Gorman Howe, whom the international media would soon introduce as The Changeling, made his way down the steep embankment, carefully keeping his balance as he navigated the slippery grass, the result of a light fall of snow. As he descended, he whispered over and over, "Torture, bind, and kill. Women, men, and children. Age is not an obstacle. Not their job, nor where they live. Feed on their adrenaline, harvest their potent adrenochrome. Feed it to the elite. Feed it to the Beast."

You shall kill, and you shall write about it. To the papers. To TV. You will brag about your work. Your awesome, admirable work. You shall begin with an Austin family of five and move on to other states, once Connor hears what we've done. We shall leave him clues. He shall drool like Pavlov's dogs, impotent in his failure. Ever useful to our cause.

When he was four feet from the bench, Eugene positioned the knife to slash his target's naked throat, hissing, "I shall be your servant. I shall be the Door. I am ready now, my Master. The number shall be nine."

"No it won't, you fucker. You move an inch, you're dead."

In the blink of an eye, Eugene Gorman Howe found himself facing not one, but a dozen different firearms, all aimed at his head and chest with extreme prejudice. The one closest to him, mere inches from his forehead, was held by the woman on the bench, whom he realized was not a prostitute, but a cop.

"What have you done to me, my Beast?" he screamed, dropping the knife on the ground. "Why abandon me now, when we have come so close? I was ready to cut the ninth. I am ready to go to Austin. Ready to model Rader... I do not understand..."

Connor, resisting the urge to punch the guy in the face to put an end to his gibberish, barked out an order to a nearby knot of detectives, including a grinning "Gin Blossom" Chase: "Get this bastard cuffed and in the transport van before the press arrive."

Howe tilted his damaged ear toward the sky for a moment and then began to laugh. "The press are *already* here, Agent Kevin Connor. Aren't they? Oh, yes. At least one of them is. I hear it on good authority that you had a little help from the Stantons and their butt-boy Benedict Arnold. The price they'll pay for interfering is going to be steep..."

Connor leaned in close as Detective Chase put Howe in a pair of handcuffs, cinching them extra tight. "I'm going to link you to every single one of them, you fuck. These eight and all the others. *Eight*, by the way. Not *nine*. So you failed. Whatever delusional mission you thought you had... Whatever this Beast you claim as your master was beaming into your sick fucking mind, you *failed*. We have the knife and, once we find your lair, we'll have plenty else as well."

Taking the pitch of his laughter up a notch, like some clown-faced comic book villain, Howe shook his head and smiled. "You can try to follow the trail. Start with the hair and teeth affixed upon my sheath. You'll only find the crumbs that I have chosen to leave. And each piece of what I've left you will make your theories more insane. I am The Changeling, Agent. The Beast may be the Soul, but I am the flesh and the bone. I am a thousand. I am one. Your defeat is measured in blood and I tell you, *you are drowning.*"

As Detective Chase, Captain Saunders, and several other representatives of the Secaucus PD were leading Howe away—the media were arriving and that's how it was done—Uriel Stanton and Ruth Anne Marsh joined Connor by the bench.

"You hear any of his bullshit?" Connor asked.

"All of it," Marsh answered. "He's completely out of his mind."

"The Changeling," Stanton said, writing in his notebook. "You give me this and a couple of hours' exclusivity and we can consider ourselves square, Agent Connor."

Connor grunted. "You can have it. Some other beat reporter will just come up with something else. Damned unusual that no one has already. Then again, this crazy bastard will be shouting his nickname every chance he gets. So have it, Stanton. But I do not consider us square …"

Before Uriel could ask what Connor meant, his cell phone started to buzz. Glancing at the screen, he said, "Sorry. I need to take this."

As he stepped away, Connor turned to Marsh. "Thank you, Ruth. You really came through for me on this. Vel-negative in all the victims' typologies gives us our signature. How he got it didn't matter, so he could get it however he wanted. Given enough time, now that we have him in custody, I'll have a trail to follow that will allow me to link him to every life he took. Dozens of cases. Dozens of families without answers. Changeling my ass. Within hours, we'll have his legal name and fingerprints. Nicknames only stick before we give the press the real ones. Then again, today might be my last day on the job."

"You kept him from getting his ninth," Ruth whispered, still chilled by the voice on the recording they had listened to in Connor's motel room four days earlier. "And he's finally off the streets. That has to count for something."

Connor nodded. "It'll be months before we know what we've got. But yeah… we dodged a massive bullet. Whether or not it actually nicked me, time will tell."

As the transport van, with half a dozen police cars front and back, pulled away, followed by several news vans, Stanton approached, his face turned pasty white.

"Uriel," Marsh said, grasping his arm. "You alright?"

"It's my brother," Stanton whispered, choking back tears. "He was picked up a couple of hours ago on the side of the Jersey Turnpike. Naked in a snowbank, in the midst of a grand mal seizure. As they were loading him into the ambulance, he was raving about a Beast... and its minion called the Changeling. Then he went comatose. Completely, utterly gone."

"I'm so sorry," Ruth Anne said, taking him in her arms.

Stanton gently pulled away. "I need to get back to Storm Haven." To Connor, he said, "I don't think this is over, Agent. Not by a longshot. We might just be getting started."

As he watched the reporter walk away, Connor thought about what the Changeling had said, and he knew that Stanton was right.

VOX ABDUCTUM

Sometime in the not too distant Present.

"Son of a *bitch*!"

Domestic Threat Early Assessment Unit Director Peter Vance slammed his hand against the top of the government-issue—and therefore grossly overpriced and underfunctioning—laser printer in front of him, wishing he had bought an extra pack of Marlboros when he had gone for a late breakfast up the street nearly twelve hours earlier.

Either that, or asked the office tech specialist, Tino "Haxx" Alvarado, to work late and help him accomplish in sixty seconds what had now taken him forty-five minutes of mounting failures to make a piss-poor attempt at himself.

Although he knew that doing so would make his goal of printing seventy pages of interviews, schematics, and witness sketches so he could go home and study them for patterns and parallels all the more impossible to accomplish, Vance poked his index finger into a random series of buttons on the evil printer's keypad.

Maybe that's why he did it. Home was where his bed was, and bad things happened when he tried to fall asleep there.

Stifling another expletive as the Hewlett-Packard POS-666 (which was, of course, not the official model name and number) began to bark and beep at him, Vance tried to gather himself together as he heard a pair of creaky patent leather shoes approaching on the supposedly sound-absorbing government-gray carpet that led to his bulletproof glass–enclosed office space.

"Unless your nickname is Haxx, go the hell away," he spat at his open doorway, meaning every word he said.

Despite his warning, the considerable bulk of the bloodhound and former All-American University of Illinois tight end that was SAIC Kevin Connor was now darkening his doorway.

"You alright, Pete? Printer trouble again?"

Wheeling his ergonomic office chair—one of the perks of being a unit director—away from the still-barking/beeping printer, Vance rifled through his desk drawers looking for a box of Marlboro reds that wasn't empty.

It simply wasn't to be.

"What the hell are you still doing here, Kev? After what you just went through in Jersey, I would think you'd take advantage of, if not the headshrinker-recommended leave of absence, than at least banker's hours for the next couple of weeks."

Sitting his impressive frame on the printer, which stifled and then stopped the migraine-inducing beeping and barking, Connor grunted. "I dislike bankers more than I do serial killers. At least the latter cut you to shreds while they're looking you in the eye. Besides, I still have piles of paperwork to wade through. There are moments I think I'm close to having it all cataloged and analyzed... then another box comes in. And this psycho's diaries make Poe look like a staff writer for Hallmark. It'll be months accounting for the carnage. Why you yelling? It was a bit much, even in matters concerning your old pal Ball-Breaker."

Ball-Breaker was the name Tech Specialist Alvarado had given the printer.

Vance leaned back in his chair. "Bitch of a headache. Haven't eaten since this morning."

Connor patted him on the knee. "Not to play mom, but call it a night, son."

"Can't. Got an influx of data to go through. Some of what I saw in New Mexico illuminated links to other incidents, other secret bases... I was in the USAF and Naval Research Laboratory databases—the ones I'm allowed to access—and I'm excruciatingly close to cracking the whole UAP phenomena, soup to nuts."

Connor raised a brow. "That's a little grandiose, Boss..."

Vance stood his ground. "So be it. Because it's accurate. I'm gonna get some coffee. You want?"

Connor shook his head. "Nah. Just makes the crime scene photos that much harder to handle."

"We make a mighty pair." Standing and stretching his arms and legs, Vance asked, "Can I get you anything at all? Bagel? Slice of pizza? There's a new Chicago-style place just opened less than a mile down the road..."

Balancing his frame on the edge of Vance's custom-fitted chair— which was far too narrow to accommodate Connor's hips—as his boss moved for the doorway, the SAIC pushed a few buttons on the computer keyboard and the printer began its work.

"I'm good," he said, turning to Vance with a smile. "And now *you* are as well. And nobody does Chicago-style pizza—"

"Except for Chicago," Vance said along in perfect rhythm. "I figured you got hooked on the Jersey version anyway..."

"God forbid!" Connor answered, following the director out the door and heading for his workstation—one of half a dozen filled with large-screen monitors and color-coded maps. Easing himself into his *not* ergonomic chair, he called out, mimicking and exaggerating Vance's usually subtle Oklahoma drawl, "Yer welcome, hoss!"

Deciding not to respond, Vance headed for the elevator, which would take him from the seventh floor, where the Domestic Threat Early Assessment Unit was located, to the building's subterranean parking garage. Placing his hand and retina in the positions needed for the bio-scan security equipment to identify him and open the elevator doors, Vance glanced back at the warren of softly glowing workstations where his team of agents identified, tracked, and almost always thwarted those wishing to do harm to the United States from within.

Kevin Connor was back at his desk, no doubt examining the details on a series of color eight by tens that would make your average citizen puke.

Riding the silent, hi-tech elevator to the parking garage, Vance headed for his car—a nondescript Chevy Tahoe painted the obligatory government black. Getting in, hitting the keyless start button, and turning on the radio, Vance gave a quick glance in the mirror and backed out of his spot.

As he headed toward the exit, an attractively husky twenty-something female voice followed up the end of a Muddy Waters blues cover by the Rolling Stones with an announcement that her faithful late-night listeners were about to hear the latest on a story that had gripped the nation for weeks.

Thank you, Lacey, an authoritative middle-aged male voice intoned. *Our lead story tonight is an update on a series of gruesome murders that has held the city of Secaucus, New Jersey, population seventeen thousand, in the grips of terror for the past two weeks. A spokesperson for the FBI told reporters today that they are confident they have in custody the prostitute-preferring serial killer who has dubbed himself The Changeling. Despite involvement from local law enforcement and at least two FBI units, The Changeling, whose real name authorities are withholding from the public at present, had eluded investigators while ritually slaughtering eight prostitutes in the northern New Jersey city of Secaucus. Complete details have yet to be released, but Special Agent in Charge, Kevin Connor, working out of the Domestic Threat Early Assessment Unit in Langley, Virginia, recently told reporters—*

A burst of static obliterated the rest of the sentence.

"What the hell?"

Pressing the preset buttons and, when that yielded nothing but continued static, turning the tuner back and forth, Vance exited the parking garage and hit the gas, hoping it was the non-descript, shielded and secure federal building that had caused the interruption at the worst possible moment.

Two blocks later, he turned the radio off. The static was beginning to make his head hurt.

A migraine was the last thing he needed.

Deciding on a convenience store whose owner he knew needed the business, Vance turned on his blinker and started to turn onto a side street.

The Tahoe's engine stuttered, roared to life in a burst of RPMs, and then stalled.

Not bothering to try to restart it, Vance gripped the wheel and whispered, "Not now. Please not now. Please!"

He then heard the familiar sound of a UAP beginning to descend from right above his car, its low, pulsing hum (*people say they are silent... they aren't!*) triggering a blinding headache, causing him to moan softly in pain.

Then his vision dimmed and he gave in to unconsciousness.

Donotlistendonottrusttrusttrustusdonotdonotfeardonotwearehere...

Wearehere...

We are HERE.

WE ARE

"Jesus FUCK!"

Vance awoke with a start, his motion to sit up in the hospital bed in which he found himself hampered by a set of loose wrist and ankle restraints and an IV in his arm.

He knew the voices. He *knew* them.

"What is all this shit? Where am I?" he asked the air, feeling his hands shaking and eyelids twitching from a lack of nicotine.

It must have been at least twenty-four hours since he had had a cigarette...

From a corner of the room, he heard the sound of a desk chair being wheeled across a patch of cheap linoleum tile.

"Director Vance, be easy. You are safe. You are in a... hospital of sorts. A private laboratory... Very well equipped..."

The voice, lightly accented, was clearly of Eastern European or German origin.

Without a clue as to why, Vance trusted it, like the voice of an old college roommate and drinking buddy.

"I was in my car..." he started, sinking into the pillow. "They had come for me..."

Standing, the tall, wiry man, dressed in a lab coat and presumably a doctor, said, "You are confused. Just lie there and rest. I will get you a glass of water."

Will sounded almost like *vill*, reminding Vance of elaborately uniformed Nazi officers in his father's favorite World War II documentaries.

Pouring several ounces of a clear liquid Vance trusted to be water into a plastic cup, the probable doctor ordered, "Drink this—all at once. It will help to settle your nerves."

"What is it? No meds... No sedatives. You put anything other than two Hs and an O in it, Doc?"

"Nothing at all. Trust me. Drink it down. All at once. Trust me."

Trust no one.

The voices again. At least three. Maybe more.

Maybe a hundred.

Reaching for the glass, Vance emptied it in a single swallow as instructed.

Probable Doctor smiled and took back the cup. "That is good. Better, yes?"

Vance nodded. "Sure, Doc. I don't know if I should be here... How I *got* here... We've got doctor/patient privilege, right? You can't tell anyone what I... Although, you have to inform my team. The Domestic Threat—"

"Early Assessment Unit. Yes, I know, and we *have* informed them. They send their very best. SAIC Connor says they are taking care of Ball-Breaker for you... I assume you understand..."

Vance chuckled. "I do. So, again... Client/patient privilege, correct?"

Definitely Doctor nodded. "Correct. I cannot tell anyone what we are about to discuss. U.S. law and the ethics of my profession forbid me. Prevent me from betraying your secrets. But, outside the laws of man, I have no reason to... Why would I?"

Vance took a deep breath. "I work for the government..."

Not the government that runs the government...

Ignoring the chorus of voices, Vance continued. "… a special organization. You wouldn't know about it. Very, very old. Older than America. Not even my supposed superiors know to whom it is I *actually* answer… And to whom *those* seven individuals answer… The Domestic Threat Early Assessment Unit is a sort of front organization—the kind of thing usually set up by the CIA. Which doesn't mean it isn't important or legitimate. My team does excellent work. They are, each of them, the best in the world at what they do. But if they knew who I am. Who I *really* am… Who some of *them* are…"

"You have a high level of clearance. You are an important man. I understand this perfectly. But, you see, I also know of these things— I have known of them for years… Lodges and quorums… Ancient objects of power… For, you see, Director Vance, I also play my role on the venerable stage on which these dramas are performed."

Vance closed his eyes, sinking further into the pillows. "Jesus-God, I'm tired. And I've already shared way too fucking much…"

The doctor tapped him on the thigh. "So sleep. I am going to take some blood, run a series of tests…"

Vance struggled against the restraints. Weakly. "You're not doing any tests," he muttered, beginning to feel consciousness slipping away. "Who'd you say you… I don't…"

The doctor's visage grew dark as he whispered, "Have any say in it, FBI Unit Director Peter Anthony Vance. Absolutely none at all."

As Vance faded away, he heard a series of hums and beeps from a faraway machine, the sounds dancing and distorting in his inner ears and cerebellum until they were indistinguishable from the sounds of the UAP that had been hovering above his car.

Through a red-tinged fog and the ache of straining eyes, Vance attempted to ascertain how long he had been gone. Judging from the position of the sun beyond the louvered blinds on the window by his bed, he had been away for several hours. Away was the accurate word. He was not asleep, nor was he merely unconscious.

Something had *taken* him. Taken him as it had—as *they* had— since his childhood. How many times? At least a dozen. To where, and for how long, he had never been able to calculate with anything close to accuracy.

In the corner of the room, through the red-tinged fog and the pain behind his eyes, Vance saw a shape with many appendages. It was several of his tormentors, crouching low and snuffling like piglets jostling for position in the slop-bin on his great-grandfather's Enid, Oklahoma ranch.

Gripping the cold metal side rails of the bed, he hissed, "Hey! Listen up, you malformed little fuckers! You keep away from me, you hear? I don't want to go to your sinister ship with you anymore, alright? I never did! Not as a boy, not as a college student, and not now! You can't just come and take me any time you—"

He felt a hand upon his shoulder. The grip was cold, firm, and, thankfully, clearly human.

"No one is taking you anywhere, Director Vance. You are safe and presently in my care."

Glancing back at the corner and seeing it was empty, Vance replied, "How long I been asleep?"

The doctor smiled. It should have been pleasant, but it wasn't. "No need for you to know. You obviously needed the rest. But now that you are awake, I wish to take a slightly different approach. To try something new. Hypnotic regression. To take you back to the night that you were brought here."

Vance shook his head. "Listen to me, Doc. I can't just take your word that you've got clearance. You need to show me some ID. Some paperwork or something."

The doctor produced a bright red lanyard from his pocket, on the end of which was clipped a laminated photo ID.

"Do you see here? Doctor A. M. Burgher. I run the psychiatric department at this facility. A branch of the Icarus Institute. Right there... my clearance is clearly indicated. You are an important patient, so they assigned you the top of the pile."

Vance struggled to focus his eyes, to read the contents as the ID rocked back and forth like a hypnotist's pocket timepiece.

Before he could do so, it was back in the doctor's lab coat.

"Now that we have settled your concerns, I must ask you a question, Director Vance. Are you familiar with Operation Paperclip?"

"'Course I am. It brought Nazi scientists and other specialists to America after World War Two, including the founder of NASA, Wernher Von Braun. But so is anyone with access to a search engine and a little curiosity about how America became a neo-Nazi shadow-state. Why do you ask?"

Doctor Burgher leaned in closer. "My grandfather, a psychiatrist, came here through Paperclip. What about Special Project DED-37? Are you familiar with that?"

Vance sat up in the bed, suddenly wide awake. "DED-37? How can you possibly know about... Jesus Christ in a poppy field... You must be one of Reinhardt's people."

Doctor Burgher nodded. "I am. Our grandfathers were recruited by the seeds of what became the Central Intelligence Agency and Department of Defense a few years later and traveled here together. We have known each other since childhood, as did they. Doctor Reinhardt runs that facility and I run this one. So you know that you can trust me."

Taking a moment to think, Vance clicked his tongue and said, "Okay. What do I need to do?"

Moving to the foot of the bed, where he had set up a small table while Vance was gone, Doctor Burgher set a metronome in motion and clicked on a penlight, which he aimed at his patient's eyes.

"Lie back and relax," he whispered, moving back to his original position. "Watch the light, and listen to the metronome. When you feel your eyelids getting heavy, let them close. Breathe in time to the beat. When you are ready, tell me about the night that you were brought here."

Feeling fully compelled to do exactly as the Credentialed Doctor asked, Vance tried his best to remember. "Working in the office... going over reports of recent sightings of UAPs... eyewitnesses, physical evidence at landing sites, interviews with cops... a couple had seen a classic saucer ... two pilots had it on radar... FAA had nothing, an eastern Ohio Air Force base denied anything in their airspace... But similar to other recent sightings... New Mexico... "

"When did you leave the office?"

"11:30... I'd been at it awhile. Needed a break. Coffee. I'm in the car, and the radio goes to static. It's exacerbating this headache I've got. Then the car goes dead. I'm... I'm not sure I can do this... I'm awfully goddamned tired..."

Doctor Burgher put his free hand on Vance's own. "You're doing very well. We are very close to answers. Please continue."

"I'm seeing this light, like it's radiating out from a door inside my head... not coming from outside... nothing to do with my eyes. It's like... like a chick of pure energy hatching from an egg that's coated in plasma... taking my thoughts as it breaks out of my skull... Jesus, I sound insane..."

"Not to me. Keep on with the telling."

"After the light subsides, I glance at my watch... It's 1:40 a.m. I've lost two hours. *Two hours*... And there's something about that time frame, the radio static, the blinding light in my head that seems familiar. Completely, coldly familiar…"

"In what way?"

Pulling his hand from beneath the doctor's and turning away from the light, Vance said, "I can't, Doc. I get it about your clearance, your role in secret programs, who it is you work with, but you gotta understand. I don't date—too afraid of pillow talk… Mumbling in my sleep… I'm deeper and way further out than special ops, way beyond Top Secret. The CIA, DHS, NSA… None of them know what it really is we do. Definitely not those blue-suited cock-blockers in the Air Force… Domestic terrorism monitoring and prevention yeah, but that ain't a quarter of it…."

Doctor Burgher chortled. "And DED-37 is so well known to those agencies, Peter? I appreciate your commitment to your oath, to staying loyal, but you can trust me."

Trust him… Trust them… You mustn't trust… You have to trust… Trust no one… TRUST.

The voices were back, overlapping and layered in Vance's mind.

"I don't trust *anyone*, Doc. Especially after what I saw in New Mexico a couple of weeks ago. Sounds paranoid, but this goes crazy deep… Way beyond that tabloid 'I married an alien from Andromeda' bullshit. I am talking actual, persistent alien contact and abduction… The type of Close Encounters phenomena DED-17 handles… Their predecessors were technical advisors to Steven Spielberg… I should not have shared any of that information with you… It's like I took a truth serum… Sodium pentothal…"

Rather than answer, Doctor Burgher switched off the penlight and then the metronome.

"Let me get you water," he said, heading for the pitcher and filling a clear plastic cup to the top. "And a cigarette. Would you like a cigarette?"

Vance felt himself smile. "Jesus, yeah, I would. It's like you read my mind."

Pulling a box of Marlboro reds from his lab coat pocket, Doctor Burgher said, "I am trained to be intuitive—so I can do what must be done. What is best for my subjects. My *patients*. For you. Here you are."

Vance pulled a cigarette from the packet, first inhaling the tobacco and then moistening the filtered tip with his lips. "You got a lighter?"

As Doctor Burgher produced a lighter from his monogrammed dress shirt pocket, Vance was sure he saw the twin lightning bolts that were the symbol of the Nazi *Schutzstaffel* emblazoned at its center. Instead of pulling away, he leaned in closer to light the cigarette. *Nicotine despite Nazis. Nicotine despite Nazis.* Enjoying the whiff of butane and taking a deep drag, he held it for what seemed an hour, saying through the slow, languorous exhale, "Christ, that's good. You think the nurses will mind?"

"Not at all. Not for such an important patient. Now for the water. Drink it down. All at once. A single swallow, if you please."

Again, FBI Unit Director Peter Anthony Vance did exactly what the nice Nazi doctor told him to.

Taking the cup, Doctor Burgher said, "Good. Now you can say what you need so badly to tell me."

Closing his eyes and enjoying another long drag from the cigarette, Vance ran his hand through his thick, graying hair. "While I was in the car, with the static and the light, I saw an alien ship, hovering above me, after the engine stalled."

Doctor Burgher nodded, taking the spent cigarette and placing it in an ashtray. "Describe to me what you saw. And please, my friend, spare me not a single bit of specifics."

Vance grimaced. "What it looked like? I don't know, Doc. I've thought about it a lot. Every time it's happened. It's incredibly hard to describe. I guess it's…"

Again the voices spoke, filling his head like a rowdy herd of Sooners before a football game in Norman:

a football field across—30 feet in diameter—blotted out the sky— whole galaxies spiraling inside—hovering—holding its position— moving at a high rate of speed—too slow to be a meteor—1,000 miles an hour—straight up in the sky—a single craft—half a dozen ships— several little ones split off from the mother—cigar-shaped— triangular—like a hub-cap—egg-shaped—like a saucer—Buck Rogers—it looked like an acorn—bright green fireballs—silver discs—like a dumbbell—luminescent—double rows of windows—dull metal—markings around the rim—hieroglyphics—reflective—no numbers or symbols—smooth–glittering…

Amid the cacophony of voices, Vance managed to say, "It had rows of lights and sounded like…" before he was once again drowned out:

blinking—rotating—shifting—swirling—stationary—red—colored—turquoise—blinding white—it was absolutely silent—swallowing sound—digesting it deep within its bowels—a low hum—guttural—had a high-pitched whine…

Then they were gone. Utterly, totally gone.

Vance licked his lips. "No doors. No windows. I was taken inside. Inside a… a… *ship*…"

Doctor Burgher whispered, "You are doing fine. Your level of recall is astonishing. Truly off the charts."

"The room itself was warm, although the tilted table to which I was strapped was cold beneath my body… From what I could see from the white-hot spill of the lights—like the ones you use in surgery—there were tubes in every hole in my naked body—my mouth, my ears, my ass… sucking out the fluids—snot, saliva, piss from my bladder… semen… They took my semen. My friggin' *semen*, Doc…"

"Don't dwell upon the memories. Just keep telling and they are harmless. Just keep telling and they will fade. We *want them* all to fade…"

Swallowing hard and craving another cigarette, Vance continued. "Felt like my teeth were floating in fluid, ready to fall from my gums… Monitors all around—bright green data on jet-black screens—numbers, letters, symbols—cascading—things I'd never seen… *Cipher codes*… I was looking for the bastards, but I couldn't see them… Just reflections in the stirrups, difficult to describe…"

"No need to try."

Opening his eyes, Vance said, "I'm not nuts."

Handing his patient a fresh cigarette, already lit, Doctor Burgher answered, "Of course not. There are explanations—scientific, spiritual, hallucinatory… Something you've seen on TV—documentaries, *X-Files*… The lies your interviewees tell you so they can get your attention… Tricks of light mistaken for flying saucers… Malfunctioning radar arrays. Swamp gas, sand cranes, weather inversions, weather *balloons*… So hard to know. To be sure."

Lies—truth—mostly truth—mostly lies—all of this is lies—all of this is truth.

TRUTH.

"The subconscious is powerful," Doctor Burgher continued. "It is responsible for eighty-five percent of all that we take in, did you know that? Waking dreams are often to blame in these cases... Nightmares, or *Alptraum* in the language of my ancestors. Did you know the word for nightmare in German is also the word for incubus? The monsters that come at night from the neural-network primordial forests of the overworked, overstressed mind. Then there is the phenomenon of confabulation. Abduction stories are as prevalent as fairy tales, as *märchen*. Travis Walton watched a TV movie about Betty and Barney Hill two weeks before his own supposed abduction..."

Dragging hard on the Marlboro, Vance shook his head. "I interviewed Walton. I've spent hours with Calvin Parker. And dozens of others. Read the transcripts of their regressions... Listened to the secret recordings of their private conversations in between formal interviews their local police departments conducted. Analyzed the lie detector data. They were telling the truth. I would swear to it in court. What they say happened, *happened*.... And I know it all the more, 'cause the very same things have periodically happened to me. They've happened since I was five, at least a dozen times. That's why I do what I do—I need to know what's been happening to me. To others. *Thousands* of others. To puzzle out the clues, to section out the memories..."

Now it was Doctor Burgher who was shaking his head. "But there aren't any. It is all just in your mind."

"It can't be! 'Cause it *hurts*. When they do those things to me."

Switching off the light by the bed, Doctor Burgher whispered, "Rest now, Peter. Later, we will go further. Together, we will make you forget."

"Peter. Peter, my beautiful boy. Time to wake up, sweetheart. Time for us to go."

Vance shifted position in the bed, the pillows blocking his view of what sounded like his mother.

My mother? Here?

Shaking his head to try to clear it of the cobwebs the mind-spiders had spun and hung while he was sleeping, Vance willed his eyes to focus on the woman next to his bed, in the spot where Doctor Burgher usually stood.

"Mom? Mom. My God... What are you doing here?"

"I'm here, too, son. Doctor Burgher called us in."

Sure enough. There was his father, in his usual denim work shirt and ever-present crimson and cream Sooners baseball cap.

Mrs. Vance smiled, taking her son's hand in both of hers. "We caught the first flight out."

Looking at his father, Vance said, "You flew?"

Shrugging his shoulders, Mr. Vance (who, Peter now realized, clearly *wasn't* Mr. Vance) said, "Doc said it was urgent."

"You've been working too hard, Peter," Mrs. Vance (clearly not his mother) said in an impressive approximation of his mother's sing-song voice. "The stress of your position… Trying to prevent terrible people from doing terrible things…"

Not-Mr.-Vance nodded. "It's heroic what you do, son. Domestic threat assessment. Thwarting those goddamned terrorists. But Doctor Burgher suggests a prolonged leave of absence—"

Not-Mrs.-Vance: "To clear your head… To keep reality squarely that, without conflating some less than happy memories from your childhood into something they are not."

Mom's no moron. But psychology isn't her strong suit. Nor are silver-dollar sentences like that one.

Not-Mr.-Vance: "Get yourself healthy. Re-focused. Re-charged. Like back when you were voted All-American. Bowl games were your bitch. Get yourself back to *that* guy. No more of your raving on and on about these crazy-ass fantasies…"

That did *sound like Dad.*

But it wasn't. Not if he flew…

Deciding for the moment to play along, Vance replied, "You have no idea whom I work for. The cases I'm privy to. The state *secrets*. And you, Mom—you know what's happened to us. All *three* of us, since I was a kid. You know damned well these aren't some 'crazy-ass fantasies'…"

Not-Mrs.-Vance's eye twitched. "No I don't, Peter. I don't know what you mean. True, your father drank. And sometimes he went too far, especially when you were small. And I should have said something, but he always took good care of us. And the Vietnam War was hard on a lot of scared young pilots like him, so far away from home… Now I understand, with Doctor Burgher's help, how you turned those terrible memories into abductions by aliens because the truth was just too hard to assimilate." Turning away to gather herself together—so Vance surmised—she turned back with a full cup of water. "Here, sweetheart. Drink this down. All at once. It'll settle your—"

Vance knocked the cup out of her hand, where it clattered to the floor.

"This is bullshit!" he yelled. "I don't know who hired you. But you're not my goddamned parents. My mother *told me* about her abduction experiences. She talked to the parish priest about them! And my father? My father hasn't gotten within a thousand feet of an airplane since his A-6 was shot down over Laos in 1968. And this horseshit about him being *abusive… Fuck* you people."

Pulling what Peter now realized was a brand new Sooners cap—not his father's tried and true, stained and frayed "rally cap"—from his balding head, as if unconsciously outing himself as an imposter, the man pretending to be Mr. Vance moved to the door. "I'll go and get the nurse."

As Not-Mr.-Vance opened the door, Doctor Burgher entered, his dark eyes wide with concern. "No need. I was listening to it all. Why would Reinhardt send me such a pair of bunglers? I've brought a sedative. If you'll be so kind as to hold him."

While Not-Mrs.-Vance retreated to the furthest corner, Not-Mr.-Vance dropped the Sooners cap, grabbed Peter's upper arms, and threw his weight against him to keep him pinned to the bed.

Doctor Burgher, hypodermic raised, began his approach.

"Get that needle away from me!" Vance screamed. "Get—"

A pinch as the plunger descended. In rolled the red-tinged fog. It had never been so thick…

Shoving Burgher against the wall, and pulling the used hypodermic needle from the doctor's hand and pressing it lightly into his neck, Not-Mr.-Vance whispered, "How the hell did your people miss the A-6 incident?"

"It must have been deeply classified. Our team is usually flawless."

Emerging from the corner with all the confidence of a seasoned contract killer—which she was—Not-Mrs.-Vance said, "We are *not*, bunglers, Burgher. *You* are. So tell your bosses… We expect to be paid. In full."

Not daring to nod with the tip of the needle pressing into his neck, Doctor Burgher said, "You will be. Use the service elevator. When he awakens, I'll say it was a dream."

Dropping the hypodermic needle on top of the abandoned Sooners cap, Not-Mr.-Vance followed his partner out of the room.

Picking up the abandoned items, the Sooners cap included, and placing them in the room's bright red biohazard bucket, Doctor Burgher turned to Vance's unconscious form. "What am I to do with you, Peter? Why won't you forget? Now you are forcing me to do things the way my grandfather and father did when they worked with Joseph Mengele…"

Opening the closet, Doctor Burgher wheeled out a cart containing a small machine hooked to a heavy-duty truck battery. Affixing half a dozen stick-on probes to Vance's chest and temples, the doctor switched on the machine, adjusting the power dial to full.

As Vance began to scream in his sleep, Burgher grinned.

For what felt like hours, if not days, Vance had been fighting against the fog and the voices, while refusing to forget what had happened to him and his family.

Switching on the machine and turning it up to full, which promptly elicited a scream of pain from his patient akin to that of a vixen having her eyes pulled out, Doctor Burgher said through gritted teeth, "Why won't you forget it all, damn you! Why do you insist on holding on to these hurtful, intrusive memories? They are not real, I tell you! They are not—"

The doctor stopped himself as he heard the commotion of raised voices in the hallway beyond the door.

A rough male voice was saying, with ample Midwestern guff, "Look here, *Nurse*—I said I'm goin' in."

Turning off the machine and wheeling its cart toward the closet, Doctor Burgher said, not looking back, "Time for me to go, Peter Anthony Vance. But we are not yet done."

As the closet door closed behind the doctor, the door to Vance's room flew open with a crash, slamming against the white concrete wall and echoing inside his head.

Entering the room, his FBI-issue Sig Sauer P226 held in front of him in a two-hand grip, Kevin Connor scanned the room for perps before turning to look at Vance. "Jesus, Pete. What the hell have they done to you?"

Behind him, a nurse Vance did not remember ever seeing said, "I'm sorry, sir, FBI or not, Mister Doe has been admitted to this facility with all the proper paperwork. You're not authorized to take him."

Holstering his handgun, Connor shook his head. "Mister Doe? Who the hell *are* you people? That's FBI Unit Director Peter Vance.

He's to be released into my custody *immediately*. Where the hell are his clothes?"

As Connor moved to open the closet, Vance whispered, "He's in there, Kev. Be careful..."

Pulling his Sig Sauer and a flashlight, Connor swept the closet with the tips of both. "Nothing in here, Pete. Except your clothes. Who is this 'he' you're talking about?"

"Listen, sir," the nurse said, a nasty note to her voice, "we have plenty of additional beds on this ward if you insist on noncompliance. All I have to do is push this button and a squad of well-armed—"

Closing the distance between him and the nurse in a flash, and pressing the muzzle of the Sig Sauer to her forehead, Connor said, "Back away from that goddamned button, Ratched! *Now!* I've got a bullet in this gun with a big old set of lips on it, and it really wants to kiss you full on French in your mouth. Now... Back. The FUCK. *Off!*"

Dropping all pretense of authority, the nurse let go of the wand that held the button without pressing it. "Anything you say."

Motioning with his head to the chair on the far side of the room, Connor told the nurse to sit and stay quiet. Turning his attention to Vance, who had managed to stand and start to dress, Connor said, "Jesus, Pete, what the hell have they done to you, brother?"

As Connor helped him into his shirt, Vance replied, "I'm grateful you found me, Kev. Where exactly am I?"

"An underground lab on the campus of Eastern Pinelands U. Been here since the sixties. Been officially closed since Hurricane Loki and the founding of Storm Haven."

Vance shook his head. "Can't be... Storm Haven? The planned city in New Jersey? Wait... Shit. Of course... The doctor was talking about DED-37. The DED program, along with The Ravenskald Group, built and wired Storm Haven. So this must be DED-47. He called it part of the Icarus Institute. We don't get much in the way of access or info for this place. Just a lot of whispers... How the hell did I get here?"

Keeping half an eye and the muzzle of his gun on the nurse, Connor shrugged his sizeable shoulders. "Hell if I know. When you didn't come back to the office the other night, I got concerned. I checked your apartment and when you weren't there, I put the word out far and wide. Coupla agents from the Newark office found your car a few blocks from here two days ago. Guys I made some connections with while I was working the Changeling case. Been forty-eight hours of frustration. Details can wait. But there are things we eventually need to talk about concerning what exactly happened to you here..."

Sitting on the bed and lacing his shoes, Vance said, wincing at the energy it took to accomplish something so easy, "Happily. But I need a couple of days."

"Looks like you've earned 'em."

"Thanks. But I don't wanna wait a second on the details from your end. How'd you track me down, SAIC Connor?"

"Understood, Director Vance. Policeman's luck. Two vics were pulled out of the Raritan River a coupla hours ago. One was still alive. Told us they were hired to play your parents, but the job went south and they got double-crossed by their employers. Died fifteen minutes later, on the way to the hospital."

Heading for the door, and wincing with every step, Vance said, "I don't suppose they gave us any names?"

"'Course not. High-end operatives never do."

"I gotta get outta here, Kev. We have to get back to the office. Pick up those papers you printed for me. Then I know where I have to go..."

Taking his boss gently by the shoulder, Connor said, "As soon as a real doc looks you over..."

"Burgher's real enough. And our priority is to find him. As soon as fucking possible. Contact Haxx and get him to start digging. Use all our IOUs if he has to. I think that Nazi doctor fucker holds the key to this entire abduction puzzle. He and Doctor Reinhardt. It all makes sense... this is the Icarus Institute. Part of it, anyway. DED-17 has a black op program called Project Daedalus. It was part of what I uncovered in New Mexico. Just like NASA, these elite fuckers love to ground their agendas in world mythology..."

"Sounds like craziness to me. Though I'm all in for finding this Burgher bastard. You're saying he's a Nazi? All the more reason to put a clip's worth of caps in his ass. Anything you want from me, you got... But those papers you mentioned... at the office... There aren't any. Nor any digital files. Haxx called me this morning... All the UAP data in the DTEAU computers was wiped..."

"Shit," Vance said. "He said something to me about Ball-Breaker. He wanted to let me know it was them..."

Five hundred miles away, in a locked room deep within the bowls of Quarry Peak Psychiatric Institute (also known to those in the know as

DED-37), third-generation Nazi doctor Albert Martin Burgher (named for Speer and Bormann) struggled against the straps that held him as the machine he had brought from Eastern Pinelands University roared to death-dealing life.

"Someone listen to me," he struggled to say, the effects of the three glasses of "water" he had been forced to drink over the previous twenty-four hours doing their work. "I do not belong here."

From within the walls—perhaps a hidden speaker, or perhaps the insides of his skull—came a sterile, monotone, inhuman answer: *You have failed us, Albert.*

"In what way? I have done nothing wrong. If it were not for me, for my work, DED-47 never would have…"

You were wrong about this subject. His curiosity over-rides your treatments. His determination to know the Truth (the Truth beneath the Truth) is too powerful for your devices, your antiquated techniques. You said you could control him. You said he would forget.

A second voice, no more human, added, *Yet he remembers… No one ever remembers. Not in such detail.*

He's devoted his life… (…devoted his life).

To uncovering the truth… (the Truth within the truth…)

You have failed. (FailedFailedFailed)

You are no longer needed. (You have become superfluous)

Superfluous.

His eyes widening to the point he was certain they would burst, Burgher again struggled against the straps, knowing it was pointless. How many patients had he restrained in this same way as he worked to erase the memories of their abductions and the genetic manipulations that were the prime interest and legacy of the Interdimensional Entities operating in America since the time of Eisenhower's Greada Treaty in 1954? The fledgling military–industrial complex (which Old Ike, his courage failing from the things that he had seen, warned against while exiting the White House) had brought his grandfather to America—given him a nice house, a luxury car, and a generous head start on his savings account—because of his work with Vril and Thule and their interdimensional brethren. His grandfather had been a lover of Maria Orsic's… Perhaps he was secretly *her* grandson as well!

"This is all nonsense!" he struggled to say, a line of spittle hanging from his lips for a moment before slinking down his chin. "I have done well! Hundreds—perhaps thousands—who remember *nothing*. Each of them doing your bidding. Each of them contributing to your *end game!* Some of them, or their hybrid descendants, sitting at this moment in the highest seats of power, bringing Order from the Chaos... Controlling the world for the Ravenskalds! You need me! You *need me*, you hear? You inhuman bastards! I demand to see Doctor Reinhardt!"

In response to this request came a wave of layered laughter akin to the sound of a drill entering the bone at the base of the skull (a sound with which Burgher was exceedingly familiar).

Then the pitch of the machine increased.

And the pain began in earnest.

"No! You mustn't. You must not take me there. I was promised. I was *promised!*"

Things change. Doctor. (ChangeChangeChangeChangeChange)

Burgher, his spittle now turning to foam as it spurted from between his clenching jaws and shattering teeth, moaned and managed to say, "It *hurts!* I was told it doesn't... It's been nothing but endless lies... If I had believed these people... I never would have helped you... You are not the only partners of the priests of the Mammon Lodge. And with darkness comes the light. The Pleiadians are soon to arrive and they will not permit you—"

The laughter/drill increasing along with the pitch and power of the machine became a sinister wave of exquisite pain that carried Burgher to the hinterlands of madness, though not much later—for the IEs meant him no malice—to a welcome and prayed-for interment in their geometric boneyards of death.

THE KITCHENER COUNTY MENACE

Sometime in the not too distant Present.

I don't know, but it's been said, Air force wings are made of lead, I don't know, but I've been told, Navy wings are made of gold…

Singing along—with a much dirtier, non-Navy-sanctioned version of the cadence—Seaman Apprentice Alfonso diMuri smiled and waved at the group of twenty sweating mechanics, radar operators, and aviation trainees struggling to keep pace with their group leader, a Chief Petty Officer, in the early morning, July-in-Ohio heat as they passed the guard shed he shared with Seaman Charlie Donovan.

"Ya gonna get ya'self in trouble one a' these days," Donovan said, punching diMuri lightly in the shoulder while mentally assessing the shapely sweatpants-hugging asses of a pair of female aviation trainees in the middle of the group. "Ya governor-who-could-be-our-next-president cousin ain't gonna be able ta help ya neither."

Such a certain truth has never before been uttered, diMuri thought with a grimace. When he had been assigned to Milton Chase Naval Aviation Training Center, located near an expansive, heavily patrolled forest just outside Pleasant Acres, Ohio, a week after basic training, he never thought that, nine months later, he'd still be standing guard duty at the facility's main gate with a dope like Charlie Donovan.

Aside from an official Office of the Governor of the State of New Jersey Christmas card with an ink-stamped signature, he never heard a peep from his cousin.

Which was truly shitty of her. Dopey Donovan was right. Rumor had it that Amorata diMuri could very well be America's next president.

And here was old Alfonso, from the very same genetic pool, an E-2 loser with no future.

"You know something, Donovan?" he said, raising his voice as five F-35 Lightning II fighter jets went screaming past the gates, "I was supposed to be a pilot…"

"Me too," Donovan answered, plunking himself down on a stool in the guard shack. "Then I flunked third grade. What's your excuse?"

"Seriously. I didn't join the United States Navy to stand sentry at some hush-hush base in Bumshit, East Ohio. I'll never bang a Kelly McGillis look-alike doin' this guardin' the guardhouse shit… I was all set up to go to Annapolis when—"

Donovan flew off his stool and put his hand in DiMuri's face as the radio started to crackle.

"Stow it, dreamer," he said, before speaking into the mic: "This is unit one, Seaman Donovan, over."

We've got a bogey rapidly incoming on the radar, an unidentified female voice reported. *A hundred feet from your position, at roughly ten o'clock. Came outta nowhere. Just above the tree line. Eyes open, fellas.*

Flipping off the safety on his M4 Carbine, Donovan asked, "Whatya mean incomin'? I don't hear or see a goddamned thing at all."

Sweeping the ten o'clock sky with his assault rifle, DiMuri shouted, "We don't have visuals, base! What in the fuck are we looking for?"

Instead of a response from the radar operator, DiMuri heard the unnerving sound of a pair of gigantic wings descending rapidly behind them.

Dropping the radio microphone, Donovan said, pointing at the sky, "What the shit is that, Al? Looks like a fuckin'—"

DiMuri couldn't hear the rest of the sentence over the sound of their M4 Carbines, which they were emptying into the sky as a grey and black, winged and red-eyed demon—seemed insane to him, but that's *exactly* what it was... a *demon* straight outta Hell—was coming straight for their asses, screaming like a fox.

As the demonic monster grabbed Donovan by the shoulders with its long, sharp-clawed toes, lifting him off the ground and skyward, DiMuri, who was slamming home a fresh 30-round box magazine into his smoking rifle, heard the voice from the radio in the guard shack. *Unit one—report! What are you two firing at?*

Hearing the sirens from a dozen high-speed vehicles approaching as the base went into lockdown, DiMuri dropped to one knee as the demon—which had released the screaming but now silent Charlie Donovan from a height of sixty feet—let out another foxlike screech as it came at him, its clawed hands extended and its oversized eyes ablaze.

"A couple of fucking joints!" DiMuri yelled, emptying his clip as the claws of the demon sunk deep into his neck. "A couple of fucking joints or it would have been Annapolis!"

By the time the cavalry arrived, half a minute later, the demon had disappeared, and DiMuri was bleeding out.

"I'm sorry, Mister Stanton, but—as I have told you numerous times—we have no record of your brother Michael ever being admitted to this facility."

Knowing that raising his voice would get him an escort out, Uriel Stanton, lead crime reporter for the *Eastern Standard*—a paper his family had founded almost a century before—took a deep breath and looked the nurse behind the reception counter squarely in the eyes.

"I was told that he was here on very good authority. So maybe your computers are glitching..."

"Perhaps *I* can be of assistance..."

Turning around at the sound of a mature, professionally trained voice that had to be a psychiatrist's, Uriel forced himself to be pleasant. "Hopefully you can, Doctor..." He glanced at the laminated ID card clipped to a lanyard partially obscuring a very expensive tie. "...Reinhardt."

Nodding to the nurse to indicate that he was now in charge, Doctor Friedrich Reinhardt, senior psychiatrist at Quarry Peak Psychiatric Hospital, motioned a second later for Uriel to join him at a table in the nearby, pleasantly appointed waiting room.

"This is very embarrassing, Mister Stanton. I was intending to call you, and here you are..." Reinhardt fiddled with his equally expensive wristwatch, although there was something about the gesture that Stanton didn't buy. "Your brother has... escaped."

"Escaped?"

"Gone missing, as it were. Sometime between group and lunch." Again, Reinhardt fiddled with his wristwatch. "I assure you things like this do not happen at Quarry Peak..."

Uriel shook his head. "They obviously do, Doctor Reinhardt, or we wouldn't be sitting here having this conversation. I'd be visiting with my brother." Much to Uriel's surprise, his comment provoked a laugh. "What the hell do you find so funny?"

At that moment, the persona that would fiddle with a wristwatch completely disappeared. "Understand me, Mister Stanton. Your brother does not have visitor privileges. He was brought here in connection with a series of horrific crimes committed by a serial killer in New Jersey after being found naked and raving near a highway last December... He had important information—the kind that could have saved several women's lives—and he chose not to promptly share it."

"My brother isn't sane!" Uriel blurted out, immediately realizing his mistake.

"Exactly," Reinhardt whispered, his voice as hard as nails. "And his progress these past many months has not been at all encouraging."

Getting his emotions in check, Uriel asked, "What about the contributions he *did make* to the case? Surely DTEAU Special Agent in Charge Kevin Connor—"

Reinhardt raised his hand to face height, effectively cutting Uriel off. "I am familiar with no such agent. And, if I was, I would not share that information with a person such as yourself. Be assured, Mister Stanton—we are not treating your brother as though he is a criminal. He has all of the amenities we offer any of our patients. Although I have to make you aware... His illness is profound. He believes he talks to a fallen angel. He professes to know things that he cannot possibly know. You should have never used his illness to try to obtain a promotion."

Uriel clenched his fists, but otherwise did not move, knowing an array of security cameras and human eyes were on him from every direction. "Listen to me, Doctor... I would never do anything to hurt my brother. It took me all these months to track down where he was. Speaking of which—your nurse-receptionist over there told me there was no record of Michael being here. How do you—"

"Explain that?" Reinhardt cut him off with a tone of complete disdain. "I simply do not have to. The State of New Jersey, with the agreement of the Federal Bureau of Investigation, saw fit to remand your brother into my custody. I have dealt with far worse cases than his. Grandeur with violent tendencies is a specialty of mine."

"That is—."

"Not an off-base diagnosis, Mister Stanton. Not in the least. Interrupt me again, and I will see you escorted out. Do you understand?"

Knowing he had no choice, Uriel silently nodded.

"The receptionist lied because that is our protocol for patients such as Michael. He has no rights while he is here under law enforcement directives and therefore his family has no rights. I said I was going to call you. I meant that. But it was nothing but a courtesy. I am well aware of the effort you have made to locate him. Admirable. You love your brother... I am truly touched. So do what is best for him. Let us find him, treat him, and make our case to the authorities regarding whether or not he is competent to stand trial for obstruction or as an accessory. Will you do this?"

Uriel had no sooner nodded his head in reluctant agreement than Reinhardt was out of his chair and moving toward a bank of elevators as a pair of imposing security guards were indicating with barely veiled hostility that it was time for him to leave.

Five minutes later, locking the doors in his dark blue Prius hybrid, he pulled out his smartphone and scrolled his contacts for SAIC Kevin Connor.

Doctor Friedrich Reinhardt might be a skilled, sophisticated liar, but Uriel had seen through them all.

Michael was somewhere in the building, and he was going to find out where.

Blaine Angeles, failed Las Vegas magician turned paranormal reality TV semi-star, made his combat-booted, skinny-jeaned way through the carefully placed debris and dumpster-extracted and fire-sale-obtained furniture used to dress the hallway of the abandoned hotel he had convinced his British producer, Sylvia Jones DeMont, to buy in his name just a few weeks before.

Waiting for the twin cues of a howling wind and sharp crack of newly purchased soundstage thunder in the Bluetooth earpiece securely duct-taped beneath his long, curly hair and signature *Supranormal Sightings* jet-black beanie (just $29.99 for ultra VIP members of Supranormal Nation on his two-hundred-thousand hits a day website and e-store), Blaine thought of the only thing that really, truly scared him…

Having to go back to doing backyard magic for snot-nosed little shit-kids in the five New York boroughs who had watched every one of the Val Valentino specials and various disgruntled wannabe illusionists' YouTube channels exposing every magic trick and illusion known to man.

He could hear their singsong Satanism in his ears despite the manufactured wind and thunder.

I know how you DOOOOO IIIIIIT! I know how you DOOOOO IIIIIIT!

Dirty little know-it-all, trust fund, prep school, Frankenstein shit-kids.

The increasing volume of the wind and thunder pulling him back to the present, he whispered, "Hour nine in the sixty-six-point-six-foot-long Demonic Hallway to the Haunted Hades Hotel in downtown Cleveland, Ohio. It's 3 A.M. The witching hour. The hour of the wolf—

when the veil between worlds is thinnest and skilled, Tibetan-trained astral travelers and lucid dreamers like myself surf between the planes on the tides of Darkness and Light. The Supranormal Sightings crew, led by me, world-renowned paranormal researcher and bestselling e-author Blaine Angeles, is determined to confront the dark, demonic entities that are responsible for over a dozen disappearances and cold-case murders in the haunted history of this two-hundred-year-old Hotel to Hell. Eight hours ago, as the sun began to set, we smashed our smartphones with hammers, melted the keys to all the padlocks securing the doors with a blowtorch, and poured a bucket of boiling water on the fuse box. There is no getting out. Not for us, and not for them. We're about to open a portal in this elevator, where fifteen-year-old Camilla Consuelos was last seen alive in 1968, before turning up three days later in half a dozen pieces in an icebox down the hall. Camilla, can you hear us?"

Not one to fuck about in post, Blaine listened in his earbud as a faint female whispering began, accompanied by all the tried and true and easily achievable tropes that kept the suckers watching—and believing—week after week. Creaking wood. Rattling windows. Knocks, bangs, and hisses. REM pods, tri-meters, digital recorders, and expensive cinema cameras all beeping, crackling, activating, and deactivating—all controlled by a newbie Google-certified sound engineer making slightly more than minimum wage.

As the sound of nails being pulled from a board filled his ear (made by two production assistants from the local community college actually pulling ten-penny nails from a two by six length of knotty pine with framing hammers), Blaine again thought of pre-pubescent, trust-fund dickbags exposing his illusions (*I know how you DOOOOO IIIIIIT!*). Then, sufficiently adrenalin-tweaked, he shouted, "Are you guys seeing this? The elevator door is vibrating. The buttons are lighting up—even though we killed the electricity—and it's starting to engage. Starting to plow a path to the recently discovered—on this very show—*tenth* circle of Hell. I feel it deep within my exclusive BA signature-soled paranormal hunter collection field boots and straight up like lightning into my supra-activated solar plexus chakra center—cleared for me by a reincarnated *sadhu* on the banks of the Kerayong River in Kuala Lumpur not 90 days ago—that it will reveal to me the truth about what was done to Camilla Consuelos... Where she went, what she met, and where her virgin soul resides."

Right on cue—as the sound engineer revved up the servos and hydraulic jacks hidden in the elevator, causing it to shake—Blaine's earbud filled with the low moans and female whispering and caterwauling produced by a recently out of work late-teens Japanese anime voice actor sitting in a jerry-rigged sound booth at the other end of the hall.

They were having dinner right after the taping.

"Camilla, is that you? You stay away from her, you hear me, you devilish, foul-footed *demons*! You. Can't. *Have*. Her! I won't let you have her again! You will not feast for another sinful moment upon her sacred soul. Her innocent, virgin soul. Camilla! Come to me. Come to your savior Blaine. I am a righteous, Angelic safe zone. Don't you try it, *demons*! Oh… you think you can *possess* me? Moloch did his damnedest. Baal? I banished that bullying bitch to a volcano in the Bahamas! Lucifer lost my number, so don't even *try* to phone me!"

The sound and other effects continued to mount in strength and volume as Blaine continued with his taunts—he was really *on* tonight… he was riffing like a master, like he had in Season 1, when nobody watched, so none of the suits and short-skirts cared what the hell he did. He'd gotten good at the once-and-done, like Pacino and Sinatra as the views and paychecks skyrocketed. But not tonight. Tonight, he'd diverted from the script right after "Angelic safe zone." Sylvia was gonna be pissed, but he didn't give a frightened fuck—*He*, Blaine Angeles (a pseudonym, of course) was the superstar of *Supranormal Sightings* and he was gonna save that virgin soul…

Though it wouldn't be virgin for long…

"Camilla… I can *see* you!" he said—picturing her in his mind, like any pro would do—especially her not-quite-big-enough-for-her-full-and-perky-breasts button-up blouse. "I *will not* let them have you! I can hear their fury. I can feel their *hate*! I can feel them try to *possess* me… Give it your wicked worst, you bestial demons of Hades! Give me all you got! Give me all you—"

Then there was a crash, the elevator door was laying on his boots, and his earbud filled with static.

Dropping his show voice and juicing up his native Brooklyn accent, he screamed, "Jesus God an' *Fuck*! What the hell jus' happened? That damned thing nearly killed me!"

As he began to lose his shit—and the crew's faces all went pale—his producer, Sylvia Jones DeMont, joined him by the remains of the elevator. "Listen closely, everyone! Let us call this horrid mistake a dinner opportunity. Forty-five minutes and we are back to work. Except for the gentlemen who cocked up the elevator! Get it fixed, quick as you can!" Leading Blaine away from the tool-belted trio already attending to the elevator, she said, "Sorry, B-A... The hydraulics must have malfunctioned."

Watching the actress voicing Camilla leave with a damned-handsome executive repping one of their newest sponsors, Blaine asked, throwing his arms in the air, "What am I paying you for, Sylvia?"

Having worked with the biggest pricks and egomaniacs at the Royal Shakespeare Company *and* BBC before conquering American reality shows fifteen years earlier, Sylvia smiled. "Certainly not for script approval. Quite the little night at the improv you were doing for us there."

Retrieving a bottle of thick green "superfood" sludge that lately was passing as his dinner—he'd put on a few pounds over the winter and it was now a meme on TikTok—Blaine grimaced... at the drink *and* at his producer.

"Leave it all in. Every melodramatic word of it. I mean it, Sylvia. I'm done with this idea that somehow I'm not in charge."

Funny how a clipped and proper British accent can produce a testicle-shriveling laugh. "Let me remind you of something, Blaine... *I* produce this show. I created *you, and* I created *Supranormal Sightings*. You do not pay *me*, yes? I pay *YOU*."

Knowing she was right and he'd badly misplayed his hand, Blaine shifted gears. "You think it's easy faking this shit? I never should have quit my magic show in Vegas..."

Again with the nut-shrinking laughter. "You didn't. Your contract was not renewed."

Gulping a foul slug of sludge because it tasted better than crow, Blaine whispered, "Are you trying to ruin me, Syl? There's still some crew around." Needing an out, he selected his longtime cameraman who was staring at a monitor. "Hey Mitch—how's the footage up to the fuck-up?"

"Bitchin', boss. You even scared *me* a little."

Glancing at the monitor, which was replaying (on a loop) the moment the elevator door came loose, Blaine said, "Save it, dude. Once everyone's back from dinner an' the elevator's ready to rock, how long 'til we go again?"

Stepping in to reassert her position as executive producer, Sylvia answered, "We'll have to splice it all in post and do pickups later this month. Unit two can shoot some B-roll with the elevator once it's fixed. We need to recast the voiceover ghost-girl anyway. This one sounds too White... even though she is, in fact, *Asian*. We need the *Hispanic* market... Ergo, we need a Hispanic *actress.* I just had a PA call her and tell her not to return."

Blaine ground his teeth and sucked down more of the sludge.

Sylvia knew who hired her. And why.

"So what's the rush with our exit?"

Handing Blaine a marked-up beat sheet, Sylvia responded, "We've got to hit the road right after dinner is done. We're due in Pleasant Acres on the banks of the mighty Ohio before sunrise tomorrow morning."

Feeling the superfood sludge coming back up from his stomach, Blaine hissed, "Pleasant Acres? Tell me you're yankin' my chain!"

Tapping the beat sheet, Sylvia replied, "It's our one-hundredth episode, Blaine. OUR one-hundredth. And the Kitchener County Menace still remains, all these many years and episodes later, your highest-rated show. *Ever.* So we're going back, just in time for Menacefest."

Crumpling into a chair and kicking off his damned uncomfortable BA signature field boots, Blaine muttered, "God, I miss Las Vegas."

Thrusting out her chin as though she were the queen of England herself, Sylvia responded, "I doubt they'd say the same. We're leaving in an hour. Get your head together. I want you at your best."

Julianna Thompson, a former anthropology and psychology of cultures professor and gifted psychic medium, sat upon her bed in her room—in actuality, a cell—in Quarry Peak Psychiatric Hospital, in rural Kitchener County, Ohio, not far from where she had spent her childhood.

As she leafed through a two-year-old copy of *People*—she wasn't allowed any *real* reading material, for fear that it might *overstimulate her mind*—Julianna suddenly sat possum-by-the-roadside still as three evenly timed finger taps were made on the HVAC register of the room—the *cell*, that is—right beside hers.

Rolling up the magazine as she rolled quietly off the bed, Julianna slid herself halfway beneath it. Holding the makeshift, clandestine speaking and listening device up to the register in front of the slate-grey vent screwed into the wall before her, she whispered, "Is that you Michael? How are you faring, my boy?"

The voice that she heard through the length of flexible ductwork between them was laced with powerful meds. "They got me on sumkinda bonzo new pharma, Jul'anna. Makin' me kinda fuzzy annnnn I usually have a *tol'rance*. An' the shock trea-menns… startin' ta—"

"Hush now, Michael," Julianna warned, backing slowly out from under the bed as she said through the rolled up magazine, "Our jailers have arrived. I'll do my best to help you. Stay strong. Do not let them break you. Or convince you you're insane."

Flapping open the magazine and sliding beneath the bright white sheet and dull gray blanket on her bed, Julianna began to read an article on a social media celebrity's apparently unexpected suicide.

Every suicide is unexpected. *If they are expected, then they can be prevented.*

They said that a lot in group.

Wiping a bead of sweat from her forehead as she heard the hi-tech security door to her room-cell being opened, Julianna looked toward the hallway and conjured up a smile.

"Good morning, Doctor Thompson. Nice to see you so happy." It was Dr. Jeffery Sayles, one of the senior members of the staff. "And *reading*. What about?"

Willing to play along while her heartbeat slowed to its regular resting rate, Julianna replied, "The epidemic of social media–driven suicides amongst so-called female *influencers* in their late teens and early twenties."

Stepping forward and taking the *People* magazine gently from her hands, Dr. Sayles responded, "Not sure how this contraband got past our crew of librarians…"

"Because they're in-house volunteers—crazy folk like me."

Pulling up a chair but not yet sitting down, Sayles replied, glancing at her chart, "There are reports being filed that you're talking to yourself. Some of the night orderlies have heard whispering coming from your room. Care to comment?"

"I don't know, Doctor Sayles," Julianna said, pleased with how their discourse was unfolding, "is enjoying the sound of one's own voice cause for concern and intervention in the infallible DSM-Six? I cannot seem to get myself a copy… Perhaps from your librarians…"

Finally sitting down, Sayles said, "Come now, Julianna… Surely you don't need the APA's *Diagnostic and Statistical Manual* to tell you it's concerning? Not a woman of your considerable accomplishments and credentials. I've admired your work since I was pre-psych undergrad at Yale. These past months, getting to learn from you, by treating you…"

"First name *and* full-on flattery, Jeffrey? And I'm not even a psychiatrist..."

Leaning forward and tapping the bed with the magazine, Sayles replied, "And yet, according to the nurses and night guards, you interact with most of the other patients as if that's *exactly* what you are... And, for the duration of your stay, I think Doctor Sayles is best..."

Careful with this one, Julianna. He just hooked you like a carp.

"What is it you want, Doctor Sayles? Group's not for an hour."

Standing up, Sayles answered, "We've been asked to bring you home, so you can do an interview."

Without fully processing what Sayles had said, Julianna replied, "I don't do interviews anymore." Then it dawned on her. "*Home*?"

Looking again at her chart, Sayles read the following: "Pleasant Acres, Ohio. A television program..." He flipped a couple of pages. "A reality show called *Supranormal Sightings*. An anniversary-of-the-initial-sightings piece. It'd be considered odd if you weren't to participate, having talked—as you claim to have—with um... the so-called Menace itself."

Still trying to process this unexpected news, Julianna sat up taller in her bed. "Don't call him that. It was a feeling, thinking being, just like you and me... Mostly me. Who made the arrangements?"

"The executive producer requested—"

"Not the *request*. The *arrangements*."

"Doctor Reinhardt, of course. Only he has the authority—"

"Thank you, but no."

Surprisingly, Sayles persisted. "It'll be good for you, Julianna. Test the strength of your progress since you've been here as our guest."

Ignoring the lie that termed her as a *guest*, Julianna asked, "By salting wounds? I was a thirteen-year-old girl made to seem a liar and a lunatic for telling the supposed *adults* what had happened to me... Your position's suspiciously unorthodox."

"I care about my patients. And, if you trust me and cooperate during your field trip, perhaps the next time you leave Quarry Peak, it will be the last. Van leaves at sunup. A nurse will get you prepped."

As Sayles exited, locking the door behind him (it really was a cell), Julianna thought about Michael.

He was just one of the reasons they were removing her.

The rest were just as evil.

Blaine Angeles, failed kiddie and Las Vegas magician and paranormal reality semi-star, opened the door to the Harmony Diner in Pleasant Acres, Ohio, laughing to himself at the old-fashioned sound of the bells hanging from the antique metal doorframe and inhaling the competing smells of their world-famous cheeseburgers and rancid cigarette smoke.

"Do these people know about the dangers of carcinogens?" he asked, stepping inside the narrow, crowded space.

Sylvia Jones DeMont, his British producer, frowned while pointing a well-manicured finger of warning in his face. "Behave yourself, Blaine. This is the town epicenter. Tick these people off and we're no place."

"Welcome to the Harmony Diner, y'all," a friendly woman in a cornflower and floral print smock with two deep front pockets and horn-rimmed glasses said in a sing-song accent from behind an old-fashioned counter straight out of *Happy Days*. Standing no taller than five foot three (including her beehive hairdo), she exuded an energy at least two times her size.

Extending her hand, Sylvia said, "Sylvia Jones DeMont, executive producer, *Supranormal Sightings*. You must be Connie Paulson."

Shaking Sylvia's hand and smiling, the woman said, "I surely am. I remember you, Ms. DeMont."

Surveying the Coca-Cola advertisements, Fountain Service sign, Seeburg jukebox, and red and white checkered tablecloths, Sylvia said, "Ten years and the place hasn't changed. And neither have you—still with the beehive and the hornrims... Amazing." Pushing open the door, she yelled to a pair of men by a Ford Explorer, "Bring it all in, boys!"

As the camera crew of two began to roll in several equipment boxes, Connie turned to Blaine. "Mister Angeles! Welcome back to the Harmony Diner!"

Forcing a smile as Sylvia elbowed him not so subtly in the ribs, Blaine said, "Yeah. Nice to be back. You gonna put me in front of the window sign, Syl? The one with the sketch of the Menace? I like the natural light. My new highlights will really sizzle in the frame."

Rolling her eyes, Sylvia replied, "Get yourself a burger, Blaine. We'll see." As she turned to survey the room so she could devise a series of shots, the British producer noticed a disheveled-looking senior hovering over the Seeburg. "Who's that by the jukebox?"

Ringing up a customer on the seventies-era cash register, Connie answered, "Godfrey Hyatt. Poor man. Used to be a—"

"He must not be seen in any of the background. Look at him. What the hell is he, Connie—homeless?"

Waving goodbye to a group of college-aged customers, Connie shook her head. "He's... complicated."

As the opening guitar melody of the Moody Blues' "Legend of a Mind" lilted out of the jukebox, Sylvia thrust a ten-dollar bill over the counter. "Let's get him some soup or something—my treat—so he can scram. Give him the change as well."

Over the admittedly pleasant sound of Ray Thomas (although she had always preferred Justin Hayward, whom she had fantasied about as a teenager) singing about Timothy Leary, eastern mysticism, and LSD, she yelled out, "Mitch!"

"Whatya need, boss?" the veteran cinematographer replied, fitting a lens onto a Canon Cinema EOS C300 Mark II camera. "Pretty well occupied at the moment."

As Ray Thomas started his two-minute flute solo, Sylvia dragged one of the decades-old tables four feet from where it stood. "I'm putting Blaine at this table here, with Doctor Thompson, who'd better be on her way. Get it lit. Moody and mysterious. She's a nut job who is currently doing a stint on a psyche ward—make sure the lighting conveys it. I also want to show the timeless oldness of the diner—*and* of the doctor. Don't wash out her wrinkles. The owner's either."

Bowing low, Mitch replied, "As you wish, Madam Producer..."

As Mitch and his assistant began positioning a standard array of lights, Sylvia spoke aloud to herself, as was her habit. "It isn't Dulce Base, or even Trans-Allegheny Lunatic Asylum, but a little file footage, a hard press on Thompson, and inventive post-production for our field segments and the Kitchener County Menace might once more bring us gold." Checking her makeup in a folding mirror she retrieved from and then threw back into her black leather knapsack, she yelled, "Blaine! Fifteen minutes to makeup! Let's make us some monsterland magic!"

Removing his combination cap and spotless white gloves, although he left the heavily ribboned jacket of his dress whites buttoned and on for the moment, Commander Trevor Carson, senior officer at Milton Chase Naval Aviation Training Center, just outside Pleasant Acres, Ohio, poured himself a generous glass of Johnny Walker Red and sat behind his desk. Pushing aside a pile of pressing reports awaiting his signature, he found himself smiling despite the dark events of the past several days at the sound of a squadron of F-35 Lightning II fighter jets screaming past his window.

"God, would I give anything to be flying with them today," he said aloud, selecting a Maduro cigar from a Spanish cedar humidor which had once belonged to Admirals John S. McCain, Senior and Junior, the grandfather and father of Senator and failed presidential candidate John S. McCain III.

Contemplating the shopping list of political ingredients that had gone into the stew of forcing such a damned decent American and former POW to select a bespectacled Alaskan Grizzly Mom as his running mate, Carson was just about to snip the end of the Maduro when his secretary stuck her head inside the doorway.

"Someone to see you," the grandmotherly archetype he had inherited from his predecessor four years earlier informed him.

Why she wouldn't retire to Mesa, Arizona, where her grandkids lived so he could replace her with a shapely piece of something better to gaze at was a daily source of irritation for the middle-aged but still randy commander.

Placing the cigar back inside the humidor and placing his cap over the glass of scotch, he replied, without an ounce of pleasantness, "Jesus, Clara... who the hell could be standing outside my door who's important enough to merit bothering me today? It's asses and elbows around here since that *thing* attac—um, *happened* to those guards... I just returned from the memorial service..."

Used to Carson's good old-fashioned misogyny—his predecessor's was much worse, and either was preferable to retirement and babysitting her daughter's four obnoxious kids—Clara merely smiled. "Uriel Stanton from the *Eastern Standard* newspaper."

"What are you telling me, Clara? It's *who* from the *Eastern Standard*? Uriel... you mean Abel Stanton's *grandson*? Christ Almighty—invite him in."

A moment later, a good-looking young man in a leather jacket, with a shock of unruly medium brown hair on his head that wouldn't have lasted thirty seconds in Carson's Navy, was approaching the commander's desk.

Putting out his hand, the young man said, "Commander Carson, Uriel Stanton... thanks for speaking with me, sir."

Not taking the young man's hand, nor moving from his position, Carson replied, "Look, Stanton. I'm going to be fast and I'm going to be frank. Your grandfather broke my nuts on more than one occasion. He called himself Holmes to my Moriarty, whatever the fuck *that* meant. What do you hope to get from me that half a dozen other reporters with more street cred and better circulation haven't? And today of all days? What do you think—that I'm feeling *vulnerable* or something?"

Giving the almost movie-cartoony naval officer his best *who me?* look, Uriel shook his head, further mussing his hair. "Not at all, Commander. Let me also be fast and frank. What I'm hoping to get from you is the truth. What the Navy is reporting about the incident earlier this week—and let me offer my condolences for your pair of fallen men—is an obvious whitewash. What the hell attacked them, sir? What was left of them by the time they were laid out on the Navy doctor's table looked a lot like butchered horsemeat."

Leaning back in his chair, Carson laughed. "You think those alien autopsy videos from the nineties are genuine as well? What the hell kind of journalist are you, Stanton? The photos you saw are admittedly impressive phonies being circulated by a group of left-wing yahoos—antimilitary pud-pullers trying to derail the latest round of funding negotiations because their drill sergeant daddies didn't love them quite enough. Here's the truth. The main gate malfunctioned, crushing those promising young sailors. Tragic. But not sinister."

"Hold on, Commander. That's the official line? Gate malfunction? 'Cause there are reports of machine-gun fire, fighters deployed, and recordings of unearthly screams..."

Assessing his foe while smiling, as his instructors had taught him at Annapolis, where he finished third in his class, Carson leaned forward, his tone both soft and even. "Accidental discharge of one of their firearms. Safety should've been on. Your next potential scoop, about fighters being deployed... This is a fucking naval aviation fucking training fucking center. *Of course* there were birds in the air! As to the screams, that gate is massive. Pulverized those men. Happened fast. Like I said—"

"Tragic. Yeah. I heard you. But here's the thing, Commander," Uriel replied, pulling a reporter's pad out of his jacket pocket. "Gates don't have massive wings, red eyes, and six-inch claws, which is the description I've been hearing. Thing's even got a name... the Kitchener County Menace. It's not the first time—"

Carson held up his hand. "The Kitchener County Menace... You have got to be shitting me, Stanton... That was nothing but a misidentified silent glider the Air Force was testing in nineteen sixty—"

Stanton leaned on the desk. "Please, sir. In the interest of fast and frank, that's multilayered bullshit. That story had legs in the late nineteen sixties because of the UFO activity in the mid-Ohio Valley tied to a secret aviation development program originating from here at Milton Chase and the clever manipulation of some paranormal researchers by the Office of Security Intelligence, but—"

Carson raised his hand a little higher just as his intercom buzzed. "Stanton, I've got a meeting. With someone *important*. I hear good things about you, son. Your grandfather would be proud. But I never cared for his Sherlock shtick, and I sure as shit won't tolerate it from you. Stick to chasing the international banks and the democracy-demolishing politico-financial deep state. That'll earn you your Pulitzer. It was funny when your granddad used to dog me about monsters. Today, the world is different. The stakes are far beyond fucking high. Leave it be, you hear me? This is not a request."

Nodding his head, Uriel exited the commander's office. A few minutes later, through a hidden security door situated opposite the desk, emerged a diminutive man in a tailored Cesare Attolini grey flannel suit.

Standing at full attention, Carson said, "Doctor Hearst. Welcome to Milton Chase, sir. Good flight in from Jersey?"

Slowly blinking his lizard-like eyes three times while running his unnaturally tapered tongue over his thin, bloodless lips, Hearst replied, "That conversation sounded... unpleasant, Commander Carson."

Once again wishing he was airborne, Carson answered, "That was Abel Stanton's grandson. He's a fucking crime reporter for the *Eastern Standard*. It's like the sixties just won't go away. But the kid's a total boy-scout."

Clicking his tongue against his teeth, Hearst replied, "Do not underestimate him and his brother, Commander. It's no coincidence he's here in Kitchener County. Only yesterday, he was looking for his brother in Quarry Peak. When our people turned him away, he called the FBI. Should he continue to press, I will leak our dossier on him to our friends in the national conservative media. People who have no use for the overeducated, antimilitary, left-wing intellectuals to whom the *Eastern Standard* caters. We have several options to suppress him... As we have suppressed his troublesome brother."

Carson felt himself relax. "I'm not sure you need to go that far. Speaking of his troublesome brother, what's the news from the Division of Eugenic Design concerning our little project? The subject is nearly ready, but I cannot get a goddamned *ounce* of info out of Vice Admiral Adler. You'd think I was a newly enlisted Seabee shoveling shit off some airstrip in Guam. I've got a meeting with the Pentagon about recent events in a couple of days and reportable progress *here* will ease the brewing shitstorm *there*…"

Lifting Carson's combination cap to expose his glass of Johnny Walker, Hearst responded, "Leave Admiral Adler to me. Let him believe he's in charge. As to the Icarus program, David Gilderson's staff at DED-17 are working with the second female EBE we captured near and partially prepped at Dulce."

Carson nodded. "What's the updated status on the initial female grey?"

"Unable to withstand the demands of the extractions. The Chaco translator has thus far proven to be more complicated than any previously recovered A-tech. Our people are working on reverse engineering the power source while a team of cryptographers work on old-school linguistic code-cracking."

Resisting the urge to sink into his chair, Carson said, "Sweet Jesus… anything at all I can file under 'encouraging'? Anything at all I can give my Defense Department bosses in the five-sided fortress?"

Again clicking his tongue against his teeth, which sounded to Commander Carson like stone upon steel, Hearst replied, "Making your life easy is not in my mission statement. Now that you've finished interrogating *me*, I have questions for *you*. How big a problem is containment for your mishap here at the base? I thought this Menace nonsense had tapered off to nothing. Hadn't been seen in decades…"

Carson laughed. Gently. Politely. "It's never *tapered*, Doctor. Not since some bullshit reality show hosted by some two-bit jag-off called *Supranormal Sightings* did an investigative special on it over a decade ago. Fully enlivened the town. This year's the eleventh anniversary of a local event called Menacefest and the fifty-seventh anniversary of the initial sightings, when the Morton Bridge collapsed."

Hearst's yellow lizard eyes began to flicker. "Menacefest? My God, Commander—Julianna Thompson was the only halfway credible witness, and she's been an inmate at Quarry Peak off and on for years. Doctor Reinhardt believes she's sufficiently cowed and no longer of any danger to the Icarus initiative or any other of our programs."

Carson grimaced. "All due respect, sir. Reinhardt hasn't done shit. Julianna Thompson is cowed because she looks and sounds like she's insane. And *that* is thanks to *us*. And now, also thanks to *us*, she's just received a pass. *Supranormal Sightings* is doing another shoot in town—an anniversary special—and she'll be on it. And man will she look looney. The producer has assured me of it. *That's* what *I've* been doing. So now it's your turn, Doctor. I need the unvarnished truth. What exactly *is* the Kitchener County Menace? I sure as shit have earned it."

Instead of an answer, Hearst moved to the security door through which he'd so coldly entered moments before. Stepping into the shadow of the doorway, he turned and shook his head. "The truth's above your pay grade. Our Subversion and Subterfuge unit will pick it up from here. You continue to be an asset——doing what you're paid to——and I'll show you the truth in time. Do not worry about Admiral Adler. He will learn to respect you, Trevor…"

Not knowing what else to do, Carson saluted. "Understood, sir. Truly."

As his yellow eyes glowed from the darkness of the doorway, Hearst said, before shutting the door behind him, "Take good care of Mary. Her time has almost come."

Within seconds of the hydraulic locks clicking into place on the security door, Carson had drained his glass of scotch and cut the tip from a Maduro cigar. Lighting it and inhaling deeply, the naval commander shuddered.

Hearst wasn't human, and Carson didn't care for such a monster speaking his daughter's name.

"I know that, Shira… but this is bigger than anything I've been working on in Jersey."

Uriel Stanton wedged his phone between his shoulder and jaw as he pulled open the door to the Harmony Diner so a multigenerational family in an impressive array of Menacefest T-shirts and jerseys could exit onto Main Street.

"I want you back here in three days tops," Shira Koury, managing editor of the *Eastern Standard*, replied from where she sat behind her desk in Storm Haven, New Jersey. "Word is the commander at Milton Chase shut you down hard this morning and that your interest in this story might not be purely professional. Governor DiMuri is less than keen on having too much attention put on her familial ties to one of the dead sailors, who had a history of drug use. He would never have been *in* the Navy, or stationed at Milton Chase, if she hadn't pulled some strings. Do you see where this is going? No one is on your side here, Stanton. You know how Micah can be when reporters decide to go rogue… even our personal favorites."

Nodding to a couple with arms full of paranormal field equipment and books about the Kitchener County Menace as they thanked him for holding the door, Uriel said, "Tell Micah to trust me. And, just so you and the governor know, I didn't mention the family thing to Commander Carson. Never got the chance. I'll see you Monday night, Shira. I promise."

Hanging up before the managing editor could respond, Uriel stepped inside the packed and cacophonous diner. If Micah Strom, the *Eastern Standard*'s longtime editor-in-chief, knew about his visits to Milton Chase and Quarry Peak—and it was clear that he knew about both—then Uriel was on to something for which it was well worth risking his career.

Stepping up to the crowded counter, Uriel smiled hopefully at a short woman in horn-rimmed glasses standing behind the cash register.

"Welcome to the Harmony Diner," the woman replied, in a pleasant small-town voice straight out of a Frank Capra film.

"Wow," Uriel said, taking in the atmosphere. "This place is… It's just like everyone says."

Handing him a menu, the woman said. "Why, thank you. Sit anywhere you like. Any place you can find a seat, that is. A waitress will be with you as soon as one's free. Smoking to the right, nonsmoking to the left."

Too enamored of the woman's accent and country manners to walk away just yet, Uriel asked, "Is it always packed like this?"

"Hardly. Word spreads when a TV crew's in town. That always brings 'em in in droves. That and our annual Menacefest, which kicks off proper tomorrow. Is that what's brought you to Pleasant Acres?"

Uriel nodded. "Yup. Well… that and a recommendation from my friend Kevin Connor that you have about the best bacon cheeseburgers in the forty-eight contiguous states."

The woman smiled a little wider. "Oh, Kevin! What a dear, sweet soul he is for saying so. I'm Connie Paulson, owner of the Harmony Diner."

Of course you are, Uriel thought. *Who else on the planet could be fit to make that claim?* Then aloud he said, "I've heard so much about you, and the diner, and the bridge disaster, and the Menacefest. I'm thinking of doing a story on it all and how Menacefest saved the town. Uriel Stanton, the *Eastern Standard*."

Shaking his hand, Connie replied, "Well, then, Uriel Stanton. Your first Coke's on the house."

Uriel smiled. "I appreciate that. I'm gonna try to find a seat."

Making his way through the closely packed tables and piles of knapsacks, duffle bags, shopping bags, computer cases, and purses between them, Uriel felt his foot catch in a shoulder strap. As he tried to extract it, he bumped into an older man with a shaggy, grey-white beard and an ancient-looking brown and orange seventies-era knit cap pulled tightly over his ears, even though it was summer and pushing ninety degrees.

Extricating his foot, Uriel said to the man, "Jesus, sir. I'm sorry..."

"Watch with your feet, walk with your eyes. Avoids a moody Tuesday...," the strange man said, moving past Uriel and heading for the jukebox.

"Huh?" Uriel said, completely confused. "First of all, it's Friday..."

"Don't mind old Odd. He's harmless."

Turning toward the sound of the older female voice, Uriel saw a woman sitting at a table by herself, a picked-over plate of fried shrimp and fries sitting in front of her, half obscured by a napkin.

"Odd?" he asked.

The woman, who, despite her age, was incredibly beautiful, with a sixties flowerchild vibe coupled with an intellectual gravitas, motioned for Uriel to sit. "His real name's Godfrey Hyatt, but the locals call him Odd."

Gratefully taking the offered chair, Uriel glanced back at the man at the jukebox. "I don't even have to ask..."

The woman frowned. "Odd can mean a lot of things, not all of them bad. You in town for Menacefest?"

Glancing at the menu although he knew what he was ordering, Uriel answered, "Yes and no. I'm really into the history of the legend. The tragedies around its time here, but how it also saved the town. And what it actually is. Uriel Stanton, the *Eastern Standard* newspaper."

The woman visibly tensed. "Oh. A newsman. I've had my fill of reporters today. I'm afraid I was too impulsive when I invited you to sit."

Uriel tried a smile. "I get that reaction a lot. Even from my friends..."

Matching his smile with one of her own, the woman said, "Well, you put it like that... You can keep your seat."

Pulling in the chair as a physical defense in case she changed her mind, Uriel said, "Not sure I understand. But I appreciate it."

"I've taken my share of guff from so-called friends. Julianna Thompson."

Uriel shook her offered hand. "Oh, wow! I've read about you. And read some of your articles and excerpts from your books. Part of my research."

"You really do want to sit somewhere else, don't you, Mister Stanton..."

Putting up his hands in a gesture of surrender, Uriel said, "I believe your story. I wouldn't have a year ago, but I reported on this very odd serial killer case last Christmas, and there have been other things. I've heard and seen some things ever since... These... Not sure how to categorize them... But let's just say the past nine months have opened up my mind."

Julianna pulled her chair in closer. "Now you're piquing my interest."

Before Uriel could speak—and he wasn't sure how much he was going to tell her—two men in white orderly uniforms a few tables away threw some bills on the table and approached them.

"It's time to go, Doctor Thompson. We promised you back by five."

Meeting the man's scowl with her high-wattage smile, she replied, "Then we'd better get on the road. Far be it from me to make trouble for an orderly." Standing up and turning to Uriel, she said, "It was nice to meet you, young man."

As she took a step away from the table, she reached for a cane that was leaning against the wall, causing it to clatter to the ground.

"Oh, damn," she said, acting the dotty senior. "There goes my cane. Damned arthritis." As one of the orderlies moved to retrieve it, she put her hand on his arm. "I've got it, Scott. Can't have you boys doing everything for me, can I?" As she squatted down to retrieve the cane, Julianna leaned into Uriel. "Our meeting wasn't an accident. *Mine the stone, climb the heights*," she whispered. Then, cane securely in hand, she stood and said to the orderly nearest to her, "Let's go, Mr. Chauffeur. My luxury chambers at your five-star resort await me, and I don't want to miss the mint upon my pillow."

As the trio moved toward the exit, a waitress who looked like she was straight out of the fifties approached the table. "Hi there. Connie sent over this Coke with her compliments. What else can I get for you, sir?"

Handing her the menu, Uriel said, "Bacon double cheeseburger, medium rare, extra cheese and bacon and an order of well-done fries. And, if you have one, a map of Pleasant Acres."

As the waitress left for the kitchen, Uriel put his head in his hand, with his middle finger and thumb gently massaging his temples, his favorite way to think. "*Mine the stone, climb the heights.* Come on, Uriel... *Mine the stone, climb the heights.*" Rubbing his temples a little harder, it came to him in a flash. "Oh shit. Of course!" Pulling out his smartphone, he scrolled through his list of numbers.

Four rings after he dialed, a gruff voice answered, "Hey. Ya got Dave. Whatchoo want?"

Having to smile at having a connected family and the greatest job in the world, Uriel said, "It's Uriel Stanton. You still monitoring things for the DTEAU near our Uncle Miltie's playground?"

"I don't know nuttin' about no..."

"Time is of the essence here, Dave. I'm working with Connor on some things. You still local?"

A moment's pause. Had he hung up?

Then a whispered response. "I am."

"Great. You still operating undercover with the laundry and cleaning services?"

"Jesus, Stanton. When did you become a journalist-operative? Kinda. Mostly. Yeah."

Uriel smiled wider. "I need you to do me an urgent favor."

Dave (a pseudonym of course) grunted. "Only if it's within my mission's parameters, Stanton. I have powerful people to answer to..."

Uriel glanced around to make certain that no one was listening. "We all do. I can assure you it is. I was at Uncle Miltie's this morning. As I said, the DTEAU is aware of it as well."

Another moment of silence.

"What's the job?"

Uriel lowered his voice a little more. "I need you to rendezvous with a van on its way back to Quarry Peak Psychiatric Hospital from the Harmony Diner in Pleasant Acres. Just left. Sing the orderlies a lullaby, and you'll find a bag of laundry in the back. I need you to pick it up and deliver it as soon as you can to..."

Of all the bad-idea illusions that Blaine Angeles had devised to try and keep up with the biggest names in Las Vegas magic, perhaps the worst was when he submerged himself in a three-centuries-old rainwater cistern on the site of an abandoned children's home and poor farm in Pennsylvania for seventeen agonizing hours on a frigid February day.

The cistern, filled to the rim with stagnant water, debris, bacteria, and myriad odors that he could smell even through the specially designed nose plugs connected to a well-concealed breathing apparatus—although, as murky as the decades-old water was, he could have been wearing a SCUBA mask—was quite possibly the tenth circle of Hell.

So he had thought. Because, after two hours of tramping through the moonlit woods a couple of miles from Milton Chase Naval Aviation Training Center, Blaine was convinced that THIS was the tenth circle of Hell.

Possibly the eleventh.

As he grabbed his shin in response to a stabbing pain from what felt like a hundred invisible thorns, he yelled out, "Fuckin'-shittin' brambles! My goddamned jeans are ruined. And these boots we sell—does anyone actually *wear* them?"

Looking as cool as Professor Challenger as he trekked through the Amazon Basin, Blaine's leather-clad producer, Sylvia Jones DeMont, replied, "Who gives a damn, B.A.? The point is they *buy* them…"

Shining his Maglite into a dense patch of nothingness, Blaine asked, sounding like a kindergartner on a ten-hour trip to grandpa's for a boring Christmas holiday, "Are we *there yet*, Syl?"

Shining her Coleman lantern onto a legal-sized piece of photocopied paper, Sylvia said, "The sketch the owner of the souvenir shop gave me is a wee bit vague. Mitch—check the GPS. How far are we from the old munitions bunkers?"

The cameraman activated his phone, surprised he could get a signal. "They're spread out for about a mile and a half, but we should be just about to the leading edge of 'em… Isn't that one of 'em over there?"

Blaine, Sylvia, Mitch, and the intern who drew the short straw for this episode—an NYU film-school dropout named Phrederico Phellini, who had flunked his senior project by just not turning the fucking masterpiece in—all crossed their flashlight beams like knock-off Ghostbusters to shine concentrated light on the spot where Mitch was aiming.

Feeling blood drip down his leg and into the top of his boot, Blaine said, "I'm guessin' it must be. How many concrete bunkers can there possibly be out here?"

From memory, Sylvia answered, "One-hundred and twenty-three, according to the old Army Ordnance maps. But this is the one with the activity. Number two. Cash Presley at the tchotchke shop was very specific…"

Shaking his head, Blaine said, "Cash Presley? That's an obviously phony name, Syl."

"You would certainly know, *Blaine Angeles*," his producer whispered back. "And so would our intern." Unslinging her rhinestone-studded leather backpack from her shoulder—she never went anywhere without it—Sylvia switched from babysitter to field general, her much preferred persona. "Unpack the tri-meters, REM-pods, cryptid caller, ghost-provokers, and all the rest, boys. That means you too, Blaine. Let's get some unaltered readings as a baseline before we calibrate the signal generators."

As Mitch and Phellini got to work, Blaine took Sylvia aside. "Why didn't you bring a second intern? I only use that crap *on* camera. I think it's making my testicles shrink. Won't you just fake it all in post?"

Pointing to a field box full of equipment with an exquisitely manicured nail, Sylvia said, "If we need to. But I've got a hunch."

"Just like your hunch about interviewing Julianna Thompson? She looked like Zombie Marisa Tomei… a poorly aged one at that. Her answers were kooky as fuck…"

Sylvia put her hands on Blaine's camouflage-jacketed shoulders. "First of all, she's beautiful. I've always had a hunch about *you*, fella… and you might just be confirming it. Second, she was credible, sympathetic, and just insane-enough sounding—especially after I do my chop and splice audio magic—to win us an Emmy. Now take this."

Despite the low light, Blaine managed to catch an up-scale digital recorder.

"What's this contraption for?"

Sylvia rolled her eyes. "It's the latest version of the voice-activated digital recorder for which you're the celebrity spokesperson. You don't wanna do baseline with the grunts? Get your ass in the bunker and try for EVPs."

Holding his ground, Blaine said with a huff, "What's with you, Syl? I am not your geek-nerd tech-bitch. Ever since Dulce, you think that we're for real. It was just a trick of the light that we saw. It wasn't—"

"Tonight perhaps we are. For real, that is. Wouldn't that be a pleasant change of pace? Now *move*."

As Blaine headed for the bunker, cursing all the way, Sylvia asked, "Mitch—how long on the infrared and time-lapse?"

"Up and running in five, Madam Producer."

"Too bad you've got a face for radio, Mitch. I'd fire his uppity ass and make you a right proper star."

"Promises, promises, boss."

Thinking that Mitch also had a face that would do for some in-the-dark companionship at the hotel later that night, Sylvia suddenly stopped.

"Hear that?" she asked.

Mitch looked up, sweeping his Maglite across the tops of the trees around them. "If you mean the sound of wings... I *absolutely* did."

From just outside the bunker, Blaine called out, "Don't you guys read the case histories? It's a sandhill crane. Maybe a big-ass owl."

Mitch chuckled. "That was military-industrial misdirection, my friend. How about you stand in front of the metal doors so I can get my lights focused, you geek-nerd tech-bitch wannabe, so we can get this done..."

As Blaine relayed a story about him and Mitch's mother on a snowy night at a ski resort, everyone froze at what sounded like a female fox having a hot curling iron inserted into her privates.

Pulling a Heckler & Koch VP9SK from her backpack and switching off the safety, Sylvia said, "That is NOT an owl... or a crane."

As she said the final word, the metal doors to the bunker slammed shut with a reverberating clang as Blaine, on the other side of them, yelled like a child in fright.

In truth, he screamed like an extra-special bitch.

Running to the bunker, Mitch yelled, "Blaine? You okay in there?"

From within the concrete structure, Mitch could hear the distorted echoes of the pained fox as it screamed, and the flap of gigantic wings.

Feeling his bladder let loose, Mitch called out, "Shit, Sylvia! The Menace monster's real! And I think it's in there with Blaine!"

Chambering a round in her pistol, Sylvia moved to the metal doors, which were tightly locked together. "Blaine, you okay in there? Blaine!"

As the unnatural sound of a rabid female fox, a pair of enormous flapping wings, and Blaine's screams continued to echo off the rounded walls of the sealed concrete chamber, Sylvia screamed as well, emptying all ten nine-millimeter rounds of her H&K into the jammed-tight bunker doors, which suddenly burst open with a shriek of twisted metal.

Then the terrible creature emerged and headed straight for Mitch.

Sitting beside the Ohio River at twilight, Uriel Stanton meditated on the sound of the gently moving water and the rhythmic click-clack of a passing Kanawha River Railroad freight train as it lumbered with its dozens of boxcars over the truss bridge to his left. Every so often, he snapped a picture on his smartphone of a tugboat pushing barges toward the big bend half a mile away, where the Ohio met the Big Kanawha at a place the Wyandot had christened Tu-Endie-Wei, "the point between two waters." Uriel looked past a tug and several barges to the West Virginia side, where a park called Tu-Endie-Wei rolled gently away in all directions from its central feature—an eighty-four-foot-high obelisk marking the Battle of Point Pleasant in 1774—a battle in which Uriel's ancestor Josiah, all of twenty-four years old, had fought and suffered a serious wound.

Point Pleasant had its own stories of monsters and disasters, different from Pleasant Acres, but in many ways the same.

Putting away his phone, Uriel reached into his grandfather's worn leather satchel—given to him by the man himself on the day he graduated with his journalism degree—and pulled out a PSB-11, or "spirit box." Setting it atop the granite and bronze memorial to the victims of the Chargin' Charles Morton Bridge disaster of 1967, he switched it on, adjusted its sweep rates and directions, and closed his eyes to better listen to the snippets of radio and bursts of static it steadily produced. After a moment, he pulled a voice-activated recorder (*not* the one Blaine Angeles endorsed) from his satchel and placed it beside the PSB-11's speaker.

Just in case.

One of five aluminum-painted bridges using "eyebars" instead of cables because they were cheaper to build, the Chargin' Charles Morton Bridge suffered a catastrophic failure due to a traffic backup caused by malfunctioning traffic lights and a stress fracture in one of its eyebars eight days before Christmas that took down the bridge and thirty-one vehicles with it in under four minutes.

Forty-seven people were killed.

Julianna Thompson's mother among them.

As Uriel leaned in closer to listen to what he thought might be a non-radio-related voice, he heard the sound of tires on the gravel pathway behind him.

Hearing the door of what he knew was a van—a very special, fitted-out Ford Transit Cargo model—open and then close, he considered switching off the spirit box and recorder, but decided to leave them on.

A minute later, a pleasant female voice behind him asked, "Are you trying to talk to the dead, Mister Stanton?"

Still watching the tugboat and barges, Uriel replied, "All the time. But I'm hoping they'll talk back. So, tell me, Doctor Thompson... What brought you back to town?"

As she moved to stand beside him, Julianna answered, "A laundry van that is definitely *not* a laundry van..."

"No one is supposed to know that."

"Dave likes to share."

Chuckling, Uriel said, "No he doesn't. It must have been your psychologist's charm."

Placing her hand in the crook of Uriel's arm as the van pulled away, Julianna said, "Glad you deciphered my clue. And thanks for sending Dave. By the way, he says he cleared this with Agent Connor, so you're square—although he would appreciate a bottle of Laphroaig Ten Year Old sent to the usual address."

Putting his hand over Julianna's, Uriel replied, "I will definitely oblige. And it was a very excellent clue. 'Mine the stone, climb the heights.' You're a patient at Quarry Peak. Or should I say, a prisoner. How'd you know I would help you? That I *could* help you..."

"A Stanton always does. It's in your DNA. Or, should I say, your blood."

Uriel's eyes widened. "How do you know that?"

"I worked with your father a long, long time ago. If the stars had better aligned, I might have been your mother." She paused a moment. "I should not have said that... The medications they give me... I never know what effect they will have..."

Indicating that they should sit on the bench behind them, Uriel said, "My father may have mentioned you. Mom's been dead for over a decade... Anyway... I'm guessing this isn't a permanent prison break?"

Julianna shook her head. "I'll soon be going back. Dave says the shot he gave the orderlies will only last an hour. When they fail to report, Quarry Peak will send some very well-trained people in search of me. I'm sure they're on their way."

Turning toward her, Uriel said, "Is it so important that they keep you there? You seem sane enough to me... Maybe Dave can arrange some kind of—"

"Careful, Mister Stanton. This is not a game. I will leave with them when they come. Quarry Peak is my home for the moment. There are reasons I need to be there. One in particular..."

Julianna put her hand over her ears as a squadron of F-35 Lightning IIs screamed past them over the river, setting the Ohio to chattering and forcing the tugboat to readjust its turn radius from the Ohio to the Kanawha.

"What a bunch of yahoos," Uriel said, shooting both his middle fingers like missiles into the sky.

"I've been hearing that sound for most of my life," Julianna whispered. "And many more provocative ones in the skies above Kitchener County. All thoughts of a romance aside, I was your father's mentor. And mine was a brilliant anthropologist named H. Tharp Ferrlington."

Uriel's eyes grew wider. "Dad *definitely* talked about Tharp. Sat on the Condon Committee and fought the whitewash hard. Then, frustrated with the lack of UFO disclosure—and all of the misinformation, false flags, and milabs—he disappeared into the Amazon in the late nineteen sixties. Dad said he was studying some type of ceremonial hallucinogenic."

Julianna nodded. "Yes. And much, much more than that. As you can imagine, being as well informed as you are—his fight against the Air Force did not come without consequences. I don't think his disappearance on November 3, 1968 was a matter of getting lost in the jungle or meeting hostile natives."

"Jesus... How did you meet him?"

"He came to Pleasant Acres when I was a teenager, when I—and dozens of others—first saw an interdimensional being."

"The Menace?"

Shaking her head, Julianna said, her tone becoming almost violent, "Don't call it that. It *menaced* no one. Sure, some people were frightened. Most of us were, myself included. At least at first. It was not of this earth. Not from this *dimension*. But equating evil with difference has led to terrible times for humanity, has it not?"

Before Uriel could open his mouth to answer—and of course he would agree—three loud bursts of static came from the speaker on the spirit box, followed by the distorted sounds of a foxlike creature and the flapping of enormous wings.

Then there was a voice. Or, more accurately, a pair of them. Ones Uriel knew so well.

There's an ancient, sacred saying in the secret halls of power: "To prevent the candle's light in the blackest hole of night, hide the gory gorilla within the plainest sight." Whistle "Onward Christian soldiers" and "Dixie" echoes back. Insert film directors and news networks into the payroll and let them say their COMIIC-determined say, prepackaged, sound-bit, and subconsciously centrifuged in contrived and cadenced ways. Do you believe in magic? 'Cause sleight of hand and legerdemain are the nefarious multinational's requisite skills for making the appearance of a Conspiracy (whether con or not, he knows) a catcher in the rye with clawed and crippled hands cradling truth-soaked lies and new world orders in its ghostly, glittering eyes. "It cannot be!" the audience screams as the hat-hare is switched for the harbinger of Hell—the shrewd and sharp-beaked Raven, attracted by the smell. And with the proper keys, as denial sits in shadow, and the shadow state sinks deep, you can almost, very nearly, decipher and decode the bloody-lettered banner hanging from its beak.

After another set of fox screams and a trio of static blasts, the PSB-11 continued its normal cycling.

Checking the digital recorder to make sure it had done its job, Uriel heard Julianna say, "Sustained transmissions do not happen through the Frank's Box. Not like that. The cycling of the stations provides an array of frequencies for entities to speak through, but..."

Sitting down beside her and grasping Julianna's hands, Uriel said, "I know whose voices those are!"

"Listen to me, Uriel. Our time is growing short. I recognize the voices as well. The first one is your brother, Michael, am I right?"

Uriel pulled his hands away. "How could you possibly know that?"

"Because they've got him drugged up in the room beside mine. We've been talking... when he's up to it... through an HVAC vent. They are doing terrible things to him, Uriel. You must do everything you can to get him released. The ethereal one, however... is that of a being so ancient and complex, so interdicted into many of the most important events in human history that—"

Julianna stopped speaking as a jet-black Chevy Suburban with blacked-out windows sped up to the bench, the driver applying the squealing brakes at the very last second to prevent an impact.

"Another gaggle of yahoos," Uriel said, standing and putting his arms in the air as all of the doors flew open in practiced synchronization.

Instead of the typical dark blue FBI or DHS jackets, all six men coming toward them wore spotless white hospital coats. Uriel recognized two of them as the orderlies from the diner, looking like they had a pair of bitching migraines.

The only one in a necktie stated, as they circled the bench, "Your extracurricular field trip's finished, Julianna."

Offering no resistance, just as she had confided to Uriel minutes before, Julianna smiled. "All good things, Jeffrey... Sorry to cause you the trouble."

Opening a Gladstone bag that looked straight out of a Hammer horror, Doctor Jeffrey Sayles replied, "Not your fault, Julianna. Perhaps it is the fault of this man here. There will certainly be a thorough investigation... But nevertheless, I do insist on sedating you." As he spoke, he prepped a hypodermic needle, which he now held toward her arm.

Instead of speaking, Julianna rolled up her sleeve, groaning softly as the needle entered a vein. Within seconds, she was losing consciousness and the orderlies were carrying her toward the Suburban.

As Doctor Sayles capped the needle and dropped it into his Abraham Van Helsing cosplay prop, Uriel grabbed his arm. "Hey! You can't just grab a person and sedate—"

Not trying to free himself, the doctor answered, "My name is Jeffery Sayles. I am Julianna's psychiatrist. So I can do whatever the hell I like. Ignore everything she told you. She suffers from delusions. As to this modified radio gadget of yours—you can hear anything you want in the radio snippets that eventually cycle through. It's like baby talk to Mommy. Don't be fooled into thinking a single word makes sense."

Playing up the lost tourist angle that was one of his favorite personas, Uriel shrugged his shoulders. "I ordered it on Amazon Prime from my hotel room last night. The locals said if I set it up at the bridge memorial, I could hear the victims' crying. They showed me photos, played me EVPs..."

Sayles let out a laugh. His bedside—or riverside—manners sucked. "Yeah. Sure. They played you, alright. It's how the town survives. Julianna's paid the price for their collective delusion and cottage industry carnival barker theatrics. You'd do well to forget the voodoo and the Menacefest and all the rest of the lies and go back to where you came from. Your newspaper editor misses you, Uriel. Go and do your job someplace other than here."

As Sayles climbed into the Chevy, Uriel yelled, "Hey! How do you know my—"

His answer was a spray of stinging gravel as the Suburban sped away.

Placing the PSB-11 and recorder in his satchel, Uriel whispered, "It's not the lies you're all afraid of, doctor. It's the truth. And if you hurt my brother, I swear to Christ—I will put that hypodermic of yours in places it was never designed to be."

Those in the know will tell you: On the Monday morning after Menacefest, Pleasant Acres, Ohio, always gives itself back over to the ghosts that call it home.

While three locals who had come out of hiding once the Menace Maniacs headed for the highway huddled around their coffee cups and puffed their cigarettes in the back of the Harmony Diner, mocking the festival and the fools who attended it, the two surviving members of *Supranormal Sightings* sat in silence at a table exactly opposite, in what an old yellow sign labeled the "nonsmoking" section.

In truth, the smoke cared not a damn for such unenforceable demarcations.

Sylvia Jones DeMont—Britain's *other* Iron Lady—felt at the moment as though her world was made of straw and the wolf was at the door.

"You should have stayed in hospital, Blaine," she said, pushing aside her untouched eggs and toast. "Your hands are shaking."

Dabbing his eyes with his sleeve, which was by now noticeably damp from hours of wiping away his tears, Blaine Angeles answered, "No way I'm going back there, Syl. They wanted to put me on the *psyche ward*, same as Doctor Thompson. Did you see what that... *thing*... did to Mitch and that intern kid when it flew out of the bunker? I never wanted any of this to be real. It was just another magic show, you know? Classic misdirection. Sleight of hand. Legerdemain, the masters called it. Not sure what that means, though… Regardless… It was supposed to be entertainment. What are we gonna do?"

Patting her star on the arm—while avoiding the salt-encrusted damp spot—Sylvia said, making her upper lip stiff, as her parents and grandparents had taught her, "We're going make the most of it, like we always have done. My phone's been blowing up. Two crew dead in a legitimate cryptid encounter. Backed up by rumors of a similar incident a few days ago at Milton Chase. The old-school networks want you. But they can suck a crumpet. *Netflix* wants you. *Supranormal Sightings* is about to go ultra-international. Random House wants you to write a book: *Mitch, the Menace, and Me.*"

Blaine chuckled. Here he was, finally in the Big Time, and it felt like breaking rocks. "It's been less than forty-eight hours, Syl. And they already have the title? This is seriously fucked up… I think the military set us up. I think we were *all* supposed to die by that bunker…"

As Sylvia began listing all the reasons why they could use every bit of it to their advantage, the decades-old bells of the door to the Harmony Diner began to tinkle as the in-need-of-a-patch screen door opened with a groan. Connie Paulson—exhausted but happy at the weekend's record turnout—smiled over the top of the morning paper at the man who stood before her.

"Uriel Stanton, isn't it? Welcome back to the Harmony. Has Julianna been…"

Saving her from having to find the words, Uriel answered, "Within an hour of her slipping her captors. Yeah. Cup of your strongest coffee and a big stack of pancakes, please. Maybe some bacon and sausage…"

Coming around the counter to place the order in the kitchen, Connie said, "I know what you did for her. Your food is on the house. For as long as you stick around…"

Uriel nodded. "I appreciate it. But I'm heading back to Jersey just as soon as I finish breakfast. Deadlines to meet, and a very unhappy editor I need to appease…"

Making his way halfway down the aisle, Uriel picked a table meant for two and sat himself in one of the chairs, putting his satchel on the other.

"If you don't mind my saying so, you look like you've seen a ghost."

Enjoying the cadence of the female British accent, Uriel turned to face the speaker. "Didn't see one. *Heard* one. Well, not a *ghost*, really… It's kind of complicated… You don't look so hot yourselves...." Looking at Blaine, he said, "Hey... You're from that show... um... Super-alien—

"—Normal," Sylvia corrected.

"Sightings." This, they said together.

Knowing that Blaine was in zero mood to talk, Sylvia said, "Yes we are. You must be a fan. This handsome fellow here is——"

"Not my thing. TV, I mean. Reality shows in particular," Uriel said, knowing he probably sounded like an asshole. "I'm strictly a news guy," he added, removing further doubt.

Blaine grunted, like someone had punched him in the sternum. "FOX is full of shit."

Uriel nodded. "As is CNBC, CNN, and all the rest. I'm a newspaper man."

Sylvia smiled. "So you're old school."

Uriel returned the gesture. "Ancient, actually. Uriel Stanton, the *Eastern Standard*."

Sylvia sat up just a smidge. "Abel's paper. Are you related? I guess you'd have to be..."

"He was my grandfather," Uriel answered, suddenly more than enamored with just the woman's accent. "Did you know him?"

Sylvia nodded. "A long time ago, when I first came to America. We were—"

Before she could finish, Uriel felt a shadow over his shoulder and heard a nearly hoarse voice whisper, "Ya dropped a quarter, angel."

Annoyed at the interruption, Uriel spun around. "No I didn't." Taking in the man's tattered clothes and dirty skin and beard, he added, "And it looks like you need it more than I do." Then he noticed the man's brown and orange seventies-era beanie. "You're... Godfrey Hyatt, right? I accidently bumped you the other day... Listen, sir, I'm sorry about what I said..."

"No need to call me Godfrey," the man answered, his light blue eyes alight. "I'll answer to Odd for a Stanton. Try a song. Jukebox over there. Lotsa messages in songs. Heard any messages lately, Uriel?"

Deciding to keep on riding the wave of weird that Pleasant Acres provoked, Uriel answered, "I certainly have. You know anything about it?"

Hyatt's eyes twinkled brighter. "I just might at that. Ya oughta listen to the Byrds."

Uriel nodded. "The Byrds are classic. Yeah."

Leaning in so only Uriel could hear, Godfrey whispered, "Decode the bloody-lettered banner hanging from the raven's beak."

As Uriel sat in silence, trying to process what he'd heard, Godfrey bowed low before moving to the table where Blaine and Sylvia sat. "Have a Pleasant Acres mornin', folks. Sorry for our loss. Oh, and Mister Angeles... Legerdemain is Middle French for 'light of hand.'"

As Godfrey Hyatt shuffled toward the door, Blaine said, "How did he know... And why did he say *our*..."

Sylvia, equal parts impressed and not surprised, answered, "That's Odd Godfrey. The homeless wonder of the riverfront. Don't you remember... worked for some hi-tech space company contracted to the military. Scored off the charts on every test of intelligence there is. Name of the company was Daimon-Metis, based in Parkersburg, over in West Virginia... One day, he just snapped..."

Coming over to their table, Uriel asked, "Did what he said—about legerdemain—did that mean anything to you?"

Blaine sat back in his chair. "Hell yeah, it did. I used to be a magician. In Vegas. I guess you knew that. Anyway, before either of you were here, I said to Sylvia that our show was supposed to be like a magic show. Classic misdirection. Sleight of hand. Legerdemain..."

As Connie brought over his breakfast, Uriel was dropping a generous tip on the table and heading for the door in a hurry.

"Okay, then," Sylvia said, chuckling. "Goodbye to you as well. Didn't even wait for his breakfast..."

Watching Connie bring the plates of pancakes, bacon, and sausage over to the chimneystacks on the other side of the diner with her compliments, Blaine said, "This town is out of its mind."

Sylvia patted him on the back, knowing Blaine would be all right. "And that particular kind of kooky will earn us hundreds of thousands of dollars."

Three hours later, as he cruised along the Pennsylvania Turnpike back to Jersey in his Toyota Prius hybrid, Uriel received a call.

Hitting the Bluetooth button on his steering wheel, he said, "Did you listen to it?"

"About a dozen times."

"And?"

"More coded messages aimed at me. Although this one is less clear than the one about the Changeling. Any idea as to why?"

"A very clear one. Michael sounded heavily drugged. And this entity that communicates through him—he likes the second-hand high."

A moment of silence. Then: "I need you to come to Virginia as soon as you can. Director Vance is mad as hell about you coopting Dave for your little stunt with Quarry Peak... and Admiral Christopher Adler is ready to ream you a new one for your visit to Milton Chase." Giving Uriel time to reflect, DTEAU Special Agent in Charge Kevin Connor continued. "You like to stir the shit, don't you Mister Stanton?"

Mouthing "Oh hell yeah I goddamned do" to the emptiness of the Prius, Uriel said aloud, "When those fuckers have my brother and continue to lie about it... and about whatever the Kitchener County Menace really is and why it killed four people in as many days, then yeah... I'm a veritable kayak paddle when it comes to stirring the shit."

Connor laughed. "I completely understand. Director Vance is doing everything he can to get your brother transferred to a facility near you in Storm Haven. One that will allow you proper access. Be patient, Uriel. This is a delicate situation..."

"Not a problem," Uriel said, resisting the urge to bang on the steering wheel with glee. "About Virginia... I'll need a reason I can sell to my bosses. They're equally ticked about my field trip..."

Connor, pausing a moment, said, "How about a piece on our facility? Very general, but it'll seem like you have insider access. A couple of canned quotes that are less canned than usual. Might send a message to some folks who need to hear it."

Uriel, not sure he was saying the right thing at the right moment, said, "The Ravenskalds."

"'The harbinger of Hell—the shrewd and sharp-beaked Raven, attracted by the smell.' We know your two families have been intertwined in a centuries-long battle of apparently cosmic proportions, and we'd like to offer our help."

Increasing the speed of the Prius as he adjusted the coordinates on his GPS, Uriel Stanton, suddenly feeling like a man reborn, replied, "I will see you in Virginia just as soon as I can get there."

PRENDICK'S ALL NIGHT FIGHTS

Sometime in the not too distant Present.

"Treat it like a friend, because it is."

"A friend that can blow a smoking hole the size of... well, whatever size it is... in a person's chest and obliterate their insides?"

"Exactly."

"You are not someone to be fucked with, Maggie Sorrus. I say that with respect."

"When we're finished with your training, Kirstine, no one will ever try to mess with you again. And if they do, they will very quickly regret it."

FBI Special Agent Magdalena "Maggie" Sorrus was glad that this unexpectedly open, but not unwelcome, exchange was not being recorded by the building's in-house security system. One of the many benefits of being assigned to the Domestic Threat Early Assessment Unit—referred to by its team members as DTEAU—was that the unit had its own gym and shooting range, and neither of them had a security camera.

"Okay, then..." Doctor Kirstine MacGregor said, switching off the safety on the Glock 17 with which she had been practicing under Agent Sorrus's supervision for the past three weeks. Taking a deep breath, she raised the pistol in the accepted two-handed hold and focused on the target. Resting her finger lightly on the trigger, she asked, "So... have you ever killed anyone?"

As Maggie prepared to empty her own Glock's clip into the head and heart of the paper target twenty-five yards away from where she stood as the alternate to a verbal response, the smartphone clipped to her belt began to vibrate.

"Safety on, Kirstine," she said, seeing the caller's name filling up the screen. "I think we're done for the day." Activating the call, she said, stepping a few feet away, "Haxx. I'm working with Kirstine on her gun skills."

"Need you up here immediately, Special Agent Sorrus."

The fact that Tech Specialist Tino "Haxx" Alvarado was using her formal title and not her first name meant it was a high-priority call. "Be there within minutes," she responded, pulling off her safety glasses and removing her Walker electronic earmuffs from where they curled around her neck. "I just have to arrange for Kirstine's early departure. We had another forty-five minutes to go."

Doctor Kirstine MacGregor—an expert in the Golden Age of Piracy and the Jacobite Revolution—was a former researcher at the Smithsonian Archives in Washington, DC. She had been under the protection of the DTEAU—and Magdalena Sorrus—ever since her abduction and subjection to memory extraction experiments at Quarry Peak Psychiatric Hospital months before. A descendent of the Highland outlaw Rob Roy and his nephew Angus, a little-known confidante of the infamous (and mostly misrepresented) Blackbeard, it was believed that Kirstine had, locked deep within her DNA, the keys to deciphering the coded journals kept by Angus and other Jacobite pirates during the early seventeen hundreds. The French pirate Olivier Levasseur figured into this, as did a mysterious wizard named Abraxas Abriendo—and it was clear that some very powerful people were highly motivated to obtain what heredity had locked in Kirstine's mind.

Those same people had subjected Maggie to similar experiments while she was working a case a few years back—although for different reasons—so her affection for and commitment to the protection of Kirstine MacGregor were understandable. Although the accomplished PhD had dated "Haxx" Alvarado once upon a time—if a spring fling in Daytona Beach could be categorized as dating—he was leaving the emotional heavy lifting to Maggie.

So, while she was protecting her, she figured she'd teach Kirstine some physical defense so she could eventually protect herself.

"Duty calls," Maggie said, seeing that Kirstine had already packed her gear. "You're not supposed to be upstairs, especially if we're getting called into action, so I'll contact transportation to take you back to your apartment in Georgetown while I'm in the elevator. Sound okay?"

Kirstine laughed. "You don't have to mother me, Maggie. Whether it sounds okay or not, it is what it is. Go save the world. I'll field strip my Glock while I wait."

Resisting the urge to hug her, which would be professionally inappropriate, video cameras or not, Maggie smiled, knowing that, in time, Kirstine MacGregor would recover almost completely from her experiences at Quarry Peak.

Almost, because, as Maggie understood from her experience— once those bastards got inside your head, you were never quite the same.

✝

By the time SA Sorrus passed the bio-scans at the entrance to the elevator and at the steel security door that led to DTEAU's offices on the seventh floor of a nondescript federal building just outside of Langley, Virginia, her field partner, SAIC Kevin Connor, was hovering his muscled bulk over Tino's chair in the gifted specialist's crowded, tech-crammed cubical.

As Tino's fingers danced with impressive speed over the pair of ergonomic keyboards hardwired to half a dozen computer towers, Connor was staring—squinting actually—at several video feeds flashing up on a trio of 20-inch, 8k screens from a variety of angles.

Standing near the other end of Tino's workstation was a female agent whom Maggie Sorrus once knew rather intimately, although she had not heard from her in years.

"Beth," Sorrus whispered, feeling herself suddenly unsteady in her heels.

Special Agent Elizabeth Donovan, the Quantico record holder for the infamous PST—standardized physical fitness test—and for the highest GPA over the twenty weeks that trainees spent at the Academy, was as beautiful as she was athletic and intelligent—with raven-black hair, light blue eyes, high cheekbones, and a radiant, movie star smile.

She and Maggie had gone through Quantico as roommates—and, for a few precious months, as lovers—until the graduation-day announcement that Director Peter Vance, head of the newly formed Domestic Threat Early Assessment Unit, had chosen Maggie for the position everyone in their class had been working extra hard for weeks to try and obtain.

Elizabeth had refused to speak to her ever since.

"Sorry, guys—working on my skills at the pistol range downstairs," Sorrus said, knowing immediately how completely lame she sounded, like Michael Keaton in *Mr. Mom*. As if that wasn't bad enough, the synchronized turn of their necks and "you kidding me?" stares from Connor and Alvarado made Maggie want to flee the scene and hide for the rest of her life in her glassed-in work space on the other side of the office.

No doubt wanting to bail her out before her ship went down, Connor said, "Our hot-shot tech guy Haxx here has found footage of a recent abduction."

"Well, actually... that's not true..." Haxx replied, his cheeks flushing with atypical modesty. "Yeah, I mean... okay, sure... I may have *found* the footage, but it was Special Agent Donovan who asked me to look for it in the first place."

"A team effort then. J. Edgar would be proud," Maggie answered, knowing the longer she waited to acknowledge Elizabeth—SA Donovan—the more the guys would want to know about what was going on after the visiting agent left.

"Good to see you, Agent Donovan," she said, smiling just enough to make it look like a professional courtesy and not what it was—the alternative to throwing Donovan out a window. "I hear you're up to impressive things in Manhattan. Everyone at the Jacob K. Javits Federal Office Building is struggling to keep up with your pace and record of excellence."

"Way to know the official name of her building," Haxx said under his breath, knowing he would pay for it later and finding he didn't care. Then, in his best professional voice—meaning the complete suppression of his natural Hispanic accent—he said, "Agent Donovan, if you could explain to Agent Sorrus what it is we've found..."

"Absolutely," Elizabeth said, looking infuriatingly at ease despite Maggie's best efforts to make her feel awkward about her presence. "As you are obviously aware, the FBI makes a habit of keeping a close eye on scientists working at the leading genetics labs across the United States. It's for their protection and for the protection of the highly sought-after IP their facilities are producing that we do so. Tino, if you'd be so kind as to switch to the primary footage... Thank you..."

It galled Maggie something fierce that Elizabeth had called him Tino instead of Tech Specialist Alvarado.

She was reasonably confident she wasn't letting it show.

"Now, what we're looking at here is the lower-level parking facility for the Brooklyn Institute of Technology. This footage is from eleven-thirty last night."

As Agent Donovan narrated, Agent Sorrus watched as a typical-looking middle-aged scientist emerged from an elevator, still wearing his lab coat and ID tag, which was too far away for Maggie to read. With his briefcase and thermal lunch bag in one hand and a set of car keys in the other, he glanced nervously around before heading for a row of cars to his right. Unlocking and getting into a few-years-old Mercedes convertible, the scientist made a quick call before starting the vehicle and heading to the ticket booth and boom barrier at the egress of the garage.

As he passed his security card across the reader that controlled the barrier, he looked panicked. Passing it more vigorously back and forth in front of the scanner, he began to yell at an unseen someone inside the tinted-windowed booth.

Thirty seconds later, three armed figures in tactical gear—one emerging from the booth and the others coming from the shadows and into the frame from different angles—had subdued the scientist, moving him to the back seat of the Mercedes, into which two of them also climbed. Sticking his arm out the window, the one who got behind the wheel raised the boom barrier with a handheld device and entered the late-night flow of traffic on Flatbush Avenue.

Keeping silent for a moment to let what Agent Sorrus had just seen sink into her mind, Agent Donovan said, "The man you just witnessed being abducted is Doctor Gregory Evans Chase, head of BIT's advanced genetics lab. He oversees a number of high-level government and defense contractor projects, including some classified experiments for the various DEDs."

"Those *cerdos sucios...*" Tino said, not bothering to hide his ethnicity nor his opinion.

"Cool it, Haxx," Agent Connor said, placing a giant hand on Tino's shoulder and applying just enough pressure to let their TS know he was serious. "The three abductors were tricked out with some serious tactical equipment. The way they moved signaled Special Forces to me. What do we know about the guy who was supposed to be manning the window?"

Donovan shook her head. "Knifed in the lung so he wouldn't make a sound. He never had a chance."

"Another case for tactical training," SAIC Connor said. Turning to Maggie, he asked, "What do you think, Agent Sorrus? You agree with my assessment?"

Making a mental note to thank Connor for his gesture after Elizabeth had left, Maggie said, "I do. There has been some concerning chatter lately in the anti-genetics community. One group in particular on which we're keeping an eye is known as the Low-Tech Alliance."

Donovan nodded. "Andy Milligan's group."

"Andy Milligan?" Connor inquired.

Maggie and Elizabeth looked at one another. After a few aborted starts, where they talked at the same time and abruptly stopped in embarrassment, Maggie said, "You came all this way, Agent Donovan. Please go right ahead."

Moving her eyes quickly side to side in order to retrieve the information from her memory, Donovan said, "Andrew Milligan is a former professor of Alternative Energies at MIT, and co-leader of the Low-Tech Alliance, along with former Manhattan public defender and environmental advocate Jack Shaw. Their focus—thus far mostly limited to letters to the editors of major newspapers, public demonstrations, and advocacy training—is The Ravenskald Group's nuclear energy and biotech divisions. They have also gotten a pretty substantial following from several fringe groups for their theory that Superstorm Loki was—if not created, then enhanced—by some kind of advanced weather-used-as-weapon technology, possibly developed in conjunction with the Air Force, Navy, and DARPA program at HAARP, so that TRG could create the planned city that is Storm Haven, New Jersey."

"They believe it 'cause it's true," Haxx said, this time under his breath.

"Anything at all to indicate that LTA has specifically targeted BIT and Doctor Chase?" Connor asked, ignoring Tino's comment.

Sorrus shook her head. "Chase and BIT both fall under the umbrella of evil entities Milligan and Shaw are committed to shutting down, but there's nothing specific. Remember… there are lots of anti-gen and animal rights groups that could also fit the bill. Some considerably more militant than LTA. This kind of military-level abduction isn't in their playbook."

"Agreed," Donovan said, her tone indicating it was time to move on. "Tino, if you would please bring up the slide show, I will clue your colleagues into the bigger reason I'm here…"

After the tech specialist had tapped a few keys, the images of two men and two women appeared on the center screen. "I'm going to give you the bare bones on this for now. I have already sent detailed files, including what you see before you, to your inboxes. I have a meeting at Quantico in an hour and then I'm heading back to Manhattan. Chase is not the only professional abducted in Brooklyn recently. Over the past three months, these four people—a city councilwoman, a real estate mogul, a supervisory nurse from a local hospital, and a Methodist minister—have also been taken by military-grade tactical extraction teams."

"Have any of them turned up?" Connor asked.

"All but one," Donovan answered. "Always under or within a quarter of a mile of the Brooklyn Bridge, and always severely mutilated, as though they were mauled by an attack dog or a larger than usual wolf." Pausing a second, Donovan added, "Given your history, I've asked for DTEAU's help on this, and Washington has agreed, as has Unit Director Vance. So then... have a look at the files, and tell me what you think."

After Donovan exited, Tino turned toward Maggie.

"Don't you dare ask me about her," Agent Sorrus replied, her tone leaving zero room for negotiation.

"I wasn't going to," Tino answered, putting his hands in the air. "I just wanted to ask if I could go downstairs to the shooting range with you and Kirstine sometime..."

Heading out of Tino's cubicle and toward her glassed-in office, Agent Sorrus answered, "Your keyboard is your weapon, so lock and load it, Haxx. We need to find links between these five abductees before Doctor Chase becomes another slab of mauled meat beneath the Brooklyn Bridge."

Stepping out of the Carrara marble shower in his thirteen-thousand-square-foot neo-Gothic mansion in Brooklyn's Cobble Hill neighborhood—the most expensive and exclusive in the borough—Cardinal Esteban Rojas, Archbishop of New York, glanced in the mirror and frowned.

His crow's feet and jagged sorrow lines were starting to return. He would have to ask his personal secretary to make an appointment with his doctor's office for a dual treatment of Botox and dermal filler first thing in the morning. After all, the Face of the Roman Catholic Church in America should not be disfigured by the marks of worry and age.

Slipping into a dark blue Zimmerli piped silk robe—even Cardinals tire of red—Rojas crossed his antique-filled bedroom with a satisfied moan. Sitting on a small round table in the corner like an old friend was a Louis XIV silver serving tray containing a Fornasetti demitasse set, a pot of espresso, a shot glass filled with anisette—at the bottom of which sat two coffee beans—and a pair of freshly made *sfogliatella*. Lowering himself into an oak and velvet chair that once belonged to Pope John Paul II—to whom Rojas was personal secretary for nearly a decade—the Archbishop poured the coffee, added most of the anisette, and sent the rest down his throat, the coffee beans clicking against his dentures with a satisfying thump.

Breaking off a piece of a *sfogliatelle*, Rojas lifted it to his lips, enjoying the texture of the orange-flavored ricotta his executive chef made daily for him from scratch. Chasing the rich, flaky pastry with a long sip of espresso, Rojas lifted a copy of the sermon he was due to deliver in a church in Brooklyn Heights later in the day, before being driven by limousine to a fundraiser for the mayor of New York at the Waldorf Astoria.

Using a red pencil to mark a change of word, addition, or deletion here or there—Rojas was known for his articulate, piously passionate without being fire and brimstone sermons—he worked his way through his breakfast, pouring himself a second shot of anisette as a reward for finishing his editing earlier than he had planned.

After calling downstairs for his secretary to take away the tray and pick up the sermon for retyping—Rojas saw computers, smartphones, and most electronic devices as the work of the Devil— the Archbishop slipped out of his robe and crossed to one of three Royal Tudor Mango wood wardrobe closets lining the wall by his bed. Throwing wide its ornately carved doors, Rojas set about selecting his clothes from the tens of thousands of dollars of tailored items neatly folded and hung before him.

Hearing the deep creak of the hinges on the bedroom door, he said, without turning around, "Ah, Sebastian... quicker than usual. I want the newly typed sermon as soon as possible. There are parts I'd like to—"

Rojas stopped short as he felt a fleeting pinch where his long, ostrich neck met his wide, bony shoulder. Thinking it was a mosquito, he thought it odd that the bite would cause the room to spin and his vision to dim as he felt himself losing balance and falling backwards into a powerful pair of arms...

It took three sets of knocks on her bulletproof office window, each one increasingly louder, for Special Agent Magdalena Sorrus to drag herself out of the pit of the past and shout a half-hearted "Come in!" without checking to see who it was.

"Sorry to disturb you," SAIC Kevin Connor—technically her supervisor, but in practice her partner and equal—said, his sheepish tone at odds with his still muscular, above-average former football-player's frame. "I just got the reports back from Ruth Anne Marsh at Eastern Pinelands U. Should be in your inbox."

Sorrus was anxious to hear what the DTEAU's go-to forensic specialist had discerned from the photographs taken of the three murdered abductees under and around the Brooklyn Bridge. Opening her email and clicking on a password-secured PDF, she input her security code and downloaded the contents to her desktop. She went through them page by page as Connor narrated over her shoulder.

"The first two abductees—the city councilwoman and real estate mogul—look like dog mutilations. Possibly Rottweiler or bullmastiff, but the bite marks and depth of the claw marks indicate well-above-average size. The Methodist minister... almost definitely cougar."

Maggie enlarged one of the more graphic bite wound photos. "Are there any cougars roaming the streets of Brooklyn?"

Connor shook his head. "Not even in the zoo in Prospect Park. This bit is even stranger... Doctor Marsh found anomalous DNA, probably left from each animal's saliva, on all of the corpses."

"Anomalous how?" Sorrus asked, searching the documents for herself as she asked. "Jesus, Kevin... she says here there were elements of hyena, mandrill, panther, and possibly one or two others. How in the hell can that be?"

"It's straight out of H.G. Wells... specifically, *The Island of Doctor Moreau*."

"We don't have enough horror in our lives without you reading the classics?" Sorrus asked, not adding her usual smile to what Connor wasn't exactly sure was a half-hearted stab at levity.

"Not me, Maggie. I'm still going through The Changeling files whenever I get a chance... there's enough horror in those boxes for half a dozen lifetimes. Some of it's unbelievable, but every bit of it is real. *Island of Doctor Moreau* comes from Doctor Marsh. She says we should contact Uriel Stanton at the *Eastern Standard* about it. Something about a relative who wrote about Moreau like he was real..."

"Peter would never allow that."

Connor leaned his backside lightly on the edge of Sorrus's desk so he could face her. "You sure about that? Our quiet little get-together last month produced an article in the *Standard* highlighting DTEAU's unique skills and list of wins that I've heard the FBI director herself pinned to her office corkboard, and the Stantons aren't new to the darker, weirder aspects of why this team was formed."

Why this team was formed... Seeing Elizabeth Donovan after so many years of silence had led Sorrus to think of little else—and how much damage was done because the reasons for her being selected instead of the more qualified candidate were a secret she was sworn not to share.

Leaning in a little closer, Sorrus whispered, "And don't forget, Maggie, that it was Director Vance who applied the political pressure needed to get Michael Stanton released from Quarry Peak and reassigned to Saint Michael's in New Jersey less than a week after the story was published."

"What can I say? You make a host of excellent points," Maggie answered. "Soon as we can, we'll talk to Uriel Stanton."

Refocusing on the details of the DNA assessment, Sorrus said, "Some of these animals are pretty damned exotic. Let's ask Haxx to focus on tracing recent shipments of these particular species, and looking for filed reports of any of them being stolen or lost... We need lists of private owners... Also zoos and circuses... Is he locked up in his tech-shack?"

Connor shook his head. "I guess the boss didn't tell you..."

"Tell me what?"

"SA Donovan called first thing this morning and requested that Haxx be sent to Manhattan to work with her team directly. He's apparently from Brooklyn. I guess I never knew that. Anyway, he was gone within an hour. Shoot him a text and I'm sure he'll run those traces for us, unless Donovan—"

"Has already asked him..." Sorrus said, finishing Connor's sentence.

Heading for the door, Connor said, "Remember what they teach us at the conferences and training seminars... we're one big Bureau family."

Clicking on the photos of the first victim and enlarging them so the bright-red carnage filled her screen, Sorrus whispered, "Of course we are..."

And families are the worst when it comes to secrets and lies.

Exiting Carlito's Sip and Smoke on Knickerbocker Avenue in Brooklyn's Bushwick neighborhood, Tino Alvarado looked around in amazement mixed with confusion as he took a big bite out of his messy tripleta sandwich. Aside from places like Carlito's and his next stop, a few blocks up, Angel Burgos' Gym, Tino hardly recognized the neighborhood where he had spent his childhood and most of his teens. Like much of Brooklyn, Bushwick, although in many ways still industrial and working class, was slowly becoming artistically diverse, trendy, and—as the glossy, Madison Avenue advertisements described it—*hipster cool.* Investment companies and entrepreneurs were converting long-abandoned warehouses into coffee shops and studios for painters, sculptors, and acting and dance troupes. Even the bars looked like they belonged in the center of Manhattan and not in this modest, down to earth, mostly Puerto Rican and Dominican neighborhood.

Taking another bite of his sandwich—which the original Carlito's grandson had piled extra high with steak, roast pork, and ham for "the local kid who got out good"—Tino hustled himself to the gym. He didn't have time to waste. He wanted to stop in and see his mother after leaving the gym before catching the L train into Manhattan later that afternoon.

Opening the door after finishing off all but the final bite of his sandwich, Tino took in the smells of leather, sweat, and bullshit—the last a result of the trash talk the occupants loved to exchange—that permeated the dimly lit expanse of heavy and speed bags, barbells, benches, and two squared circles in which fighters tested their mettle.

"Tino Pequeño! ¿*Qué pasa, hermano*?!"

Popping the last of the tripleta into his mouth, Tino waved to the man across the gym. "Nice to see you, Oscar!"

Oscar Burgos, owner of the gym and grandson of middleweight champion Angel Burgos—a Brooklyn legend who, after retirement, trained Mike Tyson and Steve "The Brooklyn Brawler" Lombardi while they were making their names—barked at a tired-looking trainee to hit the heavy bag *harder* for another ten minutes *without stopping* and crossed the gym to shake his visitor's hand.

"It's good to see you, Tino Pequeño! We hear a lot of things about you, but your mother don't say a word…"

How can she? Tino thought. *If these guys knew that I was FBI, I would never walk out the door.*

When Tino was in eighth grade, a friend of his older brother Paulo's—his sparring partner here at Burgos'—had given Tino an old Apple IIc and his love of computers was born. Picking up cans and bottles from the streets, delivering newspapers, sweeping up and emptying the spit pails at the gym—whatever money he earned went into buying parts for his computers. By the time he was a junior in high school, he was working part time at an electronics shop, setting up computers for kids at school, and getting into hacking.

At first, it was just the challenge, but then, after Superstorm Loki about wiped out the Jersey Shore and did hundreds of millions of dollars of damage to New York City, he began to hack into various government sites, including the NSA, looking for proof that what his gut was screaming—that the government had caused the storm—was true.

Of course, the *bastardos* caught him. No one fucks with the NSA—even a highly gifted hacker like Tino Alvarado. Facing forty years in a federal penitentiary under an obscure antiterrorism law, in the eleventh hour, as he lay on his bunk at MDC Brooklyn—a place he spent only a couple of weeks and never wanted to visit again, even for an hour as a visitor, *ever*—he received a visit from SSA Peter Vance. Vance was forming a low-profile unit of the FBI that needed a person with Tino's particular skills...

"What brings you back to Bushwick?" Oscar asked, after reminding a mountain of a man in the sparring ring to keep his left hand high.

"Visiting Ma," he said. "While I do some freelance work for a firm in Manhattan for a couple of days."

Leaning in and lowering his voice, Oscar said, "Listen to me, Tino Pequeño. Frankie Bank's been coming around here again as of late. You can probably smell his stench above all the others. He stayed away for a while after Paulo's 'accident' a few years ago, but he's been asking questions—mostly about you. Where you are, what you do to make a living... Thinks he can get the money he claims your family somehow still owes him even though he got his payment in full when he did away with Paulo."

Tino's brother Paulo, a very promising middleweight, had made the mistake of borrowing money from Francesco "Frankie Bank" Banquero, a local loan shark who was well connected with the infamous Five Families based in Jersey and New York. When Paulo missed his second payment after losing a fight he should not have lost—some of the guys at the gym, including Oscar, suspected someone had drugged him—Frankie Bank tampered with the brakes on his car. Oh... no one could prove it, but everyone knew it—and Paulo died on the way to the hospital after being extracted from his crumpled Lincoln with the jaws of life.

"*Madre mía*," Tino whispered. "I don't want him making trouble for you, Oscar. Maybe I should pay him..."

"Hey!" Oscar yelled, loud enough for everyone and everything—save for one swinging speed bag—to stop for a split second, before continuing slightly louder and more vigorously. Then, lower, he said, "Forgive me, Tino Pequeño. That would be very foolish. Even if you have the thirty thousand he thinks he's owed—and *Salud* if you do—it won't stop there. I have enough friends to protect your mother. Because she has *nada, entiendes*? Lay as low as you can and, as soon as this gig is finished, go back to wherever it is you live and work, *mi amigo*, and forget about the past."

Tino put his hand on Oscar's arm as the muscular old man began to stand. "First, I want you to teach me to fight. I can come here every evening for a few hours for at least the next week. I'm tired of not being able to defend myself. If Frankie Bank's on the lookout for me, I need to be prepared."

Giving Tino a doubtful look, Oscar grunted. "You know what Paulo's friends used to call you, Tino Pequeño?"

Tino winced at the uncomfortable memory Oscar was digging up. "*Puerta trasera.*"

Oscar nodded. "There are two meanings for back door, *hermano*, and they meant them both. The fights Paulo used to get into because of how he defended you… they made him even tougher. But you don't belong here anymore. You never really did." Oscar then paused a moment in deep consideration. "Tell you what. We close at eleven. You be here at eleven fifteen tonight and we will see how it goes…"

Standing up to say thank you and goodbye after nodding in agreement to Oscar's terms, Tino noticed three heavily bandaged men enter the gym. "What's with them?" he asked.

"Trio of *tipos rudos*," Oscar said, shaking his head. "Got themselves involved in some kind of crazy bareknuckle boxing that also involves fighting vicious animals in one of the local warehouses. What some *idiotas* will do to earn a peso…"

FBI Special Agent Elizabeth Donovan stood outside a prefab warehouse a few blocks away from the revitalized Brooklyn Navy Yard, in a section of the borough that had not benefited from visionary entrepreneurs and New Yorkers' hard-earned tax dollars at work.

Nursing a cup of ice-cold cappuccino grande, Donovan contemplated calling Maggie Sorrus and quickly decided against it. Quite simply, she did not have a case-related reason to do so. Both of their bosses had implemented a divide-and-conquer strategy that kept the Manhattan and Langley teams—with the exception of Tino Alvarado, whom Donovan was standing here waiting for—working separately.

As far as Maggie Sorrus, there was so much to say, and no way to begin.

"Hey there, SA Donovan," she heard Tino say as he approached her, a large cup of coffee in each of his hands.

"Tell me one of those are for me, and I can get you transferred to Manhattan."

Donovan took note of the dark cloud passing over Tino's eyes. "One of them was, but I think I'll keep them both," he answered before recovering himself enough to smile and say, "Just kidding. Cream and sugar cool?"

"Absolutely," Donovan said, carefully placing the remnants of the cappuccino grande into an overflowing trashcan. "You ready to meet some really shitty people?" Before Tino could answer, she noticed a fresh, deep bruise on the tech specialist's chin. "How'd you get the black and blue?"

Shrugging his shoulders, Tino said, "Tried to break up a fight in front of the Sip and Smoke in Bushwick late last night after visiting my mom."

Donovan didn't believe him for a second, although she said, "You might want to stick with *Mike Tyson's Knockout*. He trained at the same gym as your brother Paulo, didn't he?"

Looking increasingly uncomfortable, Tino said, "Three things. First, it's not 'Knockout,' it's 'Punch Out' with two exclamation points. Second, just because I was a hacker doesn't mean I was a gamer, and third… Tyson was before my brother's time, although they met a couple of times. How did you—"

"I did some time with the Transnational Organized Crime Unit at the start of my career. The lead investigators asked me to advise them on some of the sports betting aspects of your brother's case. Probably should have disclosed that up front. Francesco Banquero is a scumbag I'd definitely like to have on my 'got 'em' list."

Tino resisted the urge to share what he knew about Frankie Bank with what amounted to a supervisor in theory and a senior agent in reality. Instead, he said, "Let's go in and see what these guys can tell us."

Although their signage and brochures indicated they trained specialty animals for Steiner Studios at the Brooklyn Navy Yard and other film industry clients, Lights... Camera... Animals! made the bulk of their income from training guard and fighting canines.

Tino had heard about them from the three men at Angel Burgos' Gym and had promptly reported his findings to Elizabeth Donovan. He had felt guilty for not including his colleagues at the DTEAU, but only for a moment. He rarely got a chance to do field work, and the little taste he got extracting Kirstine MacGregor from Quarry Peak Psychiatric Hospital had awakened something this special assignment with SA Donovan had started speaking to in soft, seductive tones.

Entering the facility, Tino was immediately smacked in the face by a wide array of sights, sounds, and smells—all of them of the four-legged, winged, and slithering variety.

"Help you?" a tattooed weight-lifter with a bald head and two oversized hoop earrings asked, his tone indicating he had no intention to.

Flashing her FBI ID, Donovan no sooner stated her name than the thug was pulling a snub-nosed .38 from the back of his pants and firing at them.

Ducking behind a wall of fifty-pound dog food bags, Donovan called for backup and encouraged Tino to stay where he was. "Do you carry?" she asked.

"I'm not in the field that often" was his embarrassing response.

Handing Tino her FBI-issue Glock, Donovan pulled a silver Walther PPK with black grips from an ankle holster.

"Fancy shooter, ma'am," Tino said, more to calm his nerves than to talk guns while one was being fired at them.

"It was my dad's. Big fan of 007. Stay put. I'm gonna get this fucker."

Then she was gone.

As much as he wanted to see what was happening—there were now at least three handguns being fired, and lots of shouting and cursing—Tino did as he was told, touching the bruise on his chin as he gripped the Glock, and deciding he needed to get serious about his training.

Hearing the animals that filled the place going increasingly crazy— a dog he couldn't see but which was so close he could smell it was barking so loudly it hurt Tino's ears—he then heard the tattooed man cry out in pain. An instant later, Donovan was telling the suspect not to move or he would be going to the hospital or the morgue without a very important, intimate piece of his anatomy.

"Tino! Shooter's down—one of them anyway. A second suspect who must have been in the back when we came in has fled the scene. Get yourself out here. I need you to wrap his arm so we can have a chat."

Making his way to her voice while picking off the shelves the kinds of items that might be useful when field-dressing a gunshot wound—which they don't cover in hacker seminars, so he was mostly guessing—Tino rounded a corner formed by stacked rodent and reptile cages. He first saw Donovan, training the James Bond special at the tattooed man's head. As for the man himself, he was white as a ghost and bleeding all over the floor from a wound to his bicep.

"Get to work, Tino," Donovan said, before turning her attention to the suspect. "Why the hell did you go for your gun so fast? What are you people up to?"

"Like you don't fuckin' know," Tattoo Bleeder managed to mutter. "Why the hell else would ya come in here flashin' ya badge?"

"As president of the We Hate Michael Vick fan club," Donovan answered, "I like to make the rounds of scumbag ops like yours. Please speak up... I'm recording this." She hit the recording app on her smartphone and held it closer to the suspect.

"Sure, lady," Tattoo Bleeder said, wincing as Tino applied an oversized bandage to his blood-slicked arm, where the bullet had added impressive depth to a scantily clad exotic dancer's belly button. "Ya here 'cause a' the fights."

"Suppose I am. What can you tell me about them? And, remember... firing on a federal officer makes your future look like orange jumpsuits and limited gym time for many decades to come... So the more you tell me, the happier you'll be with your sentence."

After Tino dressed the wound—it was nothing of which his mother—an ER nurse—would approve—Tattoo Bleeder managed to sit up against a shelf of dog collars and leashes, which seemed to Tino wholly appropriate.

"Look," the suspect began, "we really are a mostly legit operation. Came back home a few yeaz ago after a successful decade in Hollywood. Our work is all ova the place out there—TV, movies, fashion shows—an' we thought it'd be great ta work wit' an operation like Steiner. Conquer both coasts an' all a' that. Geez... can ya maybe grab me a water?"

Tino looked at Donovan, who nodded it was fine.

"We were heah about eight months when we got an offa ta make some extra dough trainin' fightin' dogs. Mostly fuh private security fuh the wealthy. Dobermans, Rottweilers, pit bulls, et cetera. But then, dis guy… Tanks fuh the water, bro."

As Tattoo Bleeder took a break to take a long drink from a water bottle, Donovan asked, "What guy?"

"Weirdo name a' Prendick. Dresses all fancy… kinda like a high society carnival barker. Silk an' diamonds an' all. But no one evah sees his face. Keeps it covuhed wit' diff'rent animal masks. Anyhow, he convinces us ta get involved in dogfights. An' some uthah stuff. Exotic animal imports. Real cash cow. Crazy the amount a' celebrities, influencers, an' millionaire doctors' an' lawyers' wives who attend these events a' his online. Last several months it's been even weirdah… Prendick started mixin' animals wit' humans. Some a' the guys from the local boxin' gym, an' lately ex–Special Forces an' other super-toughs… Big money's changin' hands. Mostly, we do the trainin' right here, in a pen we got out back, an' the animals are picked up by vans on fight night."

As Donovan hit the end button on her phone, Lights… Camera… Animals! was swarmed with FBI agents and officers from the NYPD.

"You're gonna tell these nice men and women here who your buddy was, you hear me?" Donovan said to Tattoo Bleeder as she stepped away to take a phone call. "Agent Connor," she said, not taking her eyes off the wounded perp. "What can I do for you? Shit… When? Okay… we just had a bit of a field exercise at a dog-fighting facility near the Brooklyn Navy Yard. Haxx? He's a pro… really had my back. We are both on this hard, SAIC Connor." Pausing a second after winking at Tino, Donovan said, "Listen… if you and Maggie… Agent Sorrus… could... Perfect. I will make the appropriate requests and we'll hope to see you at the Javitz Building late this afternoon. Thanks."

Hanging up, she pulled Tino away from the mayhem so they could talk in private. "You heard who that was. DTEAU just got a report that Cardinal Esteban Rojas, archbishop of the Archdiocese of New York, who was supposed to say mass at a church in Brooklyn Heights yesterday and then attend a fundraiser for the mayor at the Waldorf Astoria, was abducted approximately twenty-four hours ago from his mansion in Cobble Hill."

"And they're just hearing about it?"

Taking her Glock from Tino's hand, Donovan said, "The Catholic Church is a world unto itself. I am sure their private police force did all they could to find him before reaching out for help. We need to get back to Manhattan. You okay?"

Tino nodded. "Fine. Thanks for what you said to SAIC Connor…"

"Listen, Tino—when you work with me, I always have your back."

"Come on now, Cardinal Rojas. Naptime is over. You have people who want to meet you."

Opening his eyes—a painful endeavor because his head felt like it was going to split in two—the archbishop of New York struggled to see his captor in the low light of the subterranean prison in which he was being held.

He had awakened hours before, only to have someone enter the cage in which his captors were keeping him and injecting him again in the neck.

"Who are you?" he asked the backlit man standing just outside his cage. "It's obvious you know who I am, but do you understand the power that I wield? I will be found, as will you, and you shall come to know the wrath of almighty God through the warriors of his Church. He shall not let me suffer. "

His captor met his threats with a dismissive laugh. "When was the last time you had a conversation with God, Esteban Claudio Rojas? Certainly not since you moved into your mansion when you became Cardinal Archbishop seventeen years ago. Because *I* spoke to him just yesterday. It was quite a lovely chat—about your days as a priest… in Argentina. You remember those days in Argentina, Your Not-So-Eminence? It was in a little parish in Lomas de Zamora, just south of Buenos Aires, was it not?"

"Who are you?" This time, the proud, cocky Cardinal Archbishop sounded considerably less proud, considerably less cocky.

His interrogator had that effect upon people. That's why he had been chosen.

"There are a few special guests I would like you to meet before we proceed. You will get to know them—I would say *intimately*, but they're way too old for your tastes—so let us say on *a whole other level*, in just a few days. For now, they wish to say hello."

As his captor whistled through his teeth, the lights became brighter—nearly blinding Rojas—and to either side of him stood two men, whose Argentinian accents as they thanked their host made his blood go cold.

What the hell was this?

The first one put his face to the bars and spoke. "*Buenas tardes*, Padre Rojas. My name is Benito Gimenez. My brother Ernesto was an altar boy in your church, Nuestra Señora del Rosario. Do you remember him?"

My God...

The second man now pressed his face against the bars. "*Hola,* Padre Rojas. My name is Amilcar Flores. My sister, Milagros, worked at your church when she was a teenager. Do you remember her?"

Rojas burst into tears while feeling his bladder release.

"Thank you, gentlemen," his captor said as they exited, after first spitting on him.

Rojas let the spittle remain where it landed, on his hand and on his cheek.

This was demonically rehearsed. How could his captor have possibly found these men... And where were Ernesto and Milagros?

"Dead," his captor said, as though he was reading his mind. Of course, he was not. The question was brutally obvious. The question was the point of all of these theatrics.

Or rather, the answer was.

"Committed suicide because of what you did, Estaban. Your selfishness. Your darkness. Your desire to possess their souls."

"I loved them," Esteban whispered.

"All of them?" his captor asked. "Because there are many. I could speak their names, but what would be the point? Of special interest is the poor girl taken from her family in 1983 after she caught your eye in the Vatican gardens while you were serving as secretary to John Paul the Second. As for Benito and Amilcar, they were in the Argentinian Special Forces before coming to America at my personal invitation. They are trained in fighting hand to hand, and with a variety of blades and ancient weapons. They are looking forward to meeting you in my fighting pit. That will happen within days."

Crumpling to the floor, where he shook in fright like the dozens of children he had invited to his private chambers over the past many decades, right up until only a week ago, Rojas whispered, a line of drool forming at the corner of his mouth, "Who are you, and why do you do this?"

Turning out the light behind him so they were left in total darkness, his captor replied, "My name is Edward Prendick. And I do it for the sport."

"Haxx! It's good to see you... New York spoiled you yet?" SAIC Kevin Connor asked as he stood in the doorway of the DTEAU's temporary command center in the Javitz Federal Building. Donovan had arranged for the space once she had spoken to her boss and confirmed that Director Vance had granted permission for Connor and Sorrus to come to New York.

Not turning around from his workstation—which looked exactly like his setup in Virginia—Tino replied, "Maybe it's best, SAIC Connor, if you call me Tech Specialist Alvarado for the duration of our time here."

Setting down his briefcase and taking off his trench coat, Connor said, "Whatever you think appropriate, Tech Specialist Alvarado," laced with just enough annoyance to fill the room with a tension thicker than fresh pea soup.

"You guys in the middle of a moment?" SA Sorrus asked as she entered.

"All good on my end," Connor answered. "Tech Specialist Alvarado was just finishing up his summary report for us. Any time you're ready, Tech Specialist Alvarado."

Ignoring the taunt but mentally preparing himself for Sorrus's inevitable questions, TS Alvarado punched up a series of images and surveillance feeds on one of his screens and what looked like a series of shipping manifests and an extensive CV on another.

"I've been working on tracking red flag incidents involving exotic animals. There have been reports of zoo break-ins along the Northeast coast, as far up as New Hampshire. A few in Ohio. Same for laboratories—meaning Northeast coast and Ohio. One incident in particular concerns me, although I don't know if it's related. Three days ago, just off I-80 in Pennsylvania, a telephone company truck struck a transport vehicle containing thirteen *Macaca fascicularis* monkeys—commonly known as the crab-eating macaque. They had just arrived at Newark International from Sumatra and were destined for an unnamed laboratory, also—take note—in Ohio."

"You know exactly which lab it is," Sorrus said, leaning on Alvarado's chair to get a better look at the screens. "I can hear it in your voice."

"I do indeed. Indeed, indeed I do," Alvarado said, making a series of keystrokes with a flourish. "But you're not gonna like it. It's the Naval Research Laboratory designated DED-67, overseen by Admiral Christopher Adler."

"Fuck," Connor whispered.

Alvarado hit another series of keys. "It gets worse. The telephone company reported the truck as stolen from their Hazelton,

Pennsylvania, facility—about fifteen minutes from where the monkey truck got walloped—within an hour of the so-called accident. Plus, only ten of the monkeys were captured. All of them euthanized within a couple of hours of capture."

"Refresh my memory about DED-67, Haxx."

"It's Tech Specialist Alvarado while we're stationed in New York," Connor whispered in Sorrus's ear.

"Whatever," she said, swatting him away like a fly. "How about it?"

"Frustratingly little," Alvarado said. "None of the seven Division of Eugenic Design facilities are public. They're all funded by private contractors, black ops slush funds, and the Afghanistan–Pakistan drug trade. We've had them on our radar for various reasons, including Director Vance's little stay in Quarry Peak and the MacGregor–Givens case. Admiral Adler supervises three of them in total. All I can tell you is that DED-67 is just about impossible to crack. There are whispers in hacker circles that they are doing some high-tech comic book super-soldier shit in there—something well beyond the capabilities of DARPA. Someone goofed and put the destination on paper—that's how I put it together."

"And where exactly is it?" Connor asked.

"Just outside Kitchener County, Ohio."

Connor kicked the metal leg of the desk. "You have got to be fucking with me. It's all of a sudden the new Area 51. And what in the fuck is the *Navy* doing with a research lab in Ohio?"

"They're going to want to get those monkeys collected ASAP," Sorrus said. "They are still on the hot seat for the death of those two sailors at Milton Chase…"

Alvarado swiveled his chair to face the two agents. "You think that thing with the sailors is connected to our thing?"

Before either of them could answer—although both their expressions said yes—SA Donovan had entered the workspace. "Glad you two are here. Special Agent Sorrus… I just got a tip on a lead I've been following, and I think you'd be perfect for where I'm headed. Ready to hit the road?"

As Elizabeth Donovan navigated her FBI-issue midnight black Dodge Charger through rush hour traffic and entered the Brooklyn Bridge, Maggie Sorrus searched for a way to broach the past, which was hanging over the interior of the car like an early-morning East River fog.

Finding no easy way and knowing they were close to their destination and might not have another chance, she blurted out, "I never meant to crush your dream. I was as surprised as anyone when I was chosen for DTEAU over you. And I know I should have called, should have reached out... Tried to explain why I took the posting. Why I *had to*... And the real reason I was chosen is so unbelievable I never thought you'd think it was anything other than bullshit."

Exiting the bridge and heading for Brooklyn Heights, Elizabeth pointed to the left. "That's Jane's Carousel over there in Brooklyn Bridge Park. It wasn't always there. It was originally built for an amusement park in Youngstown, Ohio. Sixty years later, when the place went under, Jane Walentas and her husband bought it at auction and had it transported here. But it *looks* like it belongs. It *feels* like it belongs, even though this is not where it began its life. Everyone says this was always where it was meant to be. That it found its way home. I'm like that carousel. So don't sweat it, Maggie. This has all worked out for me."

Turning in her seat as much as her seatbelt would allow, Maggie said, "That's bullshit. You just don't want to talk—"

"We have no *time* to talk. I didn't bring you here to *talk*. I needed the best. You're obviously the best, so I called your boss and got your team to help us out. I don't like losing, I don't like death, and I don't like you trying to make something right that never, ever will be." Pulling over and slamming the brakes so Maggie was thrown forward as much as her seatbelt would allow, Elizabeth Donovan said, "We're here. So focus."

Getting out of the Charger and feeling like her cheeks were as red as her hair, Maggie looked at the signage as three disabled veterans sitting outside began to whistle and catcall at the two fit, attractive agents.

"Thank you for your service, sirs," Donovan said, giving them a respectful salute and a twenty-dollar bill. "You guys split that fairly now, you hear me?" Then, to Sorrus, she said, her voice become a whisper, "Guy we want to talk to is inside. This is one of about a hundred and eighty soup kitchens and food pantries in Brooklyn. This one specializes in disabled veterans—especially ex–Special Forces. Sickens me how our government ignores the guys who fight its illegitimate wars. Do you know twenty-two veterans kill themselves in this country every day?"

Although Maggie Sorrus was aware of the statistic, she thought it best to seem surprised.

Entering the establishment, Donovan waved at a twenty-something veteran who was trying to extricate his electric wheelchair from where it had gotten entangled in a mass of burlap bags and wooden crates.

"Tobias, my friend!" Donovan said, approaching the man, who was missing both his legs at the middle of the thigh and most of his right arm. "Your new wheels giving you fits?"

"Damn straight they are, Lizzie! Appreciate the VA providin' this supposedly state a' the art chariot while my new titanium legs are bein' fabricated. They're usin' a 3D printer! Can you dig the sci-fi vibe? But this goddamned contraption… I was a Humvee driver when I was in the Marines, and navigatin' that bullet-breathin' beast through a combat zone was easier than maneuverin' this sonofabitchin' thing!"

"Let me see if we can help," Donovan said, nodding to Sorrus to move some of the bags and crates as she wrapped her hands around the handles of the wheelchair and pulled it gently backwards.

"Thank you ladies," Tobias said, smiling. "Geez, Lizzie… is there some kind a' beauty regulation for female agents at the FBI these days? I mean… damn! What a pair!"

Feeling her cheeks again begin to flush, Sorrus lowered her head and said, "Thank you, Tobias. And… and for your service as well."

As Tobias sat taller in his chair and smiled, Donovan said, "Listen, my friend. As much as we could stand here and flirt with you all day—you've certainly earned it—you know why we're here. Is he around?"

"Yeah," Tobias said, clearly disappointed. "Follow me." Pressing the joystick on the left arm of his chair gingerly forward, the veteran Marine lance corporal asked, heading down a wide aisle toward the swinging door of a kitchen, "Could one of you get that? I don't wanna scuff my new ride."

Opening the door and turning her body sideways so Tobias could get through, Sorrus took in the sight. Half a dozen men—all but one disabled or disfigured—were peeling potatoes, chopping carrots, or attending to giant, steaming pots on two immense industrial-grade stoves.

"Yo, Acres! Someone here to see ya. The lady agent I told ya about. An' she brought another looker!"

One of the men, who had three deep wounds, nearly healed, that ran from his left temple down the side of his face and halfway down his neck, looked up as Tobias called his name.

As the man put down his knife and a peeled potato, Tobias whispered, "We call him Acres because most a' his stories are so long and boring, they make our ears ache. His real name is Anthony Denham. Ex–Green Beret. He was one a' the dudes that took out the Kandahar Giant in Oh-Two. A story that *ain't* long *or* borin', if ya got the time…"

Sorrus raised a brow. "That story isn't bullshit?"

Tobias laughed. "Special Forces don't need to make shit up, Agent. 'Specially not a thirteen-foot Goliath motherfucker with a spear, flamin' red hair like yours, and *two rows* a' teeth." As Denham approached, Tobias offered his left hand. "How ya doin' my brother? Face wounds are healin' good. Some badass scars to impress the ladies. Maybe startin' with these two."

"Thank you for the introduction, Tobias," Donovan said. "Mister Denham, I am Special Agent Elizabeth Donovan with the FBI. This is my… partner at present… Special Agent Magdalena Sorrus. We are interested in what you have been doing that got you those facial wounds."

"I bet you are," Denham said, motioning them further into the kitchen and into a storage room in the back. "Listen… times are hard. Disability and all the rest don't pay the bills… I worked for a private contractor for a while after the Army cut me loose—said my head wasn't quite right after so many middle of the night assassination missions—so that dried up, and I came back to Brooklyn. I was nearly out on the street a year ago, but I have these buddies… ex–Navy SEALS. They were part of our joint mission team that took down the Kandahar Giant. Special unit no one knows about… fight some crazy friggin' shit. Anyhow, they tell me about these fightin' pits here in Brooklyn. Good money. You just show up, beat the shit outta some guys in front of a small crowd and for the cameras broadcastin' to the deep, dark 'Net and you get paid. Lotta guys like me show up. Guys whose bodies and minds are not intact enough to get in with or maintain a spot on the roster of the multinationals supplying body guards, security support—for the wealthy, you know? And for these bullshit natural resource conflicts all over the fuckin' globe. The rest of us are self-destructin'. Actin' out. Booze, drugs, beatin' on our wives and girlfriends… Our kids… Suicide rates are crazy. So, the fightin' not only pays the bills and lets off steam—it gives us back a sense of our cultivated warrior core. 'Cause that's what the government wants, ladies… mindless killin' machines, that they can later chuck back into society when we can no longer get a kill count worth our monthly pay rate. Anyhow… the worst of the guys comin' back from the Middle East are part of this secret SEAL unit… damn, they saw some evil, evil shit... fought some highly *unnatural* enemies... Their former commander runs a security corporation called Kardax... contracted almost exclusively to The Ravenskald Group. With my psyche eval on record when the Army cut me loose, I couldn't even get an interview. Very much the best of the best over there. Guy goes by the name of Lieutenant Black, but that ain't his name..."

As Sorrus worked to process all that she had heard, Donovan removed a card from her pocket and handed it to Denham. "Thank you, Mister Denham. This is incredibly helpful. One last question..."

"Hit me."

"You get those wounds on your face fighting these ex–Navy SEALs for prize money, sir?"

Denham shook his head. "Hell no. They offer a crazy bonus if you fight a fuckin' *animal*. Was a panther done this to me. But it wasn't like no panther I ever saw... Bastard had *tusks*... I'm lucky ta be *alive*, I tell you... Some of the carnage I've seen..."

"Haxx. Shit... TS Alvarado. We are in route to the suspect's home. Just exited the bridge. Gimme the broad strokes one more time..."

SAIC Kevin Connor was in full tactical gear, including a pair of glasses that fed him a continuous stream of data on weather conditions, distances to targets, facial recognition, and half a dozen other elements that would give him considerable advantage when engaging enemies in the field. He was also part of a video feed monitored by Tech Specialist Alvarado, who was sitting at his makeshift workstation at the Javits Federal Building in Manhattan working his keyboards with the fury and concentration of a master concert pianist performing at nearby Lincoln Center.

The information Alvarado had gleaned through deep web surfing and White Hat hacking had come in so quickly Connor found himself getting into borrowed gear in a Chevy Suburban with four other agents from the Manhattan office within minutes of receiving a key piece of data so they could question a suspect in the southwest Brooklyn neighborhood of Bay Ridge.

Alvarado was in his glories as he smiled at Connor through the tiny video screen in the glasses. He adjusted his headset microphone and said, "As you know, I've been looking for connections between the victims, and one logical place to pin as a possible epicenter from which to radiate out was the Brooklyn Institute of Technology, outside of which the next to last abductee was taken..."

"Entirely old news so far, TS Alvarado," Connor said, glancing at his GPS and seeing they were not far from their destination. "Clock's ticking."

"Right," Alvarado shot back. "I found a geneticist, Colin Ashe, who—after being fired from BIT by abductee number five, Doctor Gregory Chase—disappeared without a trace. I've been running cross-checks with a number of facial recognition programs—including one of my own design... Uh, sorry..., tell you about that later... But I haven't found anything that's helped me to locate him."

Connor grunted. Other than the driver, the Manhattan agents had the same gear, the same glasses, the same data and video feed, and right now Alvarado—*Haxx* for Chrissakes!—was embarrassing the shit out of him. "Then why are we headed to his house in full tactical gear in a high-speed vehicle, TS Alvarado?" he yelled.

If Alvarado was ruffled, he didn't show it. "Heat signatures, sir. I've been running infrared and thermal imaging scans via drone over his home the past four hours at the direction of Agent Donovan. There have been some anomalous spikes at regular half-hour intervals. Depth meters indicate they're coming from a basement. Also, check this out..." His face was replaced by a thermal image of the back yard of the house, where there was a barn-style shed lighting up in brilliant reds and oranges. "Gotta be a massive generator. You won't find Ashe, but *pesos* to *paella*, you'll find *something* to further the case. *Sir.*"

Fully cognizant that the tech specialist was well within his rights to have a tone, and having to switch to action mode as the Suburban came to a stop in front of their target, a modest ranch-style home that looked like it was owned by a family out of a 1980s sit-com, Connor said, "We just arrived. Stay with us as we enter."

"Will do, SAIC Connor."

Emerging from the van with the other four agents, Connor, in his senior position as supervisory special agent, directed two of the agents to the front door and the remaining two to accompany him to the back. Once the shed was in his field of vision, he directed one of the agents to open it and investigate.

Moving to the back of the house, Connor saw a bulkhead locked with a heavy chain and Stanley shrouded hardened steel padlock. At his direction, the agent beside him sliced through the chain with a set of KRC-6 pneumatic bolt cutters and, within seconds, they headed down the stairs and into the basement.

Connor felt his breath hitch as he ran the light attached to his H&K MP5 assault rifle over the contents of the space. "Excellent work you did on this, TS Alvarado," he whispered, maneuvering himself through a maze of tables and hi-tech scientific equipment as he heard the agent behind him cursing with wonder at what they were seeing. "This is not normal for a basement in a middle-class neighborhood… You seeing this freaky shit? The embryos in jars? The surgical tools? It's Doctor Frankenstein meets Doctor Moreau in here… Animal carcasses… Sketches of animal hybrids. And a sketch of some kind of bull mask…" As the two agents who had entered from the front joined their colleagues in the basement, Connor said, "We need to get a forensics crew in here. Bag and tag everything… And some tech guys to figure out what some of the machinery in the corner is for. It has to be what's generating the heat signatures. This is some pretty exotic hardware. What the fuck?" He held an old carnival-style poster in front of the screen, with "Prendick's All Night Fights" in big stylized letters across the top. "Look at this. Dated a month ago… There's a pile of them. A few dozen, looks like. Holy shit… they go back to eighteen ninety-four… Get us all you can on this, TS—"

The feed began to crackle and digitize, and the audio to cut in and out as the back yard shed exploded with a roar, fiery debris and hunks of metal pelting the back of the house and the bulkhead as the four surviving agents ducked for cover within the reinforced walls of the basement.

Eustace Grenier Dwyer-Mann—who had never forgiven his parents for giving him a name that guaranteed that every kid he ever met called him some bullshit nickname to impress their thug-bully pals or stuck-up, slutty girlfriends, like Eustachian Tube or U-Turn—settled into his custom-designed gaming chair and opened an energy drink. Taking a long swallow and releasing a belch that no one could hear thanks to the state of the art soundproofing in his basement work space—which his father thought was a dark room—*Yeah, yeah daddy, as Goth Winona says, one* big… dark… *room…* he fired up his two twenty-four-inch high res screens. Normally he would be using the third-generation VR headset developed by his father's company, Damon-Metis Corporation, but Eustace was still feeling queasy after spending too many hours the previous day in the VR headset as he spent thousands of dollars of cryptocurrency gambling and virtu-fucking in Dubai and Monte Carlo.

Reaching beneath his desk, he entered a passcode into a hidden keypad to wake up his also custom-designed (off the shelf was for punks, plumbers, and grandmas) computer tower. The guy who had built it for him had loaded it with The Amnesiac Incognito Live System, otherwise known as the TAILS OS, and a TOR browser, which operated on a VPN that was military-industrial-intelligence complex grade, thanks again to his daddy's multinational.

Not that Eustace really understood how all this privacy- and anonymity-ensuring hardware and software actually worked. And he certainly didn't have the brainpower to install it. Hell no… He had a buddy from boarding school in Princeton, New Jersey, named Tommy Sicari, who just so happened to be VP of Special Projects for The Ravenskald Group—Damon-Metis Corporation's fiercest, and really only, market competitors in the lucrative fields of advanced weaponry and psychological/physical military enhancement products. When it came to aerospace, no one could touch them—not Bigelow, Musk, or any of the other billionaires with their penis-shaped rockets and B-movie visions of colonizing Mars.

As the complex computer system came to life—red, blue, and green LEDs illuminating alien heads, ancient occult symbols, and a jolly roger on the various black rectangles and boxes all wired together beneath the glass-topped desk—Eustace Grenier Dwyer-Mann thought about his family, and their company, and most of all, how he gotten such a horrid fucking name.

Eustace Grenier—who would have slit the throat and spilled the entrails of anyone who dared to call *him* Eustachian Tube or U-Turn—was a warrior in the First Crusade who went on to become lord of Caesara and Sidon. (Eustace the much younger had no idea where either of those places were, but being lord of anything was pretty fucking cool.) In 1123, Baldwin II named him bailiff and constable of Jerusalem. Eustace's namesake had also led an army to victory in some Muslim-sounding place Eustace couldn't care less about remembering the name of.

Listening to his computer and routers chirp and beep as they connected to the coolest places on the Dark and Deep Webs—where Eustace spent an increasing amount of his time—he thought about what he would do when his father finally died. First, he would buy out his brainiac younger brother, Aaron Harman—another dick name but harder to make fun of—so he could take sole possession of the family's Second Empire Victorian, in the basement of which he now sat. Iron-gated in the center of the Julia-Ann Square Historic District, it was built in 1866 with funds his ancestors had amassed through war profiteering by selling small arms and cannon to both the Union *and* the Confederacy. The imposing house would be perfect for all the freaky shit Eustace could only do virtually at present, and he planned to hire a pair of live-in porn stars to see to his daily carnal needs, just like one of his heroes, Charlie Sheen.

He didn't like to leave the house. Not with a face distorted from a severe cleft lip and cleft palate that a dozen surgeries before he was ten and the best plastic surgeons in the world couldn't erase from his visage. He had tried a mustache, until one of the kids at the exclusive high school he attended with Tommy Sicari and the heir to the Ravenskald Empire, Samuel, started calling him Eu-stache.

Sometimes he fantasized about crushing that punk's head between a toilet bowl and the seat, which he would then sit on so he could take a massive, steaming...

A super-sexy electronic voice whispering, "My system software's all greased up and ready for your hardware, Mister Dwyer-Mann," interrupted his scatological fantasy, replacing it with a nominally less vulgar one.

Logging in to a very special account—the setup fee for which ran impressively into six-figure territory—Eustace smiled when he saw the owner of the site had uploaded a new video. Putting in a pair of Bluetooth ear buds and clicking on the play icon, he sat back in his chair, tonguing the opening of his energy drink before splashing a little of the cherry-flavored liquid onto his tongue.

After a thirty-second heavy-metal rendition of a classic carnival tune—which Eustace had heard the site owner had paid one of the top five speed-metal guitarists in the world a cool million to arrange and record—the screen went from black to red to a spinning Mesmer wheel before a mandrill-masked figure appeared in the center of the screen. Wearing a custom-cut red velvet tuxedo jacket with a matching pair of tasteful diamond brooches upon its ebony silk lapels—which glittered almost blindingly courtesy of professionally placed, high-end theatrical lighting—the man in the center of the screen placed a tall black top hat on his head and tipped his silver panther–headed walking stick toward the screen.

A beautiful touch, Eustace thought. *I've got to get me one of those, but something a little more Edward Hyde beating Sir Danvers Carew to death in the street practical, with a bigger, heavier head.*

"Greetings and good wishes," the carnival barker began. "On behalf of everyone who makes 'Prendick's All Night Fights' possible at The Coliseum month after month, year after year, decade after decade... You get the picture... we've been at this awhile now... I want to personally thank you for logging in to see what we have in store. Get ready to drool, my blood-lusting brothers and sisters... we have not one but *two* major events coming up in the next seventy-two hours. The first, two nights from now, titled "The Special," will cost you ten grand for the access code, with fifty K in minimum bets required over the course of the evening's card—and what a tremendously, spectacularly *full* card it is! We start with Man versus Man—Special Forces warriors from around the world, as always! If you're out there and think you're a modern gladiator, contact us at the secure satellite phone number on your screen... With what we pay for you to come and play, you'll be eating off fine China instead of soup kitchen Styrofoam in the blink of a predator's eye! Then we move to Animal versus Animal and the Hybrid Spectacular, with monstrosities only Moreau could imagine, which our world-class team of genetic and zoological specialists are again bringing to life for your wonder and amazement! The evening culminates with our signature Man versus Animal combat rounds and the headliner event—the champion hybrid of the evening versus our "Special Guest," Doctor Gregory Chase, until very recently head of the Brooklyn Institute of Technology's advanced genetics laboratory. Doctor Chase has unwittingly made possible our hybrid program and we wish to thank him in our own special way. Before I go, remember... I promised you *two* big events! The second, which we're calling "The Special Special," will take place the very next morning. Only those attending the first event will get details on our Special Guest for the second, but they are truly a gift from God."

As the heavy-metal carnival music started up again, twice as loud as before, Eustace activated his Crypto Wallet and began the process of transferring the ten thousand dollars that would get him the access code to "The Special."

Feeling all of a sudden aroused and a little less queasy, Eustace waited until the cryptocurrency transfer was complete before reaching for his VR headset. Punching in a code that uploaded a back alley off 1980s Times Square in the very heart of Manhattan, he virtually made his way past the tourists, vagrants, and end of the world bullhorn preachers and approached a tall, garishly made up prostitute with a purple wig and short silk skirt.

'Cause even uber-rich trust fund dudes like Eustace like to slum from time to time.

"A dead FBI agent on our watch, while we're guests in another office. I can't imagine anything worse."

The DTEAU team was in SAIC Kevin Connor's hotel room on a secure feed on his laptop. They were sitting in silence, looking at the frustrated face of Director Peter Vance. None of them was ready to speak.

After a long drag on one of his ubiquitous Marlboros, Vance shook his head through the smoke he exhaled. "I am not criticizing any of you. Nor is my counterpart in the Manhattan office. But this has gotten much more serious. And, before any of you say a word, I know we have four other victims, a missing genetics expert, and the fucking archbishop of New York. A Cardinal, for Christ's sake... So where are we at, because all the world is watching us, folks, whether they know us by name yet or not..."

As SAIC Connor and SA Sorrus brought their boss up to date on everything they were working on and where it was heading, Tech Specialist Tino Alvarado felt his phone buzz. Although he had not assigned it an ID, he knew the number. It was the Brooklyn boxing gym.

Pointing to the phone, he stepped out of the hotel room and moved a dozen feet down the hall before answering. "Oscar... everything okay? I'm at work."

"This ain't Oscar," a gravelly, low-pitched voice replied. "Oscar is incapacitated at the moment. Only temporarily. For now..."

"Who is this?" Tino asked, although the pit in his stomach and bile in his throat told him he already knew.

"It's Frankie Bank, Tino Pequeño! ¿Qué pasa, hijo de puta? Glad to hear you are working, mijo, because I am calling to collect what you owe me, on behalf of your brother. And, before you say a fucking word about being broke, let me just say, I visited your madre this morning. We had coffee and some of her chorizo y huevos. Very good chorizo y huevos, mijo. We got along real swell, especially when I told her I was an old friend of your brother's."

"How much do you want?" Tino asked, trying to control his temper and his tone. "Give me a number and I will try to obtain it."

"I don't want money, Tino Pequeño! I want your hacking skills. I need you to find out what the FBI has planned for an associate of mine, Mariano Padrino. He was picked up two days ago in Chicago on a heroin trafficking charge. He is due to be transferred to a secure facility sometime soon. I need to know when and where."

"FBI is harder than hell to hack, but I think I can do it. And that will settle the debt?"

Frankie Bank laughed. "Depends on the quality of the information, *mijo*. If it is quality, one of two things will happen… You will be debt free, or you will be too valuable to my business interests to cut you loose. If that is the case, I will make you a very attractive offer that will bring you home to Brooklyn full time and put you and your *madre* in a much better neighborhood. Big house, fancy car. A car that will be far less prone to accidents than your brother's. Get me the info, *mijo*, as soon as you can. *¿Comprender?*

"Yes," Tino answered. "I have to get back to work."

As the line went dead, Tino saw SAIC Connor coming toward him.

"Everything okay? Director Vance was not too thrilled that you bailed."

Tino nodded. "Yeah. Well… probably. It's my mother. Her health. I might need to get involved in making sure she gets the best possible care depending on the results of some tests she just had. What'd I miss?"

Connor put his hand on Tino's shoulder. "I will say a prayer for your mother. Maggie and SA Donovan are going to Storm Haven to see the head of Kardax Corporation and find out what he knows about ex–Special Forces getting involved with these animal fights. I need to spend some time with the agents who were with me at Ashe's house of horrors. We have a lot of evidence to sort through, and I'm sure they're hurting like hell. As for you…"

Tino smiled, although it was incredibly forced. "I need to keep digging on the dark and deep webs. See if I can find this *hijo de puta* Ashe."

"Yeah," Connor said, raising a brow at Tino's cursing in Spanish. "The sooner the better."

Riding the elevator in silence to the twenty-second floor of TRG Tower in Storm Haven, New Jersey, the ultramodern headquarters of one of the biggest, richest, and most politically influential multinationals in existence, SA Magdalena Sorrus felt the angry vibes washing over her from SA Elizabeth Donovan in waves. Although she had not said as much, Beth was holding DTEAU at least circumstantially responsible for the death of the Manhattan agent.

If the stakes were not so high and the time factor so critical, Maggie had no doubt the director of the Manhattan office would have instructed them to leave. Instead, he ordered the two female agents to follow up on what they had learned from the ex–Green Beret, Anthony Denham.

Taking in the amount of surveillance cameras outside the building, in the lobby, and now in the elevator, Maggie was not surprised, when, as they stepped off the elevator, a line of tiny but sophisticated cameras strung all along the hallway at a height just above the bulletproof windows across from the elevator greeted them. Their blinking red lights were clearly designed to make sure that visitors were aware they were being watched.

TRG Tower being equipped with such a high level of surveillance and next-gen technology was in no way surprising. Not only was TRG a world leader in advanced weaponry and bio-tech, Storm Haven was a preplanned, hi-tech surveillance smart city, rising like a reinforced concrete, steel, and glass vision out of a science fiction future from the mud and murky waters following the devastating Superstorm Loki that had wiped out an entire shore county and parts of two others. Consolidated into the newly named Multon County, TRG owned and administered the entire area, including its hospital, governing bodies, and security force.

If Storm Haven prospered—and it appeared to be doing just that—TRG was planning additional self-contained, corporately administrated cities in disaster-prone areas, as global warming and rising sea levels continued to worsen at an exponential rate.

Taking a right, they passed several offices with blackout windows before coming to the door they wanted. Beyond it was the founder and tactical commander of Kardax Corporation, Lt. Jacob Abel Black. Denham had said the name was probably fake and Maggie sensed the same.

After examining their FBI IDs, the secretary, without a word, indicated that they should enter the door behind her, the electronic lock of which she released by passing her hand beneath the corner of her desk.

As Maggie crossed the room, Beth by her side, she took in the large framed prints of various units in the Middle East and elsewhere around the world, along with the typical corporate motivational prints of beautiful landscapes with platitudes about discipline, commitment, service, and fortitude.

Entering the office, they saw a movie-star handsome, muscular man with cropped black hair wearing a black polo shirt embroidered in red with the Kardax name and logo—two crossed spears.

Standing to reveal baggy pocket pants and a slim waist, the man, whose utilitarian gunmetal-gray desk spoke to simple tastes bred by years in harsh conditions, offered his hand. "Agents. Welcome to TRG Tower and to Kardax. How can I help you, the FBI, and my country?"

Taking the two seats across from the desk that Black offered them before he retook his own, Maggie and Beth looked at one another, not wanting to speak at the same time. There was no fluid partnership here. No practiced back and forth. Only tension, which Maggie hoped Black wasn't seeing.

She nodded that Beth should start.

Donovan got right to the point, knowing that is what an ex–Navy SEAL commander with extensive combat experience would expect. "We are investigating half a dozen disappearances in Brooklyn, including Cardinal Archbishop Rojas, and we believe they are tied to an underground fighting operation that pits highly trained men—especially Special Forces—against a variety of exotic apex predators, including possible hybrids."

Leaning back in his chair and rubbing his chiseled chin, Black stared just over their heads for a moment while formulating his response. "I am not aware of the kidnappings. TRG is not active in Brooklyn, so it's beyond my focus. But I have heard some very concerning things about these fighting pits. You have to understand that the government and the Pentagon are failing our veterans—even the most highly trained and lethal. They come back after three or four tours after their superiors—directed by the DoD and the alphabet soup intelligence agencies who oversee all aspects of modern warfare—have commanded them to deliver lethal violence with extreme prejudice, and to witness the same every day. To have to decide if they should gun down an approaching child clutching a doll because she might be wired with explosives, or if the pregnant woman in the burka is carrying a baby or a bomb. To enter extensive cave systems and underground bunkers having no idea what might await them.

"As you can imagine, that kind of prolonged psychological pressure makes many of them incapable of assimilating back into society. Adrenaline, over time, rewires the brain. So those that don't commit suicide—and that number is nearly two dozen *a day*—or manage their PTSD and other conditions properly become action junkies. Thrill seekers. I employ hundreds of them at Kardax Corporation. It's partially why I founded it after leaving the Navy SEALs. One day, there will no longer be city police forces, but private security services. Better trained, highly experienced, and more capable of handling the kinds of situations of political and social unrest that will become an increasingly normal part of U.S. daily life. Not that you are unaware of any of this—especially you, Special Agent Sorrus. Doesn't the Domestic Threat Early Assessment Unit exist specifically for that purpose?"

Surprised, yet not, that Black knew exactly who she was, Maggie simply nodded.

"So, back to these warriors the government forgot. Kardax, and lesser private security contractors that try to copy our model, give these guys the opportunity for action that they crave, which we put to mostly positive use. This way, everyone benefits. As for the ones who go in for fighting animals for money, they are too far-gone for us to employ them. It's a very sad, very frustrating situation."

"What about Kardax employees who decide to do a little thrill-seeking and earn some extra cash on the weekends?" Beth asked.

"If we find out about it—and our job, like DTEAU's, is finding out what people do in the darkness and stopping them before they hurt themselves or someone else—their employment is immediately terminated."

"Has that happened, Lieutenant Black?" Maggie asked.

"Thankfully no," Black replied, his face a picture of sincerity. "We pay extremely well and, as I said, our guys get plenty of action, as well as generous retirement and benefits for themselves and their families, so there's no point in fighting a panther to prove yourself for 'some extra cash on the weekends,' as you put it."

As Maggie took in all that the lieutenant had said—and it was quite a lot of ugly truth in a few short, eloquent bursts—Beth stood and said, "Thank you for your time, Lieutenant Black. I am sure you're busy, as are we."

After handshakes, a few requisite pleasantries, and an exchange of cards, the meeting was over. As Beth and Maggie got into the elevator, Maggie started to speak, but Beth waved her off. It was not until they were turning out of the parking garage and headed toward the north entrance to the Garden State Parkway that Beth said, "I don't believe him for a second. He's a clever son of a bitch... Polished as a South Sea pearl. I don't know how exactly, but Kardax and TRG are somehow involved in what's happening. He was so damned careful, so impressively slick, but he let slip about the panther. Of all the animals he could have pulled from the air, he chooses the one that messed up Denham's face?"

Neither of them spoke another word on the ninety-minute drive back to the Javits Federal Building, which suited Maggie fine. She had a hell of a lot to think about, and she was feeling increasingly lost.

Special Agents Donovan and Sorrus had just returned to the FBI's suite in the Javits Federal Building when Tech Specialist Alvarado ran into the hall to greet them. "I found the fights!" he shouted, as though he were an elementary-school student on a scavenger hunt who had just found the shiniest thing imaginable.

Except, what TS Alvarado had found was possibly the darkest.

Hearing him shouting, SAIC Connor had poked his head into the hallway from his workstation. He followed the trio down the hall to where Alvarado had his setup.

"Look at this!" the tech specialist said, enlarging a video feed that revealed a tuxedo-clad man with a pair of diamond brooches on his silk lapels wearing an impressively crafted bull mask with exaggerated horns. "Recognize that mask, Agent Connor?" Alvarado asked, hardly able to stay in his seat.

"There was a sketch of it in Ashe's basement."

Leaning in, SA Donovan asked, "Is this feed live? If so, what's the origin point?"

Alvarado hit a series of keys. "Yes, it's live... but it's so buried in the dark web that there is no way to trace it back in any actionable amount of time. That's the point of the high-grade VPNs and Onion routers these dark web guys are using." Pointing to his adjoining screen, which was filled with bright green sequences of numbers scrolling through at a high rate of speed, he added, "I'm running IPs as fast as my program can handle, but it's a single needle in a million or more haystacks in order to get a hit."

"How about trying to isolate anyone accessing the feed?" SA Sorrus asked.

"Same deal. Which is sort of a good thing. I mean... no one is going to find *us* peeking in on *them* either—you follow?"

The room went quiet as the bull-masked man began to speak. "Welcome, my ravenous friends, to our virtual Special Event, which we simply call The Special! We are coming to you live, as always, from The Coliseum, as we lovingly call our custom designed fighting pit. Over the course of the next three or so hours we will attempt to settle all of the major questions that have been posed and so violently debated in the eons-old battle of Science versus God."

As the emcee gave his virtual audience a moment to let his sales pitch settle in, Alvarado's second computer beeped.

"Do you have a location?" Connor asked, as all eyes moved to the endless series of scrolling green numbers, one of which was now an eye-catching red.

Examining the data, Alvarado shook his head. "Not for the origin point. But the signal is being shared with a pay-per-view site called 'Watch 'em Die' for further broadcast reach. There are about half a dozen of these sites we've been tracking. Hardcore stuff. Makes those men eating monkey brains and animals killing people VHS cassettes from the eighties look tame. It gets extremely dark... torture, deviant sex, adrenochrome extraction, ritualistic murder. High-dollar stuff."

Again the emcee started to speak. "On behalf of the fighters—human, animal, and otherwise—I am Edward Prendick, and this is... The Special."

For the next three hours, SA Donovan and the DTEAU team—who were joined over time by the office director and several local agents—watched men fight men, animals fight animals, men fight animals, and animal hybrids straight out of *The Island of Doctor Moreau* fighting each other and the previous combinations. There was blood, gore, horrific wounds, and enough death that even the veterans among the FBI field agents found it difficult to watch for any length of time.

At the three-hour mark, the emcee returned to the screen. "I think you will agree, The Special has lived up to its name. And now... our Main Event! Our champion hybrid of the evening—a striped African hyena mixed with a bull terrier—facing off against Science personified! Bring him out, boys!"

From a cage in a darkened corner of the screen emerged a bare-chested man with a spear, a look of abject fear on his face.

"That's Gregory Chase from BIT!" Donovan said, gripping the back of Alvarado's chair so hard the plastic groaned and nearly cracked.

From the other side of the screen the champion hybrid was led to the edge of the blood-slick, gore-draped fighting pit by a pair of muscled men in Tarzan costumes and unleashed inside of it. Without missing a beat, they shoved Gregory Chase in after it. He never stood a chance. It was clear that the Main Event was not about watching a fight. It was solely about the carnage that a beast such as the hybrid could inflict upon a defenseless human body.

"Jesus Christ," Connor muttered. His vocalized thoughts were echoed by various versions of the same sentiment, punctuated by one of the male agents vomiting into a trashcan.

As they sought to find their composure, Prendick's bull mask filled the screen. "Well... so much for Science. For those attending tonight, we have a special deal for tomorrow morning's Special Special. For the modest access fee of twenty-five grand and a one-hundred thousand dollar betting minimum, you can see how God's own emissary fares against our hybrids!"

As the feed ended and the screen went blank, SA Sorrus said, "He's talking about Cardinal Rojas!"

SA Donovan nodded. "Which means we have less than twelve hours to find out where the hell this so-called Coliseum is hidden."

"At least we know who Prendick is," Connor said. "Gotta be Colin Ashe."

"Agreed," Donovan said. "TS Alvarado... I hate to ask this of you, but did you record that, and, if so, can you scan it with facial recognition software? There were Prendick's thugs in the costumes, the fighters, and I swear I saw some medical personnel."

"I am already running it," Alvarado replied, craving an energy drink and a party-sized bag of Bugles.

It was going to be a very long night and a nail-biter of a morning.

A few minutes after midnight, SAIC Kevin Connor stood in the shadows of a tree-lined street in Brooklyn's artsy Bed–Stuy neighborhood, taking a breath to let his thoughts catch up to the bullet train data stream and visual gore-fest to which he'd been subjected over the past few hours. Feeling his heart rate slow to a comfortable rhythm, he looked again at the image of a nurse in the video clip Tino had sent him half an hour earlier. Taking another deep breath, he started up the eight concrete steps in front of him, which led to a door painted an inviting hunter green.

Before he got half way up, the door opened, and an Italian-American male draped in gaudy gold jewelry and wearing a tracksuit appeared. *Jesus Christ*, Connor thought, *I cannot wait to get back to*

Langley. To complete the stereotype, the guy was wearing a pinkie ring and had a toothpick clenched in his teeth.

"Can-eye help youse wit sum-tin?" the man asked, looking bored and inconvenienced.

If he pulls out a pocket comb and runs it through his hair, Connor thought, *I will probably have to kill him.*

Pulling his FBI ID, Connor didn't managed to get a single syllable out before this ridiculous parody of a person was lowering his shoulder and charging down the stairs.

Perfect, my olive-oiled paesan, Connor thought, calling on his All-American-caliber football skills to send what was now a suspect crashing back against the first few steps, where he lay groaning and clutching his shoulder.

"Da fuck?"

Connor pulled his Sig Sauer, aiming it at the suspect's head, which drew a girlish shriek from the grimacing man. "I do not have the time nor the patience for your *Sopranos* cartoon fuckery. What do you know about the recent disappearance of Suzanne Shropshire?"

"Suze is my girlfriend. Sorta. We wennout a coupla months. She gave me a key ta her place, an' since she ain't around, I been usin' it more a' less consistently. That a crime?"

"Possibly. Depends on several factors, none of which concern me at the moment. Suzanne was thought to have been abducted several weeks ago, and we thought she might be dead. That is, until she recently turned up very much alive on a video feed documenting activities that involve at least a dozen felonies, including kidnaping and murder... I have a screen capture I need you to look at for me now."

Showing the suspect an image of the nurse that Tino had enlarged and cleaned up so it was crystal clear, Connor smiled inside as Track Suit's eyes went wide.

He was in the right place, and the suspect was ready to sing.

"I dunno nuthin'," he said, "'bout where that lyin' bitch is or what she's doin' with illegal activity. I got a text sayin' she was doin' the travelin' nursin' thing. She does that... Real good money innit..."

Connor played along. "Yes it is. Very good money. Now, Mister, uh..."

"Cozzolino. Mickey Cozzolino."

How could it be anything else? Connor thought. "...Cozzolino—I bet your friends call you Cozz... Here's the thing... I think you know at least some of what your sorta girlfriend *Suze* has been up to as of late. Now, before you respond, consider this… There are five brutally murdered people associated with this case, including a local FBI agent, so I am in zero mood for lies or clever fabrications of any sort, *capisce*?" The stress was getting to him and he simply couldn't resist blowing off some steam by playing into the parody.

"Okay, Agent. *Okay.* Suze worked for a guy named Ashe, who worked for a guy named Chase at the Brooklyn Institute of Technology, when she wasn't on duty at the local hospital. High-level stuff in a secret section a' one a' their campus buildins an' she wasn't allowed ta tell no one nuthin' 'bout it. Anyways, *how* she wound up workin' for Ashe is this… I was gettin' a few bucks here an' dere as a test subject for summa dere 'speriments. Walkin' around money, my dad usta call it. One day, while I'm waitin' ta do my ting, I see dese pills… very marketable items amongst the college an' artsy crowd, so I pocket a few a' the bottles. An' a' course Ashe finds out an' puts two an' two togetha. So now I gots ta pay him. An' I can't. So he tells me my girl Suze da nurse is gonna do some work fuh him in trade. Next ting I know, she gets carried out in da middle a' da night. Boom, boom, boom. An'… *Gone.*"

Awestruck at Cozz's use of "boom, boom, boom," Connor asked, bringing the Sig Sauer a little closer to the suspect's face, "And you didn't bother to call the cops?"

"How could I? First, I stole from da guy. Second, he knew about Suze 'cause I had brought her 'round a few times when I was part a' da tests. He acted weird 'round her. Then, outta nowhere, he starts wearing dese fuckin' *masks*… One was a crazy lookin' monkey… Another looked like a fuckin' cow wit' horns…"

"That would be a bull…"

"Yeah. Whateva. An' he starts callin' hisself Prendick. Braggin' 'bout some big doins' he was startin' at a place called the Coliseum. Fuckin' weirdo, *capisce*?"

"Listen to me, Cozz. Only I say *capisce*… *Capisce*? Did he say where the Coliseum was? Any hint of a location?"

"Nope." All of a sudden, Cozz got a very serious look on his face. "Is Suze gonna be okay, Agent?"

"She's alive," Connor said, helping the track-suited cartoon-man back to his feet. "But she's in danger. And she's involved in some very ugly dealings. Certainly an accessory to murder. So here's the deal… We're going to find her. In the meantime, I want you to turn around, go back inside that apartment, and stay there until you get word from me that you can leave. Do you understand me, Mister Cozzolino?"

Nodding, Cozz did what Connor asked.

Descending the steps and heading for his car, Connor dialed Tino.

"Any luck, sir?" Tino asked, sounding like he was struggling to stay awake.

"Talked to her boyfriend, and got the backstory. Nothing helpful as far as finding the location of the Coliseum, although more confirmation that Ashe is Edward Prendick. Shit! Prendick... from *The Island of Doctor Moreau*! How the fuck could I have missed that?"

"Got a little bit of everything on your plate right now, boss."

"Look... you keep trying to figure out where the Coliseum is. We have maybe eight hours to prevent the slaughter of the Cardinal. While you do that, I have a hunch about something. Gotta make a call. I'm stayin' here in Brooklyn. Let Agent Sorrus know." Before Tino could respond, Connor was hanging up and redialing. "Doctor Marsh... Sorry it's so late. Working a very time-sensitive case, and I had a thought. You mention to me once that an ancestor of Uriel Stanton's wrote a book claiming *The Island of Doctor Moreau* was real... That he interviewed a guy named Edward Prendick, who spent some time on the doctor's island... Prendick's the guy that narrates Wells's novel, am I right?"

From her bed in Storm Haven, where she taught forensics at Eastern Pinelands University and consulted for the FBI, Doctor Ruth Anne Marsh yawned and shook her head to clear the cobwebs. "Very good memory, Agent. Uriel's ancestor.... a great-great-great uncle, I think... is Judah Philemon Stanton. Wrote a trilogy of out-there books... Vampires, werewolves... He was friends with Watson and Holmes. Did you ask Uriel about it, like I suggested?"

Connor grimaced with embarrassment. "Been a little busy. And the Prendick connection is only now of urgent importance... Tied to animal hybridization and underground fighting rings..."

Ruth Anne yawned again. "Sorry... Was in the lab 'til late." Then she was wide-awake. "You know something, Agent... There's an animal fighting operation active in the London underground in 1894 in Judah's second book. A case he worked with Sherlock Hol—"

Hanging up and dialing Stanton's number, Connor made a mental note to call Ruth back when this was over and apologize for his rudeness. "Hey... Uriel. Kevin Connor at the DTEAU. What can you tell me about Judah Stanton and his connection to Edward Prendick?"

As Michael Stanton settled into the decades-old sensory deprivation chamber in an abandoned, nearly forgotten laboratory beneath Eastern Pinelands University, his only wish was that contact with *Him* would come quickly and without pain. Likewise, once *He* arrived, Michael prayed that he could retrieve the information his brother Uriel and the DTEAU team needed to save the life of a Roman Catholic Cardinal without the usual hoop jumping and mind games *His Highness* nearly always required.

Once he delivered the data, he could go back to his bed on the Psych Ward of Saint Michael's Teaching Hospital on the other side of the sprawling EPU campus and get some decent drugs and some blissful, dreamless sleep.

As Uriel's voice unexpectedly filled his ear buds, Michael flinched. His environment was designed to put him in a trance state, and it was doing its job. He was submerged in four feet of water in a round iron tank that his anticipated communication partner had once described as an "Orgone-producing chamber of [my] own design (extending the work and theories of Wilhelm Reich, G Harry Stine, and WS Burroughs).... A soul-clarifier cobbled together from salt, pewter, iron nails, copper plates, depleted uranium, dish soap, an assortment of coils, marmoset fur, titanium, corn husks, six electromagnets, an array of [Z]ener diodes, cormorant extract, and talc. What John C. Lilly termed a 'cognitional multidimensional projection space'— sensory deprivation chambers where whole worlds are born."

"I am going to fire it up now," Uriel said. "You ready, Michael?"

"Read me the data, U," Michael answered through a padded, waterproof microphone pressed tightly against his mouth. His eyes were covered with black swimmer's goggles. Not that he could see anything. A tight-fitting bibbed neoprene hood covered his head and neck, holding the earbuds, microphone, and goggles securely in place. "If you're gonna fill my head with electricity like some of the headshrinkers do, I wanna hear the facts and figures, brother..."

Flipping to the appropriate page in a thick binder their anticipated visitor had left behind over a decade ago, Uriel read as he worked. "'It can also be used as a psychic experience–enhancer by remote-wiring it to a decent computer, a digital to analog converter, and then to a series of magnetometers capable of feeding 8 to 12 microTesla bursts into 8 pairs of solenoids situated in a half-moon pattern on each side of the skull. Directed down through the pineal–

hypothalamic tract into the brain's right hemisphere, sending [your] melon-waves into a frenzy of theta and alpha rhythms (anywhere between 6.66 and 10.80 Hz, the latter of which will put you in a nicely suggestive state).'"

Raising his arms, Michael ran his fingers over the neoprene hood, feeling the gentle bumps where Uriel had placed the eight pairs of solenoids in the prescribed half-moon pattern on either side of his skull. "Lunchtime on the P Ward features a butterscotch pudding and a damned fine tapioca with *zero* raisins and lots of cinnamon spice. Let's get this carnival started."

Outside the chamber, Uriel heard a series of clicks and beeps as the apparatus—which looked like something straight out of re-runs of the original *Doctor Who*—came to life. It was so old and cobbled together, he kept half an eye on the brand new fire extinguisher he had bought at a twenty-four-hour box store an hour earlier before picking Michael up from Saint Michael's Teaching Hospital. DTEAU's director, Peter Vance, had applied considerable pressure in just the right places to get Uriel's twin transferred and, under the new arrangement, Michael was considered somewhere between a patient and a guest, which meant Uriel could see him as often as he wanted. However, due to his hectic schedule at the *Evening Standard*, it had been nowhere near as much as he would have liked.

Then again, showing up at two in the morning to take your admittedly insane brother for a quick trip across campus came with a truckload of uncomfortable questions that required a sixty-second call from Director Vance to the senior duty nurse on the fifth floor of St. Michael's to bring to an equally uncomfortable end.

Inside the SDC, Michael felt his scalp start to tingle as amoeba-like energy patterns in subtle primary colors began to decorate the abject darkness of the chamber.

Hiya fellas.

"Hey U… His Royal Highness is here… Do you hear him?" Michael asked, grateful that the first part of his wish was coming true.

Of course he heard me. I built this thing with a purpose—I wanted to ensure that future occupants would never be as lonely as was I during all the answer-seeking hours I spent in there over the decades. Hiya Uriel. How's tricks?

Feeling his bladder start to ache and his ears to ring, same as they always did when the Angel Falling Upward, Planner Forthright, communicated telepathically with him, Uriel only grunted in response, evoking a laugh that tickled the back of his throat and elevated his heartrate.

Listen, boys… it's been a hot minute, and I know you've got places to be… But before we begin the beguine, I just gotta say… you hafta tell Mister Beef-and-Cheese at the DTEAU that he needs to keep an eye on The Changeling. My ex-boss is restless, and that usually means some death. E. G. Howe is his chosen instrument at present and he's pissed his blade is caged. Now… to the reason why you called… The Coliseum is hidden within the Brooklyn Navy Yard, beneath the Naval Hospital, although it continues for several acres beneath a pair of buildings not far from Admiral's Row.

"That's it?" Michael asked.

Time is of the essence, and since those I hate the most are rooting awfully hard for the ugly, claw and tooth demise of Cardinal Esteban Rojas, I would consider it a great personal favor if you would see that doesn't happen. That's all I have to say. Till next time, my favorite intrepid travelers. Remember to keep the cosmic crazy hazy, my boys…

Michael found himself smiling… a rare and promising thing. Expecting to hear the almost immediate release of the airlocks on the lid of the SDC, when a couple of minutes went by and the always stress-reducing *Whoosh* of released air didn't arrive, he said into the microphone, "What the hell are you doing, Uriel? Did you forget I'm stuck in here?"

It didn't take but another second or two of silence before he began to panic. "Uriel!" he screamed, pounding his fists against the iron sides of the chamber. *"Uriel!"*

"Easy, brother." Uriel's voice was a needed balm in the Gilead of Michael's earbuds. "I wanted to call 'Mister Beef-and-Cheese' and give him the location—and the warning about The Changeling. I'll have you out of there in a minute."

Three minutes later, the neoprene headpiece, goggles, and the rest of the gear removed, Uriel started removing the solenoids from his brother's scalp. "That was way too easy…" he said, worry in his voice. "You think Planner Forthright's fucking with us?"

Michael grunted. "When is he ever *not* fucking with us, even when he's helping? You said this Special Special is happening *sometime this morning*?"

"That's what Connor told me."

Grasping Uriel's arm and glancing at his wristwatch, Michael said, "It's already four-thirty. I don't think these gruesome fuckers keep anything near to banker's hours."

"Which means the slaughter of Cardinal Rojas could happen at literally any moment..."

After Uriel had removed the last of the solenoids, Michael rubbed his scalp. "Still all a'tingle... I can see why that nutty fallen angel—or whatever the hell he *really* is—was so addicted to the ride. I actually kinda like it..."

"Terrific," Uriel said, doing his best to hide his fear, even as his nose began to twitch.

Dealing with a demon always reeked of shit.

Esteban Claudio Rojas, archbishop of the Diocese of New York, and one of the most influential members of the College of Cardinals, slowly opened his eyes, praying to God with an unprecedented sincerity that he would find himself back in his bed in his Cobble Hill mansion. *Please God*, he whispered, *let there be before me a hot breakfast on my table and my dark blue Zimmerli robe hanging from my bedpost. Let this be a nightmare from which I am able to awaken.*

Even before his eyes could focus, he knew it was not to be. The first hint was the smell. Instead of expensive colognes, myrrh, frankincense, and fresh citrus shipped in weekly from Messina, he smelled vomit, urine, and sweat—all of which were his own. The second hint was the pneumonia-inducing cold and damp of the concrete floor on which he sat.

The final confirmation was the voice of his tormentor, who called himself Edward Prendick.

"Wakey, wakey now, Your Eminence. The sun is just about risen. A little groggy, I see. Hard to get the dose right. Yes, yes... we had to give you a sedative. You just refused to *sleep*... It's nearly time to perform. Come on, now, Little Esteban... open up those eyes. How does that classic Pink Floyd rocker go? 'Is there anybody in there? Just nod if you can hear me... Is there anyone home?' Those two very well trained, vengeful fellas you met the other day are chock full of protein and steroids. They eagerly await your appearance in the pit."

Despite his tongue feeling like a wad of year-old dryer lint, Rojas managed to whisper, "It's not too late to save your soul... and theirs.

I have made my mistakes, but they were very long ago. I have atoned through good and righteous works."

Prendick, standing in the shadows outside the cell, produced an elaborate ritual bull mask replete with two-foot horns and laughed. "You have atoned, deceiver, for nothing. You have Botox injected monthly into your face because you are too vain to show your age. And your alliance to the Star Quorum—"

"I have no idea what that even—"

"My Christ, how you deceive!" Prendick yelled, slipping the bull mask over his shadowed face. "You hold one of the trio of seats reserved for Cardinals since the Star Quorum's founding in 1209 AD, do you not?"

"How can you possibly know that?"

"My benefactors are priests in the Lodges of Mammon and Moloch. I can only be so honest because you, my corrupted, lustful friend, will soon be irreversibly dead. Your politics are less than desirable in Rome. Changes must be made. Promotions granted to the worthy. Advocates put in place. At each and every turn, you and your red-dressed cohorts in the College of Cardinals have blocked the wishes of the true guardians of the Vatican."

"You mean that *bastardo* Bal—"

"Ah, ah, ah. No names. Speak of the devil and he'll arrive. My staff will be here at any moment to make you ready, and many powerful people shall witness your sanguine sacrifice. And no one will ever know the truth of why you died. Let them think it was your pederasty. Better to blemish your memory."

As Prendick walked away, Rojas began to scream.

It reverberated off the walls, and even rose to Heaven, where it filled the temples and fields.

Despite the pain that fed it, not a single angel wept.

As a caravan of FBI, NYPD, and SWAT vehicles sped toward the Brooklyn Navy Yard, supported by a trio of helicopters, Kevin Connor checked his Sig Sauer and adjusted the straps on his custom-fitted next-gen bulletproof vest.

"Are we really going on the word of a career mental patient who gets his info from a self-described fallen angel that speaks into his head?" SA Donovan asked from the front seat of the Chevy Suburban in which she and the DTEAU field agents were traveling. "My boss is about ready to reassign me to Des Moines, so your answer better be yes."

"Yes," SA Sorrus answered, putting her hand on Connor's arm to let him know she would handle Donovan's questions. "I know it's a lot to process, but he was essential in thwarting an assassination attempt on the governor of New Jersey and in catching a prolific serial killer."

"In Secaucus... also in New Jersey," Donovan answered with a frown. "Lousy way to spend the week leading up to Christmas. Aside from this fallen angel having a thing for the Garden State, the FBI, NSA, CIA, and most of the rest of the alphabet agencies at one time or another have questioned Michael Stanton. His brother Uriel's a decent reporter, and their family's done a lot for the world over the centuries, but if we get to the abandoned naval hospital and there are no fighting pits, no Cardinal Esteban Rojas, the people in this vehicle are seriously fucked—you all do get that, right?"

Instead of answering, Connor hit a video call button on his smartphone. When TS Alvarado's face filled the screen, he said, "Anything up on the feed?"

"It hasn't gone live yet. But I was just about to call you... I was able to tap into one of the attendees' VPNs. There was a built-in back door we've been exploiting to monitor the technical command center's special projects division at Ravenskald Tower for several months now. The guy who runs it is cocky, and unforgivably sloppy."

"So the Ravenskalds are somehow involved?" SA Sorrus said, peeking into the frame and thinking back on what Donovan had said after they had questioned the head of the Kardax Corporation.

"Not a surety, Agent. The feed is anonymous. And the guy who oversees special projects for TRG is named Sicari."

"No shit..." Connor whispered. Feeling several pairs of eyes on him, he said, "I'll fill you in another time." To Alvarado he said, "What are you getting from the attendee's feed?"

"There's a static screen with a shot of the bull mask that says 'Welcome to the Special Special.' The background music is the bomb... heavy metal meets carnival. Anyway... Below the mask is a countdown clock. Looks like you've got roughly fifteen minutes before the show starts."

"Great work, Tino," Connor said. "Contact me with anything new. Our ETA is five minutes."

As he hung up the phone, SA Donovan said, "It's actually about two and a half. Everybody ready?"

Switching off the safety on his Sig Sauer and giving one more tug on the straps of his bulletproof vest, Connor said, "Damn straight we are."

As two burly men in stereotypical leopard-patterned jungle outfits placed Cardinal Esteban Rojas in front of the high-end cinema cameras and professionally designed lighting that made "Prendick's All Night Fights" a premier event amongst the wealthiest of Dark Web aficionados, the most recent in a long line of "Edward Prendicks" stood beside him, running his opening monologue in his head. His stylized bull mask securely in place and the signature red velvet tuxedo and diamond brooches reflecting the light to his satisfaction, Prendick activated the wireless microphone hidden beneath the brim of his coal black top hat.

Before speaking, Prendick tilted his chin for optimal effect. The bull mask—purchased at a steep price from a holy man in Mit Rahina, Egypt, near the ruins of Memphis—was evocative of Apis, Hadad, Moloch, and the Minotaur, and he felt powerful beneath its masculine shape and considerable weight.

"Welcome, friends, to the Special Special! Before we begin the morning's fights, I would like to say a few words about how I became your host and what I am endeavoring to do for the evolution and elevation of humanity. You see, 'Prendick's All Night Fights,' from the time of its inaugural events in London in 1894, has been about much more than offering the very best in combat entertainment. Much more than just about *greed*! Although, I will be honest—we all do *love* the money that you spend! But you must not think that we squander our precious proceeds. Nothing could be further from the truth. We pay our human fighters—heroes all, in each of the countries where they have served and fought with distinction—more in a night than their governments pay them over the course of *weeks*. Men trained to kill and then cast aside as no longer fit for society. We give them back their purpose. We give them a stage to show their worth. And, should they have a gripe… Refused housing because of their income… Denied a church wedding because they brought home to America and wished to marry a *Muslim*—Yahweh forbid!… Finding it harder to secure services when an ambitious, heartless councilwoman pushes through unkind ordinances in order to line her already *bulging* pockets with contractor bribes to grease their illegal deal-making… We bring the targets of their torment before you to make their overdue recompense. Recompense in blood and tissue and bone. You have seen it these past several weeks! What a glorious recompense it has been! I *know* that you all agree! That you wish to see some more!

"This morning, we offer up a truly heinous man to face the justice of the pits. Cardinal Archbishop Esteban Claudio Rojas, until just days ago, used to live in a mansion on exclusive, lavish Cobble Hill in the city of Brooklyn, New York. He is not a man of *God* but of the *flesh*! Silk robes, silk sheets, expensive wines, expensive... *companions*, if you understand me! This decadent monster... this abuser of children within his churches... and in the confines of the Vatican gardens... represents the evil of the Roman Catholic Church. A church become so vain and secretive it pays for his monthly Botox injections to hide the guilt-lines in his face! Fitting he should be its most powerful representative in America. But justice shall be served. I have invited two Argentinian Special Forces officers from Buenos Aires to join the proceedings this morning. Their brother and sister, respectively, were physically and psychologically abused by Rojas when he was a priest. Abused to the point of committing suicide! He *admitted it* to me as he awaited his time in the spotlight. And Esteban Claudio Rojas truly *loves* the spotlight."

As Prendick spoke, the two Argentinians entered the frame of the camera, flanking the masked emcee. Each wore a sheathed knife and held a spear and a whip. As they sneered into the camera, the attendees sitting at home or at their exclusive clubs could see Rojas in the background, weeping like the children whose lives he had so soullessly destroyed to satisfy his carnal appetites.

"Now... before these two highly decorated warriors have their way with Rojas and—once they've brought him to the point of death—we witness the ultimate retribution as our champion hybrid pulls his corrupted flesh apart, as he did with Gregory Chase last night, I must tell you who I am and what 'Prendick's All Night Fights' plans to do. You see... Chase was *my* choice for the pits. *I* was the one he wronged. I was making considerable strides in my work in genetic design. Truly Nobel worthy. I was on the verge of a breakthrough in genome manipulation and hybridization when Chase pulled the funding from my work. And that is not all he did, my friends! He made every effort to ostracize me—to compare me to Doctor Moreau! As much as I admire that ambitious surgical genius despite his admittedly primitive, clumsy hybrids, which still managed to produce such beautiful carnage in 1894, I tell you this—I am no mad Moreau! I do not possess his hubris. His almost religious zeal! I do not seek to remove the evil from man—we know that is impossible—but to *harness* it! To restore order out of society's churning, ugly chaos! Tell me this, my friends: Are our lethal hybrids not beautiful? Is our inspired work not blessed? *This* is why *I* am the new Edward Prendick! *This* is why your money is so important and so very carefully spent! *This* is why we are all here this morning! So let us proceed. Without further delay, I give you the Special—"

Before he could finish with his anticipated flourish, Prendick—otherwise known in the workaday world as Doctor Colin Ashe—heard the sound of automatic weapons as his entire world went to hell.

The worst part of Tech Specialist Tino Alvarado's job was having to remain tethered to his desk, helpless and emasculated, as he watched his fellow team members engage in an all-out firefight courtesy of their hi-res body cameras.

The second worst part was trying to process the information that Prendick had shared—the only connection between the victims being that they had dishonored a veteran—a nearly impossible connection to find through the tools at Alvarado's disposal. *That's* why he had been coming up empty... *the victims weren't linked to each other at all.*

The history of "Prendick's All Night Fights," starting in 1894, would be part of the criminal prosecution case, and Tino would be tasked with providing crucial documents, deep web footage, profiles, and timelines through his highly refined research and technical skills. Somehow, an ancestor of the Stanton twins—according to what Ruth Anne Marsh and Uriel Stanton had said to SAIC Connor—played into it all from the start. That fact alone would pull them even deeper into the world of shadows and deception that was DTEAU's daily beat. But all of that had zero value to the situation at hand.

Right now, it was real-life cops and robbers, and Tino Alvarado was sitting on the sidelines.

If he was going to move forward with this gig beyond the mandatory agreement that prevented a stint in prison, he would have to do something to change that.

Clenching the arms of his office chair as SAIC Connor tackled Prendick while gunfire smoked and sparked around them, Alvarado put his attention on SA Sorrus's bodycam. If he could, he would be the pair of extra eyes she needed to keep her safe. As she cuffed one of the men in the cheap-looking leopard-print jungle costumes,

Alvarado saw SA Donovan deeper in the frame. Behind her was the kidnapped nurse, Suzanne Shropshire. Far from looking panicked, as he would expect her to, she looked almost stoic as she reached into her medical bag and took out—

"Maggie!" Tino yelled into his microphone. "The nurse has a gun. She's gonna—"

There was the distinct pop of a Glock, and Donovan was on the floor.

"Agent down!" SA Sorrus yelled, aiming her gun at the nurse and disarming and disabling her with a marksman's shot to the shoulder.

Two minutes later, the firefight was over. Alvarado would later find out that the assault team had taken out a dozen guards in the entranceway to the fighting pit, which was exactly where Michael Stanton had learned it was from his "fallen angel," Planner Forthright.

Prendick was in custody, as was the nurse and one of the thugs in the jungle get-up. The other one—whom his tattooed, earringed friend from Lights… Camera… Animals! would soon identify as the second shooter in his confrontation with SA Donovan and TS Alvarado—was dead. So were the two Argentinian Special Forces soldiers.

As for Cardinal Rojas, before the FBI agents had killed them, the Argentinians had dragged him to the cage of the hybrid striped African hyena–bull terrier and thrown him inside before closing and locking its door.

They would need dental records from the Vatican to prove it was Rojas, although no one had any doubt.

Special Agent Elizabeth Donovan died on the operating table at NYU Langone Hospital–Brooklyn five hours later, despite the best efforts of one of the top-rated trauma teams in the state.

As the EMTs were wheeling Donovan to an ambulance within ten minutes of the end of the gun battle, SAIC Connor was removing Edward Prendick's shattered bull mask from his head.

Seeing a mummy-like wrapping of surgical bandages beneath it, he yelled, "What the fuck are you doing to your face?"

"The future is surgical, Agent," Prendick replied with a laugh. "It won't all be avatars in cyberspace. If you have the money, you can be *anyone you want*—or anyone your employers choose to make you."

Thirty-six hours later, the DTEAU team was sitting in their central meeting space on the seventh floor of a nondescript federal office building outside of Langley, Virginia, which they shared with off-the-radar specialty units from half a dozen other national intelligence agencies. It was an unspoken agreement that the members of these units did not mingle, nor converse.

"Let me break this down for the three of you, as I am currently seeing it," Unit Director Peter Vance began, taking a long drag on a Marlboro. "Breaking up this fighting ring is a win. Bringing to justice the monster behind five murders and a laundry list of other felonies is a win—especially one engaged in a variety of biomedical atrocities. That said, and kudos bestowed, we need to consider the losses, which are also quite considerable. Two agents—neither from our office—were killed in the line of duty. Early word from Internal Affairs and the DOJ Office of the Inspector-General is that both field incidents were properly managed and that no suspensions will be instituted. You're all facing long Q and A sessions with both of them, and I expect you will fully cooperate no matter how unreasonable they decide to make the process. I got a call this morning from my bosses and the tone was not unkind. If you need some down time when all of this is over—after you return from the funerals in New York and have your sessions with IA and DOJ—you're more than welcome to take it. I encourage it. What you all saw in the course of completing this assignment is more than any agent should have to deal with in their career, and that is beginning to become a regular statement from me. Now… on to your reports. Haxx, you have an update?"

"It's TS Alvarado, sir," SAIC Connor said, his tone completely sincere.

"Haxx is fine," Alvarado replied. "I got all caught up in something new… Being back home and some of the folks in the neighborhood making a fuss over me… SA Donovan giving me some special attention because I was the techno-wizard shiny thing… Those guys in Manhattan need to brush their shit right up… Sorry for the language, sir…"

"No apology necessary," Vance answered. "And you're going to get your wish. The Operational Technology Division has already requested that we allow you time to conduct virtual intensives and a lecture and training tour as soon as our superiors deem it feasible. Starting with Manhattan. That'll give you some time to be home in Brooklyn with your mother. I also get the sense that you want to be in the field with Connor and Sorrus more, so I'm arranging for you to get your weapons and physical fitness training up to where they should be."

Haxx smiled. "Thank you, sir. I did get a pretty good adrenaline kick when SA Donovan and I were pinned down and under fire in that animal training facility near the Brooklyn Navy Yard."

"FBI and NYPD units were a few blocks away... nearly right on fucking *top* of the fighting pit—almost *literally*—and they had no goddamned idea," Connor said with a grimace.

"No Monday morning quarterbacking. Or, in your case, tight-ending..." Vance said, lighting a new cigarette with the old one before crushing the butt in a nearly overflowing FBI ashtray. Then to Haxx, he said, "I want you to put reassignment out of your mind. We need you here. I have a feeling this incomprehensible shit show is just the tip of the iceberg. Although, in all honestly, I am well aware that this tech training and lecture tour is going to shave major time off your mandatory assignment obligation and you're worth millions to the private sector on the open market."

"Happy to be here for now, sir," Haxx answered. "Speaking of, you asked for a report. I managed to recover Prendick's... uh, Colin Ashe's... plastic surgery records from a laptop found at the fighting pits. He's been undergoing procedures... some of which he did on himself... Been happening for months. But here's the kicker... there was a series of digital photos of whom it was he was ultimately going to look like..."

Already feeling queasy at the idea of Ashe performing plastic surgery on himself, Vance, Connor, and Sorrus—who had thus far sat in silence—collectively gasped at the picture Haxx held up.

"That's Doctor Julius Eccobukk!" Vance said, fright and astonishment competing for supremacy in his voice. "He's a Palestinian Jew—his mother's Israeli—and U.S. ambassador to the United Nations. His mediation has been crucial to the past few years of uneasy peace in the region. Have you been able to discern how long it would take for Ashe to complete the necessary surgeries?"

"About six more weeks," Haxx answered. "I have something else. As you all know, I was able to access the fighting pit feed through one of the attendees' VPNs. I was able to drill down deeper since I've been back and with my own setup and I unmasked the creepy bastard."

"Gimme a name and address, and we'll have him in custody within a handful of hours," Connor said, getting out of his chair.

Looking at the info on his tablet and then turning it around for everyone to see the picture, Haxx said, "Eustace Grenier Dwyer-Mann, oldest son of the CEO of Daimon-Metis Corporation in Parkersburg, West Virginia. I traced the signal right to the house, in the heart of the historic district. I'm emailing you the address..."

Director Vance put up his hand. "Forget it, Haxx. Completely. Delete everything you have, wherever you have it. As soon as you can."

"Wait a minute—," Connor said, his cheeks starting to flush.

"Delete it all I said. *Immediately*, Tech Specialist Alvarado," Vance reiterated, ignoring his at the moment menacing subordinate. "We cannot touch the Dwyer-Manns. You'll have to trust me on this, because it isn't the typical 'can't touch the rich' bullshit that usually ties our hands. There are legitimate reasons why that family has protection. However... you continue to keep an eye on him without having any record of it, you understand me, TS Alvarado?"

As Connor whispered about what a heap of horseshit this was, Vance concluded the meeting with a reiteration of the great job they all did and dismissed them.

As their boss headed for his office, where he closed the door and made what looked like a very serious phone call, SA Magdalena Sorrus, trying hard not to burst into tears, said to the two remaining team members, "I'm leaving for New York in an hour if you want a ride. Bring headphones or something. I don't want to talk. About anything."

Watching her walk away, Haxx thought about something he needed to do before they left. Something that would keep him up at night for weeks—especially after what Director Vance had told him about his future—but something absolutely necessary.

Best to get it over with, before he lost his nerve.

Sitting in Lucky Red's Tavern, the oldest bar in Secaucus, New Jersey, four hours later—having decided it was best to drive alone to Manhattan for the funerals—SAIC Kevin Connor set down his beer and tried to tune out the shade-throwing dart and pool players in the back. As a commercial for another startup life insurance company with a washed-up nineties actor as its spokesman ended, the reigning super-queen of nighttime cable news appeared. Her perfectly done makeup and hair, which she subconsciously touched with her fingertips as the camera zoomed steadily in for a close-up, was at odds with the solemn look on her face. "Good evening and Welcome to 'The Whole Truth with Kegan Reilly.' RWN's lead story tonight is one that will give all good Catholics pause. Cardinal Archbishop Esteban Rojas, who faithfully served New York for the past seventeen years, was found dead in his modest residence in the Cobble Hill neighborhood in the New York Borough of Brooklyn yesterday. The coroner's report, released exclusively to RWN just an hour ago, states the cause of the beloved Cardinal's death as a massive cerebral stroke."

"Horseshit," Connor whispered, loud enough to draw dagger-eyed stares from the patrons around him, who were overwhelmingly Catholic.

"Ya better watch that kinda talk in here, boyo," a man in his sixties warned from his corner stool at the bar. "Me son Daniel met His Eminence hisself. A Saint John's fan, the archbishop was, an udderwise unforgivable sin."

Thankfully, the man—whose accent sounded fake, a put-on for the tourists—went back to his Guinness as Kegan Reilly continued. "The word we are getting from our sources at the Vatican is that Cardinal Rojas will be replaced later this week by Cardinal Niccolò Balena, who currently serves as Guardian of the Doctrine in Rome, a move in line with the RCC's recent re-commitment to a more traditionally conservative stance..."

As Reilly transitioned to her next news item, Connor threw a five on the counter and headed out into the night, dialing his phone and heading to his car. "Boss. It's Kevin. Are you watching RWN? Hell yeah she's still my Midwest schoolboy crush, but this is serious. The Vatican is replacing Rojas with Cardinal Niccolò Balena. Right? And Ravenskald Worldwide News got the exclusive... I'm beginning to understand what this really was about..."

Four and a half hours earlier, Tech Specialist Alvarado slipped out the door and headed for the men's bathroom on the seventh floor. Since only he, Connor, and Vance ever used it, and neither of them were currently in the building, he knew he'd be alone.

Pulling his smartphone from his pocket, and scrolling to a number saved as The Bank, he typed a message:

MARIANO PADRINO. FROM CHICAGO FACILITY TO TIER ONE SECURITY FEDERAL FACILITY IN MILWAUKEE. VAN TRANSFER, 3 AM, I-45 N. TWO GUARDS FRONT, ONE IN BACK. LEAVE ME AND MY FAMILY ALONE.

After hesitating a moment, he sent it, deleting it from his phone within seconds.

Leaving the bathroom, he saw Maggie Sorrus waiting for him. "You ready to hit the road for home, TS Alvarado?"

Slipping his phone into his pocket, he said. "More than you know, SA Sorrus. More than you know."

A NEW TECHNIC

Sometime in the not too distant present.

Tommy Sicari, vice president of special projects for The Ravenskald Group, was feeling on top of the world. At least for the moment, and probably 'til dawn. Certainly, the three martinis he had imbibed in the last few hours had helped. Helped so much that he wanted to shout out how good he felt from the top of the building in which he currently stood, Ravenskald Tower, so that all of Storm Haven, the State of New Jersey, the Eastern Seaboard, and the entirety of the world could hear it.

Absent that reality, the two lovely, equally intoxicated ladies leaning against the hallway wall in their tight skirts and tighter blouses would do.

"Okay, now, Princess One an' Princess Two... Are you ready to enner the inner sanctum? The real nerve cen'er of what 'Solomon the Wise'—president an' CEO of The Ravenskald Group, by whom all of us are employed—proudly calls 'the New Technic'"?

His companions both screamed yes.

"Hey, hey, hey... I 'preciate the enthusiasm, an' this space is thoroughly soundproofed, but if anyone is workin' late one floor up at the Kardax Corporation, we doan' want those ex–Special Forces muscle heads comin' down an' investigatin', do we?"

"Muscles, you say?" the taller and shapelier of the two, Mona Devins, squealed, twirling her peroxide-blonde ringlets around two of her French-manicured fingers. "Maybe we *do* want a few..."

Drawing on his outsized, liquor-fueled confidence, Tommy answered, "They're all 'roided out an' limp-dicked, sad ta say. *Plus*, they got the PTSDs... Trust me—I'm responsible for runnin' their back'round checks. Besides... I'm all ya need tonight. Okay... Here we go... Now, keep in mind, I designed most a' this myself..."

Stepping up to a state of the art security door, Tommy placed three fingers on a bio-scan pad while looking into a retina scanner and saying, "Twenty-three skiddo." Pausing for a millisecond, Tommy smiled as a series of beeps and clicks filled the air, the overhead light went from red to green, and the security door unlocked.

"Super cool!" Mona said, staring in wonder at the banks of computers, servers, and security equipment arrayed around the room. "It looks like the bridge of the *Enterprise*!"

"Very good, Mona!" Tommy said, ushering in the suspiciously quiet girl whom Mona had introduced as "Angie from accounting" so he could lock the door. Activating a row of recessed lights and adjusting them down for the proper amount of ambience with a remote he grabbed from his desk, Tommy hit a second button and the glass walls that framed the control center turned a smoky gray.

"Impressive," Angie said, although her tone was screaming boredom.

"Lighten up some, Angie, would ya?" Mona said, swinging an expensive gaming chair around at what was obviously the room's command console and falling into rather than sitting down genteelly on the custom-molded, generously padded seat.

"Why twenty-three skidoo?" Angie asked, her tone still indicating she was only making conversation.

Tommy shrugged. "'Cause Solomon the Wise's office is on the twenty-third floor, and it's a cool kinda phrase. Twenty-three is extremely mystical and magical."

After the two girls stared at him, expressionless, for a moment, Mona said, "This is a very fancy setup you got here, Mister Sicari. I've never been on *this floor* before. Run of the mill receptionists aren't permitted past the nineteenth floor... Anything above is *strict*ly for executive secretaries..."

"Or, as we like to call 'em, executive leg-spreaders!" Angie yelled, sitting in Mona's lap and setting the chair to rotating with her shapely, black-stocking'd leg.

As much as Tommy loved the way Angie was warming up— apparently the drinks they had had an hour ago at the Stargazer, a trendy bar just up the street from the Tower, were finally beginning to take effect—he said, risking her re-frigidation, "Hey now. I mean it. You're gonna hafta keep it down... We doan' wan' security up here... Not before I finish conductin' my very *personal* interviews of you both for those executive positions you mentioned..."

Stopping the chair with the heel of her bright red pump, Mona said, her look both sultry and serious, "Some positions are obviously better than others, am I right? So if we were to do *real good* in this interview tonight..."

Tommy opened a mini-fridge near his desk and removed a bottle of Dom Perignon. "No worries, my girls—as soon as I pop the cork on this very expensive bottle a' bubbly, I'll tell ya how the interview is gonna unfold. We gotta get started 'cause I have a very important meet-n-greet at midnight. The interview combines the latest in kinesthetic testing, breath control, executive an' secretary liaising, wardrobe selection—an' deselection—word play, an' foreplay. Also designed by me. Get those glasses over there by the window, would ya?"

As Tommy popped the cork with a towel—so as not to spill any liquid on the arrays of computers and other devices—Mona and Angie got up from the chair as though they were cowgirls showing at a rodeo. Knowing they had Tommy's complete attention, they walked slowly and suggestively, arm in arm, to get the glasses, pausing to give each other a sensual kiss on the lips before returning.

"The interview is off to a fabulous start, ladies! Now... present glasses!"

As Tommy poured the expensive champagne—a gift from a boarding school friend in Parkersburg, West Virginia, for whom he did high-end computer work under the table and anonymously—Mona whispered, "Mmm... I like it when you show authority..."

As Tommy filled her glass, Angie added, "Me too. Soooooo, Mister Sicari... just how much authority *do* you have around here? Word is, Mister Ravenskald runs a Very. Tight. Ship."

Pouring himself a glass of the bubbly, Tommy smiled. "He does. But a captain's only as good as his executive officer, an' ladies... I'm Misters Spock and Riker combined."

Angie grimaced. "Misters *who*?"

"She's not a fan a' Star Trek," Mona said with a wink, draining her glass and presenting it for a refill.

"I like *America's Not Talented*," Angie said, again looking bored. "And I use-ta watch *X-Files*. That David Duchovny's a major fox. Get it? A *fox*?"

As the two girls laughed way too loud and long at the pun—the champagne was obviously having an effect—Tommy said, "You really hafta settle down. This room's completely soundproof, so no one in the hallway can hear a word we're sayin', but the security cameras have multidirectional mics an' are enhanced motion sensitive. I'm gonna delete everythin' when we're done—that is, after I transfer it all to a thumb drive for later an' repeated viewin'—but we really don't want the Kardax limp-dicks comin' down here..."

"Enhanced motion sensitive?" Mona purred, as though Tommy had just explained a device you would have to purchase at the adults-only store. "Like, if I stand on this console and shake my moneymaker, the Kardax hunks are gonna get a look? Angie—come on up here and let's show Mr. Tommy Sicari, Vice President of

Special Projects—and what's more special than *us*?—just how much we wanna work on the upper floors."

As Mona straddled a keyboard and several external hard drives on Tommy's desk, Angie climbed up to join her, placing her black stiletto on a computer tower so her potential employer was sure to get an eyeful of her skimpy red lace panties.

Not wanting to turn away, Tommy managed to take in the still quarter-filled champagne bottle inches from Angie's other foot. "Hey... watch the bottle. You're surrounded by wirin' an' battery packs..."

In an effort to avoid it, Angie wound up, in her inebriation, nearly knocking the bottle over.

Tommy caught it before it spilled.

"Geez, you got good reflexes, Mister Ess!" Mona said. "It's time to really start the interview and test them reflexes out."

As Tommy took a slug from the champagne bottle as the girls climbed off the console, he heard a series of pops. Looking at the wall of computer towers to his left, he saw a few sparks, got a whiff of smoke, and watched, unbelieving, as the towers burst into flames.

"What the fuck!" he yelled, both at the sight of the flaming towers and the fact that the fire suppression system wasn't activating.

"We gotta get outta here!" Angie yelled, grabbing Mona's hand and moving toward the security door. As Tommy rushed past them, she added, "Say your twenty-three whatever-the-hell-it-is and get this fucking door to open! *Now*!"

Punching in the five-number code that allowed egress from the room, Tommy let loose a string of curses he first learned in middle school as the door light stayed red and the hydraulic locks failed to release.

"What the hell is going on?" Tommy said to the air, suddenly stone cold sober. "The security door won't open. Lobby security's *gotta* see us. The Kardax guys upstairs *hafta* smell the smoke!" Looking up at the security camera above the door, Tommy waved his arms and yelled, "Help! Hey, somebody help us in here!" Then, as the flames began to spread dangerously close to the trio, he asked of no one, "Why aren't the sprinklers coming on?"

As the girls began to scream, pounding on the security door until their fingernails snapped and their palms were bruised and numb, Tommy felt the hairs on the back of his neck begin to tingle as the office filled with flames...

Uriel Stanton, lead crime reporter for the *Eastern Standard*—a major daily newspaper founded by his ancestor, Uriah, almost a century earlier—stood just outside the door of the two-story home where he lived, holding his breath as he slowly slid the key into the lock.

As much as he loved the convenience of renting an upstairs room from a kindly retired schoolteacher whose sole purpose at this point in her life seemed to be to dote on her overworked tenant, getting home at one a.m. was always a risky affair.

He never knew if she would be waiting for him in her bathrobe and hot pink curlers, more like a mom than a landlord-*cum*–cook and laundry lady, wondering where he was and expressing how worried she'd been.

Luckily, she must have been sound asleep; he made it up the stairs and into his room without catching even a glimpse of a hot pink curler as it went around the corner.

Locking the door behind him and switching on the light, Uriel spread his arms in an attitude of utter submission as his cat, a four-year-old Highland Lynx named Orson Welles, looked at him with a Charles Foster Kane my-empire-is-crashing-down-around-me look of derision.

"Easy there, Orson," Uriel said, grabbing a can of tuna from off the kitchen counter. "Not like you went without food or water for twenty-four hours... More like twenty-two. And a half..."

As helpful as his landlord, a retired high-school composition teacher named Mrs. Evelyn Hudson could be, she was allergic to Orson and avoided their rooms like the plague.

Uriel had fallen in love with the sea captain's–style dwelling as soon as he saw it, and the location really was perfect, although the beautiful irony of having a landlady named Mrs. Hudson—seeing as the uncle of the founder of the *Standard* had been friends with Dr. Watson—would have made him sign the lease no matter what.

Sensing that all was forgiven as Orson attacked the bowl of tuna he had placed on the floor—the Highland Lynx was softly purring as he ate—Uriel lay down beside his feline roommate and said, "I really am sorry, Orson. Shira's got me chasing half a dozen different stories. Why Ruth thought it was a good idea for me to adopt you is honestly beyond me... No offense... I'm just around less and less and the thought of Mrs. Hudson in a Hazmat suit... Yikes." Sitting up, Uriel noticed a flashing red light on a side table in his living room, which doubled as an office.

Not that he used it as either.

"Well look at that, Mister Welles… A message on the antiquated answering machine. And to think I nearly threw this nostalgic piece of primitive technology away due to peer pressure…"

Getting up and crossing to the answering machine—Mrs. Hudson's previous tenant had left it and a red rotary phone when she'd moved and he just couldn't resist the romance of it, though just a couple of people had the number—Uriel pressed *Play* and sat back in an estate-sale wingchair that would have gone perfectly in 221B Baker Street.

You have… One. New. Message. Message one, today, 2:48 p.m., the electronic voice reported.

Uriel smiled at the sound of the familiar voice of his longtime friend, Tommy Sicari.

Hey, U. It's the Big T, feelin' not so big on this rainy day in Jersey. Hopin' ya get this. You gotta be the last non-senior-citizen on our globally warming planet that still has a home phone and answering machine. Good thing, though. Cell's too easy to hack. Look… I know I've been a shit, but I need you. There's heavy at TRG. Super uber heavy. I can't talk to Sam-o… He didn't want me workin' for his old man in the first place. If I get outta this with all my parts and pieces, you just might win a Pulitzer. This is crazy big, my friend. I'm talkin' New World Order. Or, more specifically, TRG's New Technic. And that douche bag Dwyer-Mann… Eustace… The son I went to boarding school with—not the cool, successful one who hates our friggin' guts. Talk about toys in the attic… He nearly fucked me good. Anyway… meet me at the Stargazer 'round midnight and I'll get you up to speed. I'm gonna be entertainin' a couple of girls from the secretarial pool right after work, but it'll be the old in an' out, if ya get what I'm layin' down. That weirdsville fucker Eustace gave me a bottle of top-shelf bubbly, and it's beggin' to be tasted. Okay, brother. See ya tonight. And, again… I'm sorry for bein' so scarce and not so great when I do find time to appear so you can see my handsome face… This really is big, my friend…"

As Uriel, concerned for his friend and intrigued by what he had said, put his finger on the play button to listen to the message again, he was startled by a knock on the door.

Crossing the room, fully expecting it to be Mrs. Hudson asking where he'd been, or offering him some food, Uriel heard a male voice say, "Uriel, you in there? Open up. Your landlord let me in."

Unlocking the door, Uriel motioned his visitor inside. "Samuel. Hey. I'm on my way downtown to meet Tommy at the Stargazer. I'm already running late. Supposed to be there at midnight..."

Samuel Ravenskald, the only son of one of the world's richest and most powerful men, shook his head. "He isn't going to be there, U. There was a fire at TRG. Twenty-first floor. Technology Wing..."

"Shit," Uriel said. "Anyone hurt?"

"Worse than hurt. Three bodies, burned so bad they can't... Two females and..." Samuel started to cry. "They're going to need dental records. But they're pretty sure it's..."

Laying his head on Uriel's shoulder, Samuel began to sob with such intensity his upper body shook.

Putting his arms around his friend, Uriel thought, *Jesus Christ, Tommy. How heavy did it get?*

✝

The next morning, just after sunrise, in an office stuffed to maximum capacity with books, maps, and artefacts accumulated over decades at the Eastern Museum of Meso-America on the campus of Eastern Pinelands University, Michael Stanton tried to shake off the previous evening's psychiatric drug cocktail and concentrate.

Sitting on a three-hundred-year-old rug that illustrated the *Popol Vuh*—the Mayan creation story starring the Hero Twins Hunahpú and Xbalanqu—Michael stifled a yawn and focused his mind on the rhythmic sounds being produced by three bamboo flute players and a percussionist beating a drum and shaking a gourd rattle at precisely 73 beats per minutes. They were sitting in front of him in a semi-circle around the rug's perimeter, playing softly but with passion.

As for the bpm, Michael knew that it was *precisely* 73 because, whenever the percussionist diverged, even by a beat, the quartet's director (and third flutist), Professor Abraham Wharton, stopped the musicians and made them start again.

As the hypnotizing beat and melody danced inside his head, he saw Professor Wharton slowly move his flute from his mouth and begin to chant: "*Sanco tupanché, tecco du mané, té-liggo, té-liggo nupanché. Sanco du mené, heelo du ché ché. Sanco tupanché, tecco du mané, du mané, du mané. Vibra sume ché ché. Sanco tupanché, tecco du mane...*"

Without being fully conscious he was doing so, Michael responded, "*Sanco du mené, heelo du ché ché. Sanco tupanché, tecco du mané, du mané, du mané. Ché.*"

The two men repeated the call and response for several minutes, until Michael started to see and feel a mass of blue, electric light swirling around his body. As Michael's extremities began to tingle, Professor Wharton brought the session to a close with a conductor's upward sweep and vigorous closing of the hand.

"That is all for now," he said, as the percussionist and two flutists rose from their chairs and placed their instruments in a carved wooden trunk. "Take your flute with you and practice it, Marika. Your tones were sometimes sharp. You are holding tension in your embouchure and throat. Michael must experience the full effect of the incantation, understand?"

Taking her flute out the trunk and placing it in her backpack, Marika said, "Last time I practiced in my dorm room my roommate fell asleep curling her hair and nearly burned her face off."

"All for the cause, my dear," Wharton replied with a smile. "Of course I am kidding. I suggest you only practice while *alone*."

The percussionist waved goodbye to the two flutists, asking Wharton after they had exited, "Was my time-keeping any better today, Professor?"

Wharton rose, placing his scarred, weathered hands on the young lady's shoulders. "Drumming is definitely better. Rattle... not so much. Keep on using the metronome, Gia. I chose you for a reason. Have faith and don't stop practicing!"

After Gia had left, Wharton locked the office door and carefully prepared two gourds of yerba mate in the accepted, ancient manner while Michael studied the images on the rug on which he sat.

"I am guessing the twins are kind of like U and me?" he asked, running his fingers over the faces of the brothers.

"Kind of," Professor Wharton said, handing Michael a gourd. "You have certainly had your share of trials, although I fear you have not yet experienced even a glimpse of your own particular Xibalba. Soon, though, that will change—an obvious fact after your recent, unexpected encounter in the sensory deprivation chamber.[1] Hence, the urgency of getting the warding exercise up to its full potential. Iblis

---

[1] Michael's encounter with an unexpected visitor in the SDC is related in detail in Section 5 of *The Cannon and the Quill, Book Four: All the Devils Are Here.*

is our most dangerous enemy, Michael. I cannot impress that upon you enough."

Taking a sip of the earthy tea, which tasted and smelled like eucalyptus, through the silver bombilla sitting in the gourd, Michael nodded. "After what he did to my cranium, I am already fully convinced. Can't you tell how seriously I am taking these sessions? Speaking of... That incantation... it's used to open and close the obsidian mirror, am I right?"

"Partially," Wharton answered. "Sorry to be so dreadfully noncommittal this morning. When you say 'open and close,' it is far too general. The mirror has several functions. The incantation will open and close it for divination—visions of locations and events in the present and the future. But its true purpose—and why it is so sought after and dangerous—is to open and close something else. As for you... because you have a genetic attachment to the mirror, the incantation will work the same way on your energy field. It will protect you from the djinn that claims to be Iblis, Michael. And, if you so choose, it shall even protect you from *him*... from the other one, I mean..."

Taking another sip of the mate, which was helping his head to clear, Michael said, "He has a name, Professor. He can be an asshole, but he's also come through for us—and for DTEAU. My last session in the sensory deprivation chamber with *him* was quick and clean. And our ancestor's books... the obsidian mirror was how he often came through with his clues and communications. And it's also how he helped Judah P. and his nephew Uriah with destroying Edward Hyde..."

"I know well enough his name," Wharton said. "I was the one who bestowed it upon him. The one that you and Uriel know him by, that is... His real names are a secret." Sipping thoughtfully on his mate, he added, "But he wasn't there when Iblis harmed you, was he? Of course not... There are only two beings in the whole of the Universe that conniving bastard fears, and Iblis is one of them. I want you to be very careful, Michael. They are treating you well at the teaching hospital... Having you brought here so early was accomplished without question, but the drugs they have you on... They make you incredibly vulnerable."

"I am just shy of being a licensed pharmacologist by now, Professor. I am being careful with my dosages... and so are the staff. Not like at Quarry Peak, or some of those other places..."

"That's all over now. I promise. Now, before you finish your tea and the orderlies return to collect you, I have some excellent news. Your father is coming home."

"Feels like it's been years instead of months. I know Uriel misses him a lot."

Offering a grandfatherly smile, Wharton whispered, "I am sure he is not the only one who does."

After decades of speaking louder than normal over the constant din of the bullpen of the *Eastern Standard* and half a dozen other newspapers at which he worked, starting as a cub reporter and rising to his present position of editor-in-chief, Micah Strom could yell with the best of them when angry.

"People are starting to look, Micah. Keep it down to a normal growl, and I will happily keep on fighting."

Shira Koury, the *Standard*'s managing editor, knew all about Strom's reputation for being an old school, stereotypical movie and comic book EIC, given to long rants, pointed threats, and always smelling of cigarettes and whiskey.

It's why, nearly three years earlier, she had taken the job even though she had already received slightly better offers from the *Chicago Tribune* and *Washington Post*. Strom might be a poster boy for toxic masculinity, but he also had more integrity and commitment to the original aspirations of the Fourth Estate than the rest of the EICs at America's ever-dwindling list of major newspapers combined.

She even looked forward to fights like the one they were having now.

Shooting a glare out into the bullpen to keep the curious at bay, Strom said, lowering his voice, "I'm trying to save the *Standard* from the scrap heap or a very hostile takeover, and all of our jobs in the process, Shira! We can't afford the kind of heat the kid is bringing down!"

"Look, Micah. Your time as editor-in-chief hasn't been easy, God knows, but you're a fixer. You did it for the *Sentinel*, the *Post*—and in time, you'll do it here. You're panicking. It's unbecoming in a crafty old bastard like yourself."

On most days, Shira's deftly administered mix of sympathy and honesty would bring Micah's growling down to an almost purr.

Today was not one of those days. "The shareholders are out of patience, Shira. The kid's ancestor founded the *Standard* with

Ravenskald dollars—against his Uncle Judah's warnings—and Solomon is all but majority shareholder. If our position is weak, stock is cheap, and he might just spend a little money to improve his position on the Board. He is really up my ass to put the kid on ice. We print far too many retractions. We back the kid in his hunches and we indulge him like no one else in the bullpen. He's wrong as often as he's right. And he ain't much for naming names."

"You finished for now?" Shira asked, getting up from her desk and closing the door. "You just described Woodward and Bernstein. As for the rest of it... I don't care about jealous reporters in our bullpen— he makes them all work harder. And, yes, Uriel is sometimes unable to meet the standard of evidence to back his theories, but he is rarely, if ever, *wrong*. Uriah Stanton's uncle had damned good reason to warn his nephew off the Ravenskalds—they all but owned Uriah's father—and they have only gotten more powerful... more corrupt. This surveillance-state city is just the start of Solomon's plans for America. I will speak to Uriel the first chance I get about some of the ways we overindulge him... Time away from the office, his expense account... But if you want to save this paper, then you have to know his reporting—not to mention his connections with the university, the FBI, and with Ravenskald's son and at least one upper-level employee—are why we aren't already out of a job and editing articles for some hipster trust fund blogger."

"God for-fucking-bid, Shira!" Micah said, although it was accompanied by a grumble-throated laugh, signaling the crisis, if not the conversation, was over. "Look... The kid's got classic chops, the requisite nose for the news, as we used to say in the Woodward and Bernstein days. But investigative hot-shots are bygone personalities. Newspapers are nearly dead, and the Internet's a cesspool. As soon as he wins a Pulitzer, he'll go off and write a book. A *best-selling* book with a big fat advance and lots and lots of royalties and that will be that."

"Why must you be so goddamned cynical?" Shira snapped.

"To balance out your Pollyanna optimism!" Micah shot back. Pausing for a moment so things didn't escalate to their earlier levels, he added, "The scrutiny is getting intense. The stockholders have had it with him. Less maverick, more mundane. That's the orders from our overlords. That's the only way to save it."

Opening her door so her boss would understand that the conversation was over, Shira got the final word. "If what you say is true, Micah, then journalism's already dead, and we're presiding over its grave."

Eustace Grenier Dwyer-Mann hated to be outside.

Nature was for punks and faggoty forest guides. Summer camp fucking and pot smoking were acceptable of course, but mostly the stuff of eighties teenage comedies. Eustace had been to several summer camps—his parents hated having him home when boarding school was out—and the pickings were always slim.

There was only one place—despite his sizable trust fund, which allowed him to physically travel anywhere in the world—where he could find plenty of action, totally on his terms. That was the world of Virtual Reality, which made it no small irony that Virtual Reality was the reason he had been forced to leave his technologically and psychologically secure basement and make the four-mile journey from his home in the Parkersburg, West Virginia, Historic District to Blennerhassett Island.

Well... not Virtual Reality, per se. But Virtual Reality on the Deep-Dark Web.

His summoner hadn't given him a choice. When certain people call, you answer, despite the inconvenience.

Besides, he had been aching to take a ride on his brother Aaron's newly restored 1951 Vincent Black Shadow Series C.

He had gotten to Blennerhassett Island nearly before he had left. That's how fast that jet-black fucker could go.

He had no sooner removed one of his old dirt-bike helmets, which his father had gotten done up as a hyena head by a well-known airbrush artist for Eustace's seventeeth birthday, as a way to get him out of the house more, when he heard the distinctive sound of a 1970 BSA Lightning approaching.

His summoner had arrived.

It was time to bullshit, bargain, or bribe his way out of the unfortunate mess he had found himself in after the FBI had brought down Prendick's All Night Fights.

He would much rather be in his VR headset, gambling, fighting, or fucking in Dubai.

Soon enough, he thought. How long could a scolding from his father's biggest and truthfully *only* rival actually take?

"Nice bike, Mister Ravenskald," he said, as friendly as a disfigured psycho like himself could manage to seem.

Pulling off his boringly unadorned helmet, Solomon Ravenskald, CEO and Chairman of the Board of The Ravenskald Group, turned off his bike and stretched his arms.

"Aaron inspired me to get it out of storage when he made his most recent purchase. It's not quite the rocket that Black Knight is, but I think it'll keep up. My mechanic is excellent. I am surprised you ride, Eustace—and that Aaron let you borrow it."

Eustace shrugged good-naturedly. "My brother and I are just full of surprises. Don't worry about 'keeping up,' at least today... they go the same speed when they're parked."

Eustace had heard about Solomon Ravenskald's laser-eyed glare and lack of humor. Now
he was experiencing them both for himself.

"We won't stay parked for long. I wanted to meet you here to offer a little history lesson. What do you know about the mansion that sits behind you?"

Eustace found himself too unnerved by the 'won't stay parked for long' comment to attempt a sarcastic response. "We used to tour it every year when I was little. It's the Blennerhassett House. A sort of wealthy guy named Harman from Ireland bought it so he could live there with his wife, who also happened to be his niece. Crazy kind of Jerry Lee Lewis marrying his cousin kind of thing..."

Solomon Ravenskald's eyes continued to bore into Eustace.

Fuuuuuuuck.

"Place burned down in 1811 and was rebuilt in the 1980s. He got in a lot of trouble because he was part of some secret conspiracy with Aaron Burr."

Eustace was tempted to mention the *Got Milk?* commercial, and the guy with the mouthful of peanut butter but he thought if he did he might end up with a mouthful of broken teeth.

"It wasn't 'some secret conspiracy,' Eustace." Solomon sounded like a boarding school headmaster. "It was a plan to break off part of the United States and form a separate country. Burr was assisted by nearly a hundred others, foremost amongst them General James Wilkinson, Harman Blennerhassett... and both my ancestors and yours."

"No shit?"

Eustace couldn't help himself. It just came out. That was exactly the kind of information that could have gotten him occasionally laid at summer camp...

"Our ancestors were part of Lundberg's 60 Families, which he tried to expose as villains in 1937. Along with families like the Rockefellers, Du Ponts, Vanderbilts, and Astors, we *built* this country, Eustace. And the Ravenskalds and Dwyer-Manns are the most powerful of the lot. *That* is your birthright. And even more so your brother's..."

Suddenly Eustace realized for whom his brother had been named.

Solomon continued his lecture. "Yet you sit in a basement watching violent videos and engaging in virtual sex on the internet. It disgusts me, Eustace. *You* disgust me. I normally would not care how you spend your empty hours to any greater degree than if you were a cockroach, but your degenerate lifestyle has recently cost me time, money, and personnel."

Eustace now understood *exactly* where this was going. He started to worry he would piss himself.

"I heard about the fire," he whispered.

"It was a very costly accident."

"Tommy Sicari's death, or Tommy Sicari?"

"I was referencing the equipment and the technology center itself. Tommy turned out to be an utter disappointment. Just another degenerate cockroach."

Eustace was now almost certain he was going to piss his leather leggings.

"I didn't mean to get him in trouble. I never thought it would be—"

Solomon put on his helmet. Not closing the visor, he said, "That is the first adult thing you've said since I arrived. Reparations need to be made, Eustace."

"Whatever it costs, sir, I will pay it."

Solomon laughed. "I don't need your father's money, Eustace. If I did, I would have bought Damon-Metis Corp. a decade ago. I have a very important associate who needs your skills with the internet. He's moving an asset into the field who could use your specific talents in the undertaking of his work. We are going to meet him at his home in New Haven—here in West Virginia, not Connecticut—this afternoon. You'll feel very much at home there. He has a Queen Anne Victorian similar to your father's with lots of secret rooms holding lots and lots of secrets. Sound familiar?" Glancing at his Cartier Santos-Dumont wristwatch, he said, "We are falling behind my schedule. Try to keep up."

Closing his visor and kick-starting his BSA Lightning, Solomon glanced in his mirror and sped off southwest toward Mason County.

Starting the Vincent Black Shadow, Eustace was glad it was only a fifty-mile ride.

At the rate Solomon Ravenskald was traveling, they'd be there before they left.

☦

Three days later, Solomon Ravenskald, in a tailored Armani suit, was heading to his limousine for the twenty-minute drive back to Ravenskald Towers after the conclusion of Tommy Sicari's funeral when a caustically shouted "Hey!" stopped him in his tracks.

Unaccustomed to being addressed in such a manner, he nearly kept walking, although curiosity at this rare event compelled him to see who it was.

"How dare you—" he said, as he was turning around. Then he saw the speaker. "Uriel. You're the last person I would expect to address me—or anyone else—in such a manner."

"I am not in the mood for niceties," Uriel said, approaching with a slight portside list that cued Solomon to the fact that he had been drinking.

Confident that his three bodyguards were close enough to the pair that they could intervene should Uriel become more than verbally aggressive, Solomon decided to be diplomatic. "Understandable. I know you and Tommy were close. I am sure my son is just as upset and inebriated as you are. Stopped off at the Stargazer between the church and the cemetery, did you?"

"This has nothing to do with our toasting our dead friend over a couple of beers," Uriel said, wisely keeping better than arm's length from Solomon. "I am pretty fucking positive that Tommy's death was not an accident. I have it on very good authority that you knew that he was involved in something you didn't like. Something that would have put TRG in the FBI spotlight. And that he was onto something else... something in which you are personally involved..."

"Uriel!"

Solomon looked away toward the sound of his only son's voice.

"What the hell are you doing, man? You said you'd play it cool... I can hear you from across the parking lot." Standing shoulder to shoulder with his longtime friend, Samuel said to Solomon, "Hey, Dad. Never mind us... we drowned our sorrows over our loss and Uriel here's obviously keen to point a finger..."

Turning to face his friend—who was at this moment nothing more than a representative of his family's most hated enemies—Uriel got nose to nose with him before whispering, "Keen to point a fucking finger? Are you serious with this shit? You heard the recording on my answering machine. Tommy was going to tell me something the other night, and your father here killed him before he could."

Solomon put a hand up as his bodyguards advanced several steps toward Uriel. "You need to sleep this off. Our families have rarely seen eye to eye... And I know that Samuel did not want Tommy working for me. I should have listened to him. We were going to fire him. With good cause. One of our security officers found cocaine in his desk. He was in debt and playing fast and loose with his stock shares to get out of it. There was no reason for him to have two secretaries with him in the technological command center unless he was up to no good. I had a call last week from the SEC. Worse still, he was involved in illegal internet activity with Quentin Dwyer-Mann's youngest son. That disfigured sicko, Eustace. So, of course he would make up a bunch of lies about all the evil things I'm doing at TRG rather than tell his supposed best friends the truth about his personal failings. If there was ever an Icarus flying too close to the sun with a pair of stolen wings it was Tommy Sicari. Be honest—how often have you bailed him out? Loaned him money? Given him a ride home when he'd had too much to drink—something I am going to arrange for the both of you, in a minute."

"No need for that, Solomon. I will give them a ride."

Another voice Solomon recognized. "Joshua! Look how fit and tan you are! No doubt all that brilliant Amazonian sun and rigorous digging. When did you get back?"

Doctor Joshua Stanton, Professor of Archaeology at Eastern Pinelands University, shook Solomon Ravenskald's offered hand, although he didn't want to. "I wanted to be here for the funeral service, but my plane was delayed. Got into Newark late this morning. Hello, Samuel. Uriel. Sounds like an intense discussion you're all having."

"Just the grieving process in action," Solomon said, his smile looking to Uriel like a jackal's. "Our grief-stricken sons have been drowning their sorrows a little too vigorously and intoxicated minds in intelligent young men are given to wild conspiracies and speculation."

Joshua moved so he was standing next to his son. "I have never known a Ravenskald to be the subject of wild conspiracies and speculation... I find that rather puzzling..."

"Keep your sarcasm to yourself, Joshua," Solomon said, his gaze and tone turning cold. "You're no angel either. If you want to carve out some time, we can trade revelations for our sons. I will even let you share the first one."

"Look, Dad," Samuel said, used to playing the role of peacekeeper when it came to the always-uneasy interactions between their families. "Emotions are running high. I have plenty of questions about Tommy's death, same as Uriel. But they'll keep. He hasn't seen his dad in months and Joshua, you do look pretty great, but also pretty jet-lagged. Let's do this another time... or maybe not at all."

Pausing a moment, Solomon nodded. "Point taken. Good to see you, Joshua. Uriel. Samuel... if you want a ride to the university I can stop there on my way to my office."

Looking to Uriel, who nodded, Samuel answered, "Sure, Dad." To Uriel and Joshua he said, "Talk to both of you later," before following his father and his bodyguards to the limo.

Once the limo had pulled away, Joshua took Uriel by the shoulders. "Are you crazy? You don't try to bully Solomon Ravenskald. Not *ever*. Especially not intoxicated. You know damned well of what he is capable of doing when crossed..."

Uriel nodded. He was sobering up just enough to become embarrassed. "I can tell that statement isn't hypothetical. You're damned right I do. Tommy left me a message the day he was killed. On my machine. He was worried about someone intercepting it. He wanted me to meet him at the Stargazer, but of course he never made it. He said there was something heavy happening at TRG—and something about Eustace Dwyer-Mann. He mentioned something he called the New Technic."

Joshua released his grip on Uriel's shoulders. "I will see what I can learn about Tommy's murder, although I'm sure your FBI contacts will be able to help you as well. Don't look so surprised—I was in the Amazon, not on the moon. And I have plenty of contacts of my own."

"So you agree that motherfucker took out Tommy."

Joshua nodded. "Yes. And many others over the years. There's never proof, of course—his network is extensive and he's made a high art of covering his tracks. He employs the most experienced agents of chaos in the world. The Ravenskalds always have. That's why the battle has waged for a millennium. And that's why there are lodges and councils in place to fight him on much larger, safer fronts than a parking-lot confrontation. You need to keep control."

Ignoring the admonishment, Uriel asked, "What do think Tommy was talking about? Artificial intelligence? Weapons development? Biomedical manipulation? Is that the New Technic?"

"It's part of it. But there's more. Mind control, physical enhancement research for the Department of Defense and the so-called DEDs, weather manipulation... And the Cyton D-23 nuclear generator project."

"We're meant to stop this, Dad. That's what it means to be a Stanton."

Joshua smiled. "Wow. Talk about sharing revelations... I am suddenly realizing that what happened here today was my doing. I have been saying those words around you and Michael since you were little. Now you're reminding *me...*"

"So what do we do?" Uriel asked.

Joshua thought carefully for a moment. "I need you to get inside what's left of the technology center at TRG. Call Solomon's office and apologize. Mea culpa as hard as you have to. But let him agree to you visiting him at Ravenskald Tower."

Uriel nodded in understanding. "I can definitely do that. I'll arrange an interview... offer a sympathy piece on the tragedy. Then I'll try and get inside the tech center. What is it you're trying to find out?"

"I need some residue. On a napkin or a handkerchief."

"What for?"

"I'm not sure," Joshua said, "but I'll know when I find it."

"I'll do my best, Dad," Uriel answered, giving his father a hug. "It's really good to have you home."

Eugene Gorman Howe, known to the world as "The Changeling," was so fucking happy to be home.

Even if it did suffer the stink of the law enforcement personnel who had ransacked it in his absence.

"*West Virrrrrginnnnnnia... ass-fucked momma,*" he sang while switching on a newly installed camera surveillance system in his New Haven—make that New Heaven—Queen Anne Victorian, "*take me hooooooooome... rutted roads.*"

His time in a maximum-security facility for the criminally insane after that bastard Kevin Connor from DTEAU had thwarted him—he and the Voice of the Beast *both*—in Secaucus, New Jersey, the previous Christmas season had been hard. Not because of his fellow inmates, or the guards—no one dared fuck for an instant with a confessed carver–killer of eight prostitutes (although it should have been nine). Not to mention the sixteen others whom Special Agent Connor had managed to link to Eugene during his trial and conviction because of the teeth and hair he had used to decorate his knife sheath. No. It wasn't because of any of them... but because of the silence.

The Beast had not spoken to him for a single moment from the time of his arrest to the time of his unauthorized release by Xavier Hearst and members of the Kardax Corporation.

"That only scratches the surface, Ay-gent Connnnn-nnnor," Eugene said as security camera feeds blinked to life one by one on a flat-screen monitor. "And I am only getting started." Seeing the cellar of what used to be his mother's house—before she expectedly died—come to life on the screen, Eugene switched on the remote lighting system technicians from TRG had also installed, illuminating a chained figure sitting in a computer chair, asleep.

Eugene found the guy's hair-lip irritating to look at, but Hearst had been clear—unless Eugene wanted to go right back to his cell and the Silence, he would work with whomever Xavier Hearst ordered him to.

Switching on his new computer's external microphone, and picking up an old label maker filled with a roll of blue labels, Eugene said, "Wake up, Eustace. Hey—I just realized... Eustace and Eugene. We have nearly identical names! And apparently we like the same kinds of games... although I hear you don't get out much and live it all in *fantasy*. Basement to basement, man... hope you're cool with the digs. This is a temporary situation. The police are gonna come back here, sooner rather than later. So we gotta get busy and put rubber to the road."

Opening his eyes and looking into the lens of a ceiling-mounted camera, Eustace Dwyer-Mann said, "You don't have to chain me up like a hostage in the basement, dude. I'm not going anywhere. Mister Ravenskald wants me to help you, so I'm going to. I *want* to."

"Else he'll wear your balls for bracelets—and I will be the jeweler," Eugene said, enjoying the pun between *jewels* and *jeweler*. He wondered for a second if Eustace had noticed and realized he didn't care. He had work to do, and until it was begun, he knew the Beast would not come back. It wasn't enough to be in the house and on the property where he had logged his first three kills—his mother's abusive dago boyfriend, then his bible-beating aunt, and then, at last, his mother. He had to *earn* it. With blood. Plans had been made before his arrest, but he could tell those plans were scrapped. He'd receive some new instructions, and the Eu-dude in the basement would use the fancy, expensive computer system Hearst had provided to help him. Address searches, photographs, satellite imagery of homes and neighborhoods, license plate numbers… everything was digital now.

A serial killer's delight.

"Okay, Mister Eustace," Eugene said, missing his knife, which had been confiscated upon his arrest, "I need you to find me a real estate open house in the area. Limit it to only Wood and Mason counties—"

Eustace, having wheeled himself to what he had been surprised to find when he woke up here a few days ago, was his entire computer setup from home, said into the camera, "Wood County is where I'm from."

"*I do not fucking CARE!*" Eugene screamed into his mic, wincing at the feedback as it bounced back from Eustace's speakers. "*I don't care. IdontcareIdontcareIdontcare. You understand me you malformed, ugly piece of ferret shit? DO. YOUR. FUCKING. JOB. We are not pals, friends, butt buddies, or even colleagues. YOU. WORK. FOR. ME. SO WORK!*" Taking a breath, he said, "The last male fucker who interrupted me in this house wound up kissing a grinding wheel. Although it would do wonders for that repulsive hair-lip of yours, it would probably render you unable to work. But do not fucking test me."

Eustace, his hands trembling as they hovered over the keyboard, whispered, "I'm sorry I interrupted. Open houses in Mason and Wood counties…"

Enjoying the delicious energy from Hair-Lip's burst of fear, diminished as it was because of the wood and plaster between them—having gone so long without killing, he was too doubtful of his self-control to risk being in the same room with his helper—Eugene continued his instructions. "I need the time when they end, so I can show up just before and be the last one there… alone with the realtor. This way, I have about an hour to do the bleed that fills my need. Make sure they're women, H.L. The more gaudy makeup, the bigger the hair, the better. Look at their always stupid-looking, Glamour Shot phony-as-fuck photos online. I have some practicing to do, and I prefer to do it with whores… Perky titties earn you a bonus …"

Putting down the label maker after pressing the button that cut the one he had made while talking to Eustace, Eugene took a hunting knife that had been left for him by his benefactors from the top of the table where his computer sat and began sharpening it on a leather strop. He began to laugh as Eustace burst into tears as he searched for matches for Eugene's request.

Perhaps the Beast wasn't speaking, but Eugene felt him all around him now, pleased as pie at his protégé, and itching to watch him kill.

The Beast would ward the house against intrusions for a time, which was fine.

Eugene had lots of places to be, and plenty of girls to gut.

But first, he needed Hair-Lip to help him make a video.

Samuel Ravenskald stood on the opposite side of the street from his Cape May, New Jersey, home, enjoying the sounds of the seagulls floating on the updrafts of air created by the waves from the roaring ocean only a block away.

Once he and his guest were finished at the house, he would suggest they have a picnic on the beach.

Holding his finger to his lips as he turned to face his guest, Samuel crossed the street and stood behind a multigenerational cluster of eight vacationers—a grandmother with a walker down to a sleeping infant in a stroller—half-listening to a tour guide outfitted in a gingham dress and white bonnet reminiscent of the days of the American Revolution.

"And here we have an exquisite example of the Italianate style of Victorian architecture here in Cape May," the tour guide said, shooting the newly arrived pair a look that said, *You can't take this tour for free.* "Built in 1872, it was personally designed by the wealthy industrialist Jabez Ravenskald as a secondary home for his family, as were most of the houses on this street. The Ravenskalds owned several of the iron blast furnaces and glass-blowing operations in central and southern New Jersey and built the villages that sprang up around them. This structure is unique in that its tower is sixty-six feet high—which is exactly one foot taller than the tower atop the house of Mister Ravenskald's rival in the gas and oil business at the time, Armand Sicari. We'll be visiting that house next. It's right up the block there—the one that's blue and gray. Then I'll be showing you some stunning examples of the popular Queen Anne style... You go on ahead. I'll be with you in a moment."

As the tour group moved up the street, glancing at their guidebooks and taking photos of several homes not an official part of the tour, the tour guide said to Samuel, "Good morning. The tour is more than half over, but if you want to continue, the price is the price."

"Oh, hey... Hiya," Samuel said, throwing the tour guide a charming smile. "Great outfit, by the way. Very authentic. Especially with the tennis sneakers peeking out from underneath."

Pulling her skirt down a little more to hide her footwear, the tour guide said, "You can take the tour for free. Just don't go on Yelp or Rate-It and report me. I need this gig. It's paying for nursing school."

Samuel put up his hands. "Your secret's safe with me. Walking these streets several times a day would be brutal in period footwear. So... the restorations to this house are going phenomenally well, wouldn't you say?"

Relief in her voice, the tour guide answered, "The Historical Society is thrilled with the progress so far, and they can be a difficult gaggle of blue-hairs. Oh... please don't tell any of them that I said that..."

Samuel turned his smile brighter. "Like I said, your secrets are safe with me."

"And you are?" the tour guide asked, suddenly noticing Samuel's looks.

"The floor restorer. This is my assistant, Aurora. The owner of the house—Solomon Ravenskald's son... his name at the moment escapes me... isn't here today. Aurora and I are taking some measurements. She's new. I'm training her."

Slightly less smitten now that she knew that the man before her, although attractive, was only a floor restorer, and not wanting her group to get too far ahead—the best way to get a lousy review on Yelp—the tour guide said, "Well... Have a pleasant day."

After she had moved out of earshot, Samuel's guest, Doctor Ruth Anne Marsh, raised a brow and asked, "You always pretend *not* to be *you*, Samuel?"

"Only in Cape May. That's the basic point of a two-hour drive on the Parkway. Anonymity."

"Yet you outed *me*. Kinda. Your *assistant*? And what's with the name Aurora?"

"I had to. I couldn't very well tell them a world-renowned pathologist was slumming with a lowly restorer of floors. Besides... you *look* like an Aurora. Have I never mentioned that?"

Ruth Anne smiled. "You haven't." She paused a moment, stepping closer. "Since you brought it up... Why *am* I slumming with you?"

Taking her hand in his, Samuel said, "Because I just lost a close friend under horrible circumstances, and you happen to adore Cape May."

"Both true…"

"But there's more. Being a pathologist, disease-riddled systems hold a particularly strong fascination for you. And our triad of families—Ravenskald, Stanton, and Sicari—we're as thoroughly diseased as they come. And Tommy…" Samuel paused as his voice broke and his eyes filled with tears. "I'm sorry, Ruth. This wasn't how I wanted this weekend to go. I've got wine and beluga in the fridge and, come nightfall, all the houses are lit up for the evening walking tours. I thought we'd have a picnic on the beach and then take one of the ghost tours… Cape May is chock full of ghosts, a good percentage of which—according to the more salacious guidebooks and collections of local ghost tales for sale in every tourist trap in town—my ancestors were ruthlessly responsible for creating."

Stepping up onto the second front porch step so they were looking eye to eye, Ruth replied, "I'm glad you asked me here. I want to help you, Samuel. I do. You and Uriel both."

Samuel frowned. "We certainly could use it. But not in the same way, if you understand what I'm saying. I won't have some weird lovers' triangle come between us. Not with the strain of our family names already creating so many problems all the time."

Putting her arms around Samuel's neck, Ruth whispered, "I thought there might be something happening between Uriel and me this past Christmas, during and after the serial killer case, but there wasn't. Uriel has a single mistress—his job." To better make her point, Ruth leaned in and kissed him.

Feeling himself go weak in the knees, Samuel asked, "You taking advantage of me, Aurora?"

"Only if you want me to."

In that moment, listening to the sounds of the ocean and smelling the scent of her skin, Samuel couldn't think of anything he wished for more.

✝

SAIC Kevin Connor kicked the wall of his office, releasing a puff of dust as the drywall cracked, burst, and then caved around his shoe. As he listened to the voice on the other end of the call, he was tempted to drop the smartphone into the hole and call it an afternoon.

"What do you mean it was a professional extraction?" he asked instead, hearing the protective cover of the smartphone strain as he squeezed it in frustration. "From a maximum-security facility? Were Nicolas Cage and Michael Bay involved?"

Connor knew he'd be reprimanded before the day was out for such extreme sarcasm on an official call, but he didn't really care. One of the most dangerous, deranged serial killers the FBI had ever encountered had almost magically disappeared and no one was exactly sure how he was able to pull it off.

"Have you managed to keep it quiet?" he asked, not apologizing for his snark but softening his tone. "At least that's something. Howe has victims all over the country… I'm just beginning to get a handle on how extensive his kill list is… And we need those areas on high alert. He may have unfinished business in Secaucus, for instance. And he certainly has it with me. I'll contact the other FBI offices here in Jersey in addition to the State Police and Captain Saunders in Secaucus. Has anyone been by his house? West Virginia. How do you people not know that?"

Connor put his phone on mute as his boss, Unit Director Peter Vance, entered his office.

"On a call, boss."

"About the Changeling. … I'm fully aware. Ease up on those guys at the prison, will ya? I was just on the phone with *my* boss and *her* boss. Whoever got him out has money to buy the best. It must have been planned for a while."

Nodding his head, Connor took a breath, unmuted his phone, and said to the equally pissed-off warden on the other end, "Look. I may have been out of line. Most important thing is to catch him before he kills again. And he will. And very soon. I'll contact who I need to in West Virginia and get them over to his property ASAP."

Hanging up without a formal goodbye, Connor tossed his phone on his desk and leaned heavily back in his chair. "Sorry about the wall."

Vance shrugged. "I'll get maintenance on it tonight. No one needs to know. I get Manny Jets tickets several times a year. You gonna be okay?"

"The Changeling won't wait very long. And I doubt he went back home, although I'll get the local PD to check. Howe could be almost anywhere, and I know he's hungry as hell for blood. So no. I'm really *not* okay. But I can do my job. This fucker is mine, Pete. No one knows him better."

"I agree," Vance replied. "Do whatever you have to, and ask for what you need. I'll do everything I can to back you."

Doing a quick database search for the number of the New Haven, West Virginia, police department, Connor dialed his phone and reminded himself to be nice.

The way he was feeling, however, he'd be lucky to manage civil.

Uriel Stanton felt his heart increase its rhythm as the elevator at Ravenskald Tower descended from the twenty-third floor to the twenty-first.

To the site of Tommy Sicari's horrific, burning death.

Standing shoulder to shoulder with him, in an obscenely expensive suit, was the man who was responsible.

As the elevator came to a stop, Uriel said, "I appreciate you taking the time to talk with me, Mister Ravenskald. I can't imagine how busy you must be with all of this. And the threats from the environmental groups concerning your plans for a nuclear generator here in Storm Haven..."

As the door opened, Solomon ushered Uriel out. The smell of smoke, melted plastic, and a variety of chemicals hit Uriel in the face.

"Anything for a friend of Samuel's. And Tommy's, of course," Solomon said, not seeming to notice the odors. "We could use some positive press. Trailblazers are always misunderstood and mistrusted, Uriel. Like the now-celebrated prophets of old. Groups like the Low-Tech Alliance, although honorable in their desire to do some good in a weary world, are misguided in their approach. To say nothing of their lack of imagination and trust in people who are clearly smarter and more capable." As though thoroughly bored with the subject, Solomon said, "I've been watching your progress. It's impressive. But not surprising—you've got news ink running through your veins..."

Placing his hand on a bio-scan pad and lining his eye up with a deep blue beam of light, Solomon said his name, and the door to Tommy's operations center opened with a series of clicks and beeps.

"I don't mind letting you into the control room, Uriel," Solomon said, switching on a set of halogen work lights. "But I have another appointment I need to get to, so let's be quick. Obviously, this is to allow you another moment to mourn your friend. Understand something though—you are no longer here in an official capacity, as a reporter for the *Standard*. Am I clear?"

Nodding his agreement as he stepped inside the burned out room, Uriel pulled a handkerchief out of his pocket—purchased that morning—and, placing it over his mouth and nose, he said, "Ugh... the smell is really something, isn't it? We definitely don't have to linger..."

"I honestly don't notice. It's a scent I know rather well from my visits to Kamdesh and Wanat in Afghanistan. There's something about the combination of electrical wiring and charred flesh that seems perfectly natural once you've experienced it enough."

Solomon, who was heading for the door, spun around as he heard a table falling over, followed by Uriel cursing.

"Jesus! Sorry about that. It's unsettling in here," Uriel said, stepping back toward the door as he slipped the now residue-covered handkerchief into his pocket. "I tripped on some fallen debris."

Solomon's face was a mask of impatience. "Perhaps we should go."

"Yeah," Uriel answered, following Solomon out the door. "Thanks again for speaking with me, Mister Ravenskald. I promise to present TRG and this unfortunate tragedy in the best possible light."

As he waited for the elevator that would take him back to his suite, known as Solomon's Temple, the CEO of TRG said, "It's Solomon. It's wasteful for our families to be at war. So let me offer some advice. Tommy Sicari made the fatal mistake all wannabes make—what he was getting himself involved in all sounded so much better to Tommy as an *idea* than as a set of required actions. The Sicaris have always been the broken cog, the weakest link in our longtime family triad. They have always had bigger egos... bigger mouths. Tommy's way was family tradition. My ancestor competed with a Sicari—for a brief period of time—for supremacy in the West Virginia gas and oil industry. They always finish third, if they finish at all. You look upset. Get over it, Uriel. You're a Stanton. He wasn't. Never could be. Sooner or later, the Sicaris burn while the Stantons—and the Ravenskalds—continue to thrive."

Then the elevator opened, and Solomon was gone.

Fifteen minutes later, sitting in his car, Uriel stared at the now greasy black section of his recently purchased handkerchief. Dialing his phone, he waited for his father to answer.

"I got the sample from the control room. And some very arrogant and unsolicited advice."

"I have no use for Solomon's advice—nor should you," Joshua Stanton said from his office in the Eastern Museum of Meso-America. "As for the residue... excellent work. As soon as you can, drop it off at the EPU forensic pathology lab. Ruth Anne anxiously awaits it."

Assuring his father he would make it a priority and telling him again how happy he was to have him home, Uriel dropped the handkerchief into a freezer bag and headed for Ruth Anne's lab, his mind spinning with all that Solomon had said.

Glancing at his phone two hours later, Uriel saw that he still had a few minutes before he was officially late for his meeting with Shira Koury, managing editor of the *Evening Standard*. He could see her through the window of the Stargazer Bar and Grill, in the booth unofficially reserved for members of the newspaper's ever-shrinking staff.

Thinking about Tommy and all the hours they had spent there—usually with Samuel Ravenskald—Uriel entered the crowded bar, exchanging hellos with half a dozen people between the entranceway and where his boss was waiting, a warm beer and tuna melt sitting ignored in front of her.

"Shira. Hey." Uriel slid into the bench seat opposite, trying his damnedest to not look guilty. "I made sure to be on time. Wow… look at you. I never thought I'd see my boss in blue jeans and a Yankees cap. You look good. Relaxed."

"My brother's having a get-together for the playoffs. I promised I'd stop by. Thanks for coming, Uriel. I have some news, and I wanted you to hear it first. The *Evening Standard*'s in danger. Micah's trying to lure additional investors to keep Solomon Ravenskald from becoming the majority shareholder. But it's a lot of wining and dining. He needs time. Which means we've been ordered to play it safe—especially you."

Uriel smiled. "But you have no intention of doing so."

"I don't. And here's why. I came to Storm Haven because the *Standard* is still the poster child for free and fair reporting. Ravenskald has tried to bully the other shareholders, but they believed in what your family was doing and enough of them still do to block his bid for now. Your grandfather Abel is a legend. And your great-grandfather is the reason why a minority female from a bad neighborhood in Chicago majored in journalism at Loyola. Micah's doing his best. We have to do our part to back him. What I want from you is caution. If necessary… subterfuge. We won't solve the world's problems in a month, a week, or even a year—and if King Solomon takes over, we'll no longer get the chance. Both of us will be fired and no one in the business will even return our calls."

Uriel paused to order an iced tea from the waitress hovering at the edge of the booth. When she left, he asked, "You promise to have my back if I do exactly what you're asking?"

Taking a slug of her beer, Shira nodded. "I believe in what you're doing. Someone's got to push. And your instinct for sniffing the truth is like no one's I've ever worked with. But I won't be able to run any obvious interference. You are, for all intents and purposes, on your own. If something blows up, the paper must come first. Agreed?"

"It's how my grandfather would want it."

Leaning in, Shira asked, "So. What are you working on?"

"The fire at TRG. A few hours ago, I interviewed Solomon Ravenskald. He's expecting a positive piece. That's how I presented it. First draft's in your in-box."

Shira frowned. "Tell me it's what he's expecting."

"For now. Absolutely. But only to buy me time. When will Micah have an answer from the hopefully new investors?"

"He's holed up with them in a fancy mansion in Parkersburg, West Virginia, for the next several days."

"The Dwyer-Manns."

"Exactly. Quentin would love to ruin at least one of Solomon Ravenskald's relentless grabs for power before he dies. So... we good?"

Sipping his iced tea, Uriel smiled. "We are."

"I'm not sure why I'm here, Detective. The place looks deserted and you sounded as though it was urgent. So enlighten me."

SAIC Kevin Connor had just flown from Newark to Charleston, West Virginia, where he obtained a car and drove an hour to the Changeling's home in New Haven (*aka, the middle of nowhere*, he thought).

He had done so at the request of the smug Mason County detective standing before him.

"Happy to," the detective replied, thoroughly unimpressed with Connor's size, rank, and tone. "Yeah, it is deserted. But not too long ago someone ran a helluva lotta computer an' electric wirin' through this place. Shavin's from the drill holes in the beams in the basement are fresh."

"But there's no computer equipment?"

"Not a broken Gameboy..."

"Doesn't make much sense. He only escaped a couple of days ago. Why go through all the trouble? And why did you drag me to West Virginia to tell me you've discovered wood shavings?"

Kevin had been to this house several times since the arrest of the Changeling on Christmas day the year before. It gave him the creeps, as did the mostly wooded acreage on which it sat.

Especially a cave half a mile away.

"Because he left you a present." The detective handed Kevin a thumb drive. On it was a blue label with raised white letters reading `KConnorPiggie`.

Taking the drive, Connor asked, "You guys got a laptop I can use?"

Sitting in his car half an hour later, the thumb drive deep in the pocket of his raincoat so he could get Tech Specialist Alvarado to examine it, Kevin replayed in his mind the video file it contained.

It was easy enough to do. Although it was eight minutes long (a minute, no doubt, for each of the eight women Howe had slaughtered in Jersey), it was nothing more than an eight-second segment repeatedly looped of Howe smiling as he shouted "Come and get me, Kev! Come and get me, Kev!"

Starting the car and heading to the airport—although he wasn't going back to Jersey—Connor knew that, every night, as he tried to fall asleep, until he (re)captured this psycho, he would see that insane smile and hear those taunting words for hours on end.

The worst part was, he knew the Changeling knew it too.

Dr. Ruth Anne Marsh dismissed her Advanced Forensics class with a smile, reminding them that they should all be studying for the upcoming exam.

Seeing Uriel standing in the back of the lecture hall, she shut down the overhead projector she had been using to show her students techniques for obtaining evidence from under a victim's fingernails and in the ears, nose, and mouth, and waved him down.

"Pretty graphic," he said, giving her a quick kiss on the cheek.

"Pretty important in forensic examination," Ruth replied, pulling a folder from her briefcase. "They will certainly see much worse. And, if they've been paying attention, maybe they'll one day find a hidden piece of evidence so the cops can catch a killer. Speaking of evidence—I'm impressed. You did a great job getting residue on that handkerchief."

Not bothering to take the folder Ruth was offering, Uriel asked, "Was it arson?"

Opening the folder, Ruth replied, "Absolutely. But it's complicated. Whoever did this sure as hell knew what they were doing. Plus, they knew Tommy's habits. An aerosol-based accelerant is present in the sample you obtained. One that even a seasoned insurance investigator might miss. If I had to guess, whoever applied it was very thorough. It was most likely activated from either timed or remote-detonated fuses. Considering how wired that building is for security, I would go with the latter."

Shaking his head, Uriel said, "Agreed. I felt watched the whole time I was there. These fuses... they could have been hidden in computer towers or in a server setup?"

"Absolutely. But here's the thing. I don't disagree that Solomon Ravenskald ordered this done. He may even have alerted the fire chief so his crews were ready to go. That's the benefit of owning everything—every person—in a self-contained surveillance state like Storm Haven. That said... you don't have any way to prove it. The detonators, if they were in computers or servers, are long gone. I'm sure he was able to keep investigators away from that equipment by citing IP concerns should there be salvageable drives or motherboards. And, even if we had them, there's no proof of where they came from. Ravenskald has lots of enemies. He could easily claim corporate espionage, if he hasn't already."

Before Uriel could answer, Samuel was at the door, a bouquet of white carnations in his hand.

"Private meeting?" he asked.

"Not at all," Uriel said, as Ruth slipped the folder back into her briefcase. "I was just telling Ruth about my interview with your dad."

"Fun, fun, fun I bet," Samuel said, handing the flowers to Ruth, and kissing her lightly on the lips.

Uriel, suddenly uncomfortable about the display of more-than-friends affection, said, "Well... I can see you two have stuff to do, and I've got a pressing deadline."

"We're driving down to the Cape," Samuel said, putting his arm around Ruth's shoulders. "I've got a lot to think about and Ruth likes the ocean."

"You guys have a splendid weekend," Uriel said, heading for the door before they noticed how awkward he felt. Reaching into his pocket for his car keys, he remembered the mini recorder in his pocket. "Hey," he said, turning around. "I know you want to beat the traffic, but there's something I need you to hear."

Ruth put her hand on his arm as he approached. "No need to make this weird. I mean, you and I are clearly just friends, and—"

Uriel waved her off. "It's not about your dating. Yes we are, and I hope you'll both be happy, wherever this may lead." He pulled the recorder from his pocket. "I pulled the tape out of my answering machine. Maybe the two of you will hear something on Tommy's message that I'm missing."

Uriel pressed play on the recorder. An electronic voice exclaimed, "*You have one new message. Message one, today, 1:23 pm.*"

"I have no idea what that is. I grabbed the tape around 3:30, just before I left my apartment."

Turning up the volume, Uriel placed the recorder on Ruth Anne's lectern.

Hello, Uriel. I can see the look on your face, and man is it ever precious! You were expecting to hear the voice of your barbequed hermano I bet. Sorry to disappoint, but I think you're gonna love this.

"That's your brother... and the... other voice," Ruth whispered, getting a quick nod from Uriel in return.

Human life is worth less than you think. People die all the time, in all kinds of ways. For all kinds of reasons. Most of them, in the final analysis, are avoidable. Man-made. Unkind. Whether it's from engineered food additives, unnecessarily prescribed and dangerously untested pharma, environmental contamination, murder, car accidents, gain-of-function viruses, or the physiological toll of a level of stress never meant to be borne, people die. And all those so-called "natural causes" are really not natural at all. So who's to say what's moral when it comes to man versus man and the sanctity of life? Who's to say that "Do unto others" means "Live and let live"? Maybe it means drop your socks, grab your cocks, and make your final charge. What other motivational mind-speak can I use to make this clear? Beat your plowshares into swords, take and hold the high ground, and babies... lock and load! Maybe it means taking the right-handed hammer of slavish idle industry and switching it to the left for urgency and usurpment. The contaminated veil with which you drape your shameful faces is wearing worn and thin. You cannot trust your neighbor. He won't grant you any favors. He's too self-involved. Protecting his patch. The government—and the government that runs the government—is out for count. Body count. Reduced population count. 'Cause you're only so much fodder—for factories, for armies, for delivering packages and chemical concoctions passing as food to one other in the blink of an eye in your unhealthy hybrid deathtraps. But you're nothing but rats in a cage. Rodents bred for research in the reprehensible realm of the New Technic. And the lab's about to burn, dear brother, just like Tommy Sicari's playhouse. And when it does, it'll look suspiciously like the unavoidable and wholly dire disaster the Hollywood and not-really-news news networks, pedophile priests, and pasty politicians you gullible fuckers so masochistically love to trust will tell you really isn't their fault. Only then, when all the moldy bread and syphilitic circuses that have blinded you since you were born are burning at last from your eyes will you finally see the evil these puppets exist to peddle. That's useless information in the moment that you die.

The tape beeped and then was blank.

"What the fuck was that? Your brother and *who?*" Samuel asked, his face a mask of confusion.

"Tommy's message is gone," Uriel said, ignoring Samuel's questions. "My only proof is gone…"

"Proof of what, Uriel?" Samuel said, his face a contorted mask of anger. "You know what… I don't want to know. It's that conspiracy mind of yours. Yours and your mental brother's… and whatever roommate he got to read along with his shitty little fictions. Ruth… you ready?"

Thinking it best to leave with Samuel as quickly as possible before tempers got out of control, Ruth nodded, grabbing her briefcase and following him out the door.

Watching the couple disappear down the hall, Uriel pulled his smartphone from his pocket, opened his recording app, and, hitting play on the recorder, listened again to the message before he sent it to Kevin Connor.

DTEAU Director Peter Vance pulled his rented four-wheel drive into a rutted and muddy quarter-mile pull-off wondering if he'd somehow gotten lost. His smartphone was no help—he had lost the signal miles ago. Then, just as he was committing to turning around, he saw a hunting cabin at the edge of the woods surrounded by a dozen stately maples.

Sitting on the porch—staring deeply into nowhere—was SAIC Kevin Connor.

"Hey Kevin," Vance shouted as he pulled in. "I nearly didn't make it. Thanks for the head's up on the four-wheel drive. Jesus, this is remote. How did you—"

Kevin motioned to a quad sitting beneath one of the maples. "Left my rental at the foot of the mountain. That belongs to my uncle. He keeps the cabin in shape since neither my sister nor I visit here much anymore. It was really my father's place…"

Craving a Marlboro but not wanting to spoil the cabin's idyllic setting—the gentle slope of a mountain not far from Beecher Falls in Canaan, Vermont—Peter sat on a stump across from Kevin. "How's your father doing?"

"He hardly knows who we are. We didn't have any choice but to put him in the nursing home. Debbie's always angry with me. Says I don't get home enough, which I don't… Feels like she's left holding the bag. She took mom's passing very hard. Not that I didn't. But I have work, and with my nephews both at college…"

He stopped talking as his voice began to break.

"Your father's a hero, Kevin," Peter said, upping the manly to manage the awkward moment. "Best test pilot the Navy ever produced."

"And they wiped his memory for it. Don't give me that fucking look, Pete. He was part of the reverse engineering program at S4. They couldn't erase him like they tried to do to Bob Lazar, so they erased his *memories*. Fucking pricks."

Peter wanted nothing more in that moment than to tell his best friend that he was just frustrated by a horrible disease inflicted on a parent, giving it a cause that he could, if not mitigate, then seek vicious vengeance for.

But, having seen more than his share of what the US Government and the COMIIC—the Corporate Oligarchy Military–Intelligence–Industrial Complex—had inflicted on American citizens, including members of the military, he knew it would be nothing less than betrayal.

Passing his supervisor a mason jar filled half full with a clear, strong-smelling liquid, Kevin said, "Thanks for coming."

Accepting the mason jar, which he knew contained a batch of Kevin's uncle's infamous, dangerous moonshine, from which he took a sip, Peter replied, "When you use words like 'life and death' and 'emergency', it doesn't leave me a choice."

Kevin chuckled. "I hope you didn't think that I was talking about *me*. Yeah, I'm tired and frustrated and frankly pissed as fuck, but 'life and death' and 'emergency' apply to the *work*, not to me..."

Pete took another sip of the moonshine. Pulling the wrapper from a pack of Marlboro Reds, he asked, "Mind if I smoke?" The booze was igniting his nicotine addiction beyond his ability to fight it. "Give me a minute before you fill me in." Lighting a cigarette and taking a drag, he said, "This place is beautiful. Your dad built the cabin by hand I think you said?"

Kevin nodded, handing Peter an old coffee can for his ashes. "Built it after he quit flying planes. Got a nice check from Ben Rich at the Skunkworks for his consulting work and he put it all into buying the land and bringing in some specialists to help him cut the wood and pour the footings. But he did most of it on his own. He spent a lot of time here. Saw some weird shit over the years..."

"Such as?" Peter asked, stubbing out his cigarette and immediately lighting another. "Bigfoot? Whitley Strieber cabin in the woods alien-type encounters?"

Kevin knew Peter's history. He wasn't busting balls.

"A little of each. You ever get abducted in the woods?"

Peter shrugged. "Maybe. As a kid. They came for me in my bedroom mostly..."

"Weird how we can talk about all of this insanity as if it's perfectly normal."

"Because it is. That's why we're part of DTEAU."

Kevin stood and sniffed the air. "Storm's coming. It's getting cold. Let's go inside. I've got a fire going. Won't take but a minute to get it blazing. How about some coffee and a nip? Brandy or Bailey's?"

"Brandy for the first, Bailey's for the rest."

Kevin laughed. "You're the boss."

For the next eight hours, the FBI special agents and close friends talked about Eugene Gorman Howe, the latest recording from Michael and Planner Forthright that Uriel had sent, the New Technic, and the fact that Eustace Dwyer-Mann going missing and Tommy Sicari's death were definitely not a coincidence.

No matter what road they traveled, it led to Ravenskald Tower.

As a nearby grandfather clock chimed at 3 a.m., Kevin said, his speech markedly slurred from the liquor they had consumed, "Uriel got Ruth Anne Marsh a residue sample from Sicari's control room at the Tower."

"Any evidence of an accelerant?"

"On the nosey, boss. Exotic and expensive. Damned near untraceable if not for our Ruthey's genius. It was a professional hit. I wish Uriel had made a copy of Sicari's phone message…" Finishing his fifth cup of generously spiked coffee, Kevin poured several fingers of brandy into his empty mug. "I wish you'd let me track down and question that psycho fucker Eustace. The way the Changeling's place was wired, I know that shit's involved. That's a dangerous combination…"

Opening his second pack of Marlboros, Peter said, "Maybe Tommy Sicari refused to get involved, and that's why he was killed."

"Maybe. But it's definitely more than that. Uriel said Tommy was talking about some very heavy stuff at TRG. The New World Order. The New Technic. The Dwyer-Manns… The Ravenskalds… They can't have immunity, Pete. That's not what I signed up for."

Taking a long drag and holding the smoke in his lungs for several seconds, Vance finally answered, "I didn't either. So how we fulfill our mission is about to fucking change."

Ruth Anne Marsh had been walking the beach in Cape May for hours, thinking about her career as a forensic pathologist and professor and the positives and pitfalls of consulting for the FBI. Although the field experience and chance to bring murderers and rapists to justice were essential to her mission as a teacher of future FPs and to her sense of purpose, cases like the serial killings in Secaucus had begun to take a toll.

She was beginning to have nightmares.

Uriel's friendship—although he'd signaled at times he was interested in more, he was married to the *Standard*—and Samuel's increasing role in her life romantically had been keeping her grounded and sane. But the increasing tensions with their families—evidenced by the confrontation the previous afternoon at the university—were causing more stress than comfort and, as she watched the sun begin to set over the Atlantic Ocean, she worried where it would lead.

Taking one last glance at the sunset, Ruth entered the imposing Italianate Victorian that Samuel had recently purchased from his father. Although the outside looked like something out of a horror film, with its odd angles and sixty-six-foot tower—which, according to Samuel measured *exactly* sixty-six point six feet high, a creepy little detail—the inside was friendly and warm.

Entering the foyer, Ruth took off her sandals and shouted that she was back.

When Samuel didn't answer, she walked down the narrow central hallway next to the staircase. Seeing a light on in the study, she entered, undoing the first two buttons on her blouse as she said, "Nothing like the salty air and sand to get Aurora feelin' frisky!"

She suddenly stopped at the third button, and retreated a step toward the door.

Samuel was sitting in a wingchair by the fire. In one hand was a glass of amber liquid. In the other was the report from her briefcase detailing the findings of the residue from Ravenskald Tower.

"Have a nice walk?" Samuel asked, the light from the fire making his eyes look demonically red.

"Samuel... I can—"

"Shut up, Ruth. Okay?" Tossing the folder full of papers at her face, he yelled, "What the fuck have you done?"

Then he was out of the chair, and Ruth began to run.

ABOUT THE AUTHOR

Joey Madia is a novelist, screenwriter, playwright, actor, historical educator, storyteller, and director. He has written narratives and designed the puzzles for Escape Rooms in North Carolina, Scotland, and the Mothman Museum in Point Pleasant, West Virginia, based on literature and historical events. Many of his plays and screenplays are based on true stories or historical events. He is founding editor of www.newmystics.com, a literary site created in 2002 that houses the work of more than 140 writers and artists from around the world. His website is newmystics.com/joey.

You can reach him through Facebook, Instagram, Twitter, TikTok, his Amazon Author Page, Goodreads, Stage 32, Film Freeway, Reedsy Discovery, and IMDb.

Made in the USA
Columbia, SC
23 December 2022

74851377R00117